MOHAMMED & SUSAN

Samantha Kane

MOHAMMED & SUSAN

www.samanthakane.net

First published in the United Kingdom in 2018 by Diversity Books Ltd.

A CIP catalogue record of this book is available from the British Library.

ISBN: 978-1-9164187-0-7

www.diverstybooks.com

Typeset by
Born Group London, 90/92 Pentonville Road, London, N1 9HS

Printed and bound in Great Britain by Clays Ltd, Elcograf S.p.A.

*This book is dedicated to my readers, my cats,
and to animal lovers*

To stop hating, it was necessary for me to understand.

Pierre-Joseph Proudhon

1

The sound of drilling penetrated the morning somnolence of an upscale Victorian mansion adjacent to Kensington Gore, undergoing extensive refurbishment. From behind the mesh-covered scaffold a cacophony of voices emerged seemingly in competition with one another; a veritable babel of languages thrown together in this illustrious corner of London. The local residents looked on unimpressed. Since homes were transformed into investment opportunities, there had been no respite from the intrusive noise of heavy machinery: drills that made one's ears ring; diggers that shook the earth beneath one's feet; and the high-pitched cutting sound of electric saws. Neighbours would pull aside their blinds to gaze at the scene of this nuisance, hoping someone would observe their sour expressions: a silent protest designed to inform these nomadic builders that their presence was most unwelcome. Amidst this clamour of competing languages, a concrete mixer pulled up, attracting the attention of several workers, who descended one of the ladders that connected the different levels of scaffolding. The mixer's flexible trunk was thrust through an aperture in the façade, emptying its load of liquid concrete into the foundations. Adding to the noise, the rush hour traffic provided a continuous din, a steady backdrop to this multi-faceted symphony. Here a courier on a motorbike bibbed his horn; there a driver in a white van whizzed past, deftly weaving between office workers who proceeded mechanically, transfixed to their mobile phones.

Suddenly a loud voice rang out, and the noise from the site was brought to an abrupt halt. Moments later, a flurry of immigrant workers, probably of Middle Eastern origin, made a bold exodus from the building, scattering like ants into the adjoining streets. Another group quickly followed, albeit with less urgency, speaking among themselves in what appeared to be Polish. Finally, an English site foreman, wearing a hard hat and high-vis jacket, exited with determination onto the pavement. The remaining workforce surrounded him, while he spoke in urgent tones into his phone. Something serious had occurred that required the presence of the police. When, a few moments later, the imminent arrival of an ambulance and several police cars was heralded by the wailing of sirens, passers-by stopped and gaped to see the reason for the commotion. With the arrival of the cavalcade, a number of policemen entered the building, some in regular uniform, others in plain clothes. The area was promptly cordoned off, and onlookers thrust away from the site. Paramedics hastened inside.

The senior officer introduced himself to the site foreman, who appeared to be more shaken now than previously.

'Detective Inspector Davidson. . . You are. . .?'

'Nick Harris. I'm the site foreman.'

'Right. Tell me from the beginning, what happened.'

'A terrible accident. . . One of my labourers has fallen through a pane of glass on the first floor into the basement. We've just had it filled with concrete. He wasn't moving. Is he dead?'

'I don't know yet. We'll have to see what the paramedics say.'

The foreman lit a cigarette. His hands were shaking. Davidson, however, displayed no signs of emotion. Whether the death was suspicious or an accident, he had seen it all before. He had grown old in the force. Now in his mid-fifties, he had developed a slight paunch; he had sparse, greying hair, cut short. His grey, badly fitting, polyester suit, declared that he had no pretensions regarding his appearance. He had gone beyond all that. Years of observing the shadier side of life had instilled in him a less-judgemental, even philosophical, outlook on the human condition. In a staid and serious manner, he began:

'Take me from the beginning, then. So, Nick, you arrived at the site this morning. . .'

'Yes, just before eight. . .'

He paused in his account as Davidson was called away by the paramedics, who confirmed that the individual was deceased.

Harris could tell that the news was bad. He hadn't expected any other outcome, and felt somehow responsible. He should never have employed immigrant labour, he pondered. The need to cut costs had led him to jeopardise the safety of his team.

Sergeant Wood approached Davidson. He was old school, a relic from another age, one of those individuals who refuse to move with the times. He had learnt policing in another era, and adhered to a type of probity too often reviled nowadays. A tall, wiry, middle aged man with thinning hair, he dressed in what might be described as a functional way. In his mind, there was always a quicker way to do things, which modern policing had complicated with layers of bureaucracy. He admired Davidson in whom he saw a similarity of outlook. Ambling stiffly over to Davidson, who turned to Nick:

3

'Just hold on a minute. I'll be back in a moment.'

The two detectives descended a ladder into the basement. Face down in the setting concrete lay a body, surrounded as by a halo with shards of glass. Wood thanked the paramedics, who gathered up their apparatuses and departed. Turning to Davidson:

'Shall I arrange for the forensic guys to come down?'

'Yes, get them down here immediately. I don't want anyone interfering with the scene.'

'Right, gov,' the officer dutifully observed, and ascended the ladder into the brilliant morning sunshine.

'Oh yes,' Davidson shouted, 'tell Harris to come down here.'

'Right, gov,' came the reply.

Harris appeared to have recovered something of his equanimity. He was now concerned about the impact this accident would have on his business; whether he might be in trouble with the authorities for his lax attitude to health and safety. Accordingly, he was very guarded in what he said, responding to the detective's questions in as few words as possible. He didn't want to implicate himself in anything.

'I want the names of all the people who work on the site,' he began perfunctorily, 'I need to interview everyone. And that includes your immigrant workers too. . .'

'I don't think they'll be particularly obliging, inspector. I mightn't see them again after what's happened.'

'I know. But do your best. Is there any CCTV coverage?'

'No, officer.'

'And the deceased. I take it you know what his name is? That you've got his particulars?'

The detective knew the true state of affairs, so after gaining the little information he could, he didn't press Harris any further.

4

The forensics arrived. Dr Chalk, who seemed to be in charge of the team, was a hearty, laid back fellow, with a red face. He had that perennial imperturbability often portrayed in fiction. Such types do really exist. Leaning over the prone body of the deceased, he quipped:

'We'd better get him out of there soon, or he'll set in the foundation!'

The body had been turned over by the paramedics, and displayed the shell of a nondescript, heavy-set man somewhere in his forties. While Chalk was carrying out his investigations, Palmer, a younger detective, was outside interviewing those workers who had not fled the scene.

One person stood out, Susan Green, an architect who had been visiting the site. She was an attractive lady, probably in her early forties, medium height, with shoulder length dark hair. From her accent, it was clear that this immaculately dressed woman was of foreign origin, albeit her English was faultless. She was on the first floor and the only witness to the whole incident. She explained to Detective Constable Palmer that she noticed a man on a ladder painting the big window on the first floor. Somehow, she related, he appeared to drop his bucket of paint onto the floor. He then descended the ladder, walked toward the barrier that separated the wooden floor from the glass roof to the basement, and put his leg over the barrier, then stood on the glass roof that didn't take his weight which led to his demise.

'Do you know why he did that?' Palmer queried.

Susan paused for a moment, the began in a considered manner:

'No, I don't. . . Sorry.'

'Where were you at the time of the incident?'

'I was on the other side of the glass roof that connects the two buildings and illuminates the basement.'

'OK, Miss Green. Do you mind just waiting here while I have a quick chat with the governor?'

Susan nodded, while Palmer entered the building, where Davidson was still interviewing Harris by the entrance lobby:

'Gov,' interrupted Palmer, 'can I have a word?'

Davidson took him to one side. Palmer conveyed what he was told by the architect.

'Yes, I know,' affirmed Davidson, 'the foreman explained the whole thing. Ahmed – that's the deceased – was an Iraqi immigrant. He was painting the window, dropped his paint, then thought he'd take a short cut across the beam around the glass roof to the other side of the connecting building to get more paint, but lost his balance and fell. Forensics found clear footprints of white paint from the bottom of the ladder toward the glass barrier, and on the other side of the glass barrier. He shouldn't have been there in the first place. Unfortunately, it appears he's the author of his own misfortune. So, you can let Miss Green go. It's just an accident. We're done here.'

'Just too lazy to go down one ladder and up another!' Wood commented sardonically.

Palmer left his colleague and returned to Susan, who had envisaged having to endure a long, drawn out process of interviews before free of the matter. Thus, she was pleasantly surprised when Palmer returned, gave her his card, and said he'd be in touch if he needed any further information. Whilst relieved, there was something within Green that was somehow dissatisfied with the outcome; an urge to tell her story.

Susan promptly departed. Zigzagging through the heavy traffic, she marched north toward Hyde Park. So much was going on in her head that she needed to walk things off. Her unabating, brisk pace carried her through the entrance to Kensington Palace Gardens, across the Serpentine Bridge, into Lancaster Gate, and onwards to her apartment in Notting Hill Gate. But the walk had done her no good. Her thoughts were racing; her mind a vortex of emotions; old memories bubbled up, memories that could break one's heart; memories wherein beauty and love were intermingled with shame and hatred; memories where love and death were exquisitely interwoven.

'Oh God!' she muttered aloud, 'How, after so long, could this have happened?'

She paced up and down like a caged tiger, cradling her head in her sweating palms. In a single moment, when life had seemed so sure, these terrible, insurmountable feelings had been flushed from the subterranean depths of her psyche into the bold, searing light of day. But there was more. Something within forcing up through her subconscious: the image of one emerging from the past. That face constructed of all that was evil, bigoted and violent. God! How she hated that face.

She sat for a moment, then hastily got up to pour herself a glass of whisky, and at once drained it. She poured another, and sat at the dining room table. But she couldn't relax. Once again, she paced back and forth. It couldn't just end like that. She reached inside her handbag and took out Palmer's card.

2

Back at the police station, Palmer entered DS Wood's office:

'What is it, Palmer?'

'I don't know sir. It's about that death on the building site this morning. There's something about that architect woman just doesn't sit well with me. I think she knows more than she's letting on.'

'Have you got any evidence of that?' Wood commented in a noncommittal way.

'Nothing solid. It's just a hunch. I know the governor's ready to write it off as an accident. . . But, still, something seems amiss. I mean, she was alone with him on that floor. . . No one took a proper statement, and the other Iraqis who knew the deceased made a run for it. It all seems rather fishy.'

Wood was not altogether convinced. If you keep digging into things, there's nothing that wouldn't sound problematic. You spend years investigating suspicious behaviour and in the end you become cynical. You lose that ingenuous quality that's willing to take an incident at face value. Nevertheless, Wood was impressed by Palmer's inquisitive disposition and was willing to humour him a little:

'OK, then. I'm due to close my report on the incident, so I'll give you the task of finding those Iraqis to interview. Search the address of the deceased; see if you can find something more solid to identify him and inform his next of kin. Does that seem fair to you?'

Palmer was content with the outcome:

'Yes, sir. Thank you, sir.'

Early the following morning, Palmer arrived at the station unshaven and dishevelled. He had spent hours reading statements, making various enquiries, and speaking again with the site foreman about how he found his workers and their whereabouts.

He returned to DS Wood's office:

'Morning sir.'

'What's happened to you? You look like you haven't slept.'

'Not much, sir. A long night.'

'So, then,' queried Wood, 'any progress?'

Palmer seemed excited.

'Actually, sir, we've located the house in Shepherd's Bush. Me and DC Smith will be paying it a visit this morning. Just to have a look around and interview the workers.'

'Good man,' concluded Wood with a furtive smile, 'but when you and Nicola have finished galivanting around, there's more important work to get on with here.'

Shortly thereafter, the two detectives drove through the iron gates of the police station. It took them only a few minutes to reach their destination, from opulence to apparent poverty. Arriving at a rather tired looking property, they rang the bell. After much persistence, the door was opened by a scruffy individual of foreign origin, who looked somewhat rattled at the presentation of the detectives' warrant badges.

'Don't worry, this isn't an immigration raid. We're just here to ask you a few questions.'

'How many of you work on the Kensington site?' Nicola queried.

Fearing that he might get in trouble for working cash in hand, their interlocutor remained silent, and looked quizzically at the detective, as if he couldn't understand.

'Look, don't mess us around,' Nicola added, 'you know perfectly well what I'm saying.'

'Three . . . maybe four,' the immigrant replied.

'Do they all live here?'

He hesitated, then guardedly replied:

'Sometimes. . . They come and go.'

'We need to speak with the other workers who live here about what happened yesterday.'

Palmer was getting a little agitated at their tardy progress:

'Can we speak with them?'

'OK, OK. . . Just one moment. Come with me.'

They followed the young man upstairs, who knocked on the occupants' respective doors, who then congregated in the kitchen.

'OK guys,' Palmer commenced, 'do any of you know a man named Ahmed?'

They mumbled to one another in Arabic.

Nicola glanced at Palmer, who turned to the scruffy young man:

'What are they saying? Please speak in English.'

Jassem, the eldest of the group, whose command of English was superior to the others,' offered:

'When a dead man's name is mentioned, we recite a verse from the Quran. It means, "God rest his soul in peace."'

'You knew the man, then? When he came here, to England, and how he found out about the job on the Kensington site?'

'None of us knew him very well,' Jassem commenced, 'he hasn't been here that long. There's an Iraqi who

10

operates an estate agent. He brought him here only about a week ago. There was something strange though. He was offered a job that would have kept him busy for the whole year. That's not something anyone would usually refuse. But he was more interested in taking on this painting work in Kensington, that would have only lasted a couple of weeks. It all seemed strange. And it wasn't because the Kensington job was well paid. In situations like this, when something can't be explained, we call it maktoob.'

'What's that?' Palmer asked.

'It means that this was his fate. That it's written.'

Before leaving, Palmer turned to Jassem and asked:

'Just one more thing. Did the deceased, Ahmed, know Susan Green, the architect?'

One of the group, a young man who had previously remained silent, spoke in Arabic to Jassem.

'We don't really know.'

'Could you please tell me what your friend just said? Can you translate for me?'

Somewhat reluctantly, Jassem said that his friend spoke of the English woman speaking Arabic.

'And how does he know that? Has he met her? Can you ask him for me?'

Jassem and the young man spoke together in Arabic. Turning to Palmer, he related:

'The lady, Susan Green, asked him to carry a heavy square of glass to the first floor. He couldn't understand her with his poor English. She got frustrated with him and explained what she wanted in fluent Arabic, with a Baghdadi accent.'

'That's interesting. Thank you.'

The two detectives left the building.

'There's more going on there than meets the eye,' Nicola commented.

'But, really . . . What do you think?'

'I think we're both busy and have more important things to get on with.'

Palmer was clearly more enthusiastic than Nicola.

'But, before we lay this matter to rest, we need to just have a look at the deceased's address. Perhaps we can visit that Iraqi estate agent, and give our architect friend another visit in a day or two.'

'That sounds like a lot of unnecessary work. Why don't you finish things up yourself? I've got plenty to be getting on with.'

'Fair enough,' concurred Palmer, 'you get on with what you're doing. I'll catch you up.'

The deceased had resided in a hostel near Commercial Road in London's East End. Among the few possessions he owned was a worn prayer mat and a copy of the Quran, wrapped in a piece of clean cloth. On the wall of his room was a black and white photograph, probably of him with relatives, and some cheap prints showing stereotypical images of the Middle East. Clearly, Ahmed had been home-sick. Hanging in the wardrobe were a few brightly coloured shirts, the kind of thing that might have been fashionable in another time and place. But what attracted Palmer was a book written in English, stowed away in a draw. Why would a man, he asked himself, who apparently spoke very poor English, have such a book? Perhaps the title, written in bold letters, had attracted him: *Mohammed and Susan.*

Palmer flicked through the pages, then quickly shut the book to read the back cover. Something caught his eye and froze him with shock. The author was none other than Susan Green, the architect. Palmer left with the book and went straight home. He couldn't wait to read it. Here, perhaps, was the key to the mystery. Even while driving he couldn't resist glancing at the book laying on the passenger seat, arriving at last at a bachelor pad in North London. He quickly changed and had a shower, prepared a quick micro-wave meal, and sat down with the book, the title of which promised to take him on a journey of discovery, to a warm climate in a faraway land. He opened the book at the first page.

3

My name is Susan Green. However, I started out life as a boy, Sami Ali. This is my story. I was born in Baghdad, Iraq. Like me, Iraq has undergone many changes, and my country of birth and I have both evolved along the pattern of the phoenix, destruction giving way to rebirth.

In 1958 my father, Kamal Ali, a member of the teaching profession, moved from the land of the Hanging Gardens, Babylon, to Baghdad. He was a poet and revolutionary, and embodied his revolutionary ideas in his poetic effusions. A man of his idealistic nature was bound to encounter opposition, and so he did. In 1963, my father was dragged from his bed in the night by Saddam Hussein's secret police and interrogated for six months, for having written a small work of poetry with an allegedly Communist subtext. So little in those days, at least in Iraq, was required to land a person in trouble! But for all these imputations, Kamal was a good-natured and harmless man and, most importantly, he was very funny. It was these qualities that brought the attention of many young ladies, among whom was my mother, an English archaeologist visiting Iraq on sabbatical leave from the British Museum in London, who was engaged on excavation work in Babylon.

She befriended the young history teacher, Kamal, who taught at a school near Babylon's ancient ruins. Kamal compared the teacher to a kind of prophet, endowed with the ability, not to foretell, but to mould, the future. The role of a teacher, he urged, demanded infinite probity and hence must remain inviolable to corruption and intrigue. At public gatherings, his speeches and poetic recitals were eagerly awaited, and regarded by his fellow teachers as the model of sophistication and rhetorical fervour. Carried away to oratorical heights, Kamal's voice would boom like an oracle, his arms gesticulating wildly in the air; his large, honest eyes gazing heavenward as if seeking approbation from above. All those present were utterly mesmerised, and almost forgot the discomfort caused by the hard, plastic chairs that previously had not given them a moment's peace. It was as if they had been transported beyond the harsh political realities of life to a land where chickens fly ready-roasted in the air and the soil yields its produce freely, like the days before Adam's Fall; where love and friendship are the sole determinants of human relations. Looking to history for inspiration, he frequently pondered why a country blessed with a great civilisation like Iraq had suffered so great a decline? At the same time, he admired the British and the European nations for their inventions and strange, post-modernist cultures, their understanding of democracy, law and order. During the day he was often seen taking his young students to field trips to the ruins of Babylon, where his frequent panegyrics found concrete – or rather baked clay! – embodiment in the archaeological remains (like a lost civilisation once inhabited by Titans) left by the great kings Hammurabi and Nebuchadnezzar. Here a love-struck king had immortalised his passion in the famous Hanging Gardens.

It was during one of these field trips that my father first met the eyes of a young, pretty bespectacled English lady.

She was slim, impeccably turned out, with her hair neatly styled in a bouffant. Like my father, Pamela Green was an idealist (some would say 'a dreamer') who shared his love of Iraq. Their discussions on history, politics and the education of the Iraqi youth ultimately gave way to amorous flirtation, secret assignations and whispered endearments. In him she confided her past, troubled relationships with men of her homeland, the last of whom she described as a 'cold, emotionless drunk.'

She was a war orphan, with little to tie her to England other than her career. In Kamal she saw an Eastern knight 'full of promise'! Kamal's love was reciprocal and profound, but he equally loved Iraq. It was only natural, then, that the young archaeologist should accept the romantic teacher's invitation to settle down in Iraq, thereby resolving their respective loves in a union that fused all their desires. In 1959 they were married. In those days, when marriages were customarily arranged by a khataba or matchmaker (whose role it was to bring two people together at the instigation of their parents), this was truly unique, and came as a shock to Kamal's parents. A year later, I was born; the year after that witnessed the birth of my brother, Zayed.

Our family lived in a small suburb, developed about eight miles south of Baghdad, in the countryside know as 'The Land of Saffron.' Uniquely inhabited by those in the teaching profession, it was known locally as 'Dur Almulamean' or the 'Teachers' Houses.' A pretty suburb, on one side it was flanked by radiant yellow fields of wheat, swaying gently in the blistering heat rising from the earth; on the other, a small village, strewn with traditional single-story mud huts, was separated from the new villas by a bumpy dirt track. Passing through the entire length of the suburb, the track weaved its way through a tangle of partitioned date groves,

16

orange trees, arable land, and terminated in the slow-moving waters of the Tigris.

My parents were among the first to move into the new suburb, which at that time was witnessing the construction of a multitude of villas. They lined the road, dazzling the eyes with their pristine whiteness. Each villa embodied the desire of its owner, reflecting, in concrete, the psychological edifice of his mind. Some of the villas were as large and magnificent as palaces; some, small and robust; some of two stories, others of three. Among these, our villa was somewhat unassuming. 'Always stick to the mean' was my father's much-used maxim. It had two ample stories, a roof terrace, and a swimming pool at the rear. Throughout, the floors were covered with marble, the walls painted brilliant white. My parents had very few possessions in those days, being young, and having myself and my brother to care for. But, for a very modest price, they obtained some Art Deco furniture from a family of expatriates returning from Iraq to Europe. These items they distributed sparsely throughout the villa, at least giving the impression that it was occupied.

A heavy wooden door opened onto our garden, separated from the dirt track by an imposing iron gate. I was too young at the time to remember how quickly this little oasis sprung up, but my earliest recollection is of a medium-sized garden, partially overtopped with a trellis-arbour inter-woven with grape vines. Heavy, abundant clusters caught the head of unwary visitors, and fell softly onto the dusty driveway. To the left of the arbour the garden was shielded from the heat of the afternoon sun by a wall of trees bearing a variety of fruits: oranges, figs, pomegranates, and lemons. Struggling for life amid the trees, a small patch of grass, aided by an indomitable sprinkler, defied temperatures that rose up to fifty degrees. Bees buzzed greedily around the

17

jasmine and rose flowerbeds that bordered the garden. It was a fine place to live, especially to grow up in.

My mother never objected to our father and grandparents raising us as Muslims. Hence, one of my first memories is when I was five years old and my brother, Zaid, was four, I remember being present at a magnificent celebration. The entire community, dressed in their party clothes, turned out for the occasion. All our relations attended, even my auntie, who lived a hundred miles away in Twerig. They filled the house and the garden; some even had to make do with the dirt track. Peals of laughter cut through the continuous din of conversation. Women rolled their tongues, giving forth a piercing and shrill cry, so common among Middle Eastern celebrations. Framed by a tangle of fruit trees, a brass band had set up, where the trombone, tuba and horns sought frantically to maintain concord. One of the trombonists had laid his instrument aside, and could be seen kicking his legs out amongst a group of young ladies, who were tossing sweets over their shoulders, high up into the sky. An aroma of spit-roasted lamb drifted across the company, filling all with a hearty desire to eat. It was all so much fun!

Unlike the other guests, my brother and I were dressed in simple white dishdashas or gowns. We hadn't the faintest idea what these celebrations were all about, but scurried around, chasing and playing with our relatives' children. My brother got into a scrap with a young ruffian, which caused his little dishdasha to rise up and display his little winkle. Everyone laughed. After this, we rummaged through a pile of presents that had been accumulating since the party began. We tugged at their brightly coloured wrappings, leaving some completely exposed and strewn across the floor, awaiting the unsuspecting foot of an aunt or uncle to flatten them. Then I upset a table of cups, which scattered in shards on the tiled floor. It seemed that we could get away with anything that day; as if people were tolerating our horseplay for a greater end. What this end was, however, it was best we did not know beforehand. Several times I asked my father why a bed had been set up in the living room. He didn't seem to want to tell me, instead hurrying me on to join the party and enjoy myself. But, all was soon to be revealed.

The large congregation filed noisily into the living room, dancing and clapping as they entered. The band stopped playing. Our parents then lifted my brother and I gently onto the bed, encouraging us to lie down and look up at the ceiling. This, of course, was very difficult, what with all that clamour going on. We were, understandably, desperate to know what was about to happen to us.

'What's going on?' my brother urged.

'I don't know!' I replied. We looked despairingly into each other's eyes. Then my brother started to cry.

A clearing opened in the crush surrounding the bed, to let through a trim little fellow dressed in a white cotton suit. He carried a small brown leather case under his arm, from which he extracted a cloth with an assortment of sharp instruments bundled inside.

'They're going to kill us!' Zaid screamed. We clasped ourselves together and rolled into a ball.

'Don't be worried children,' the little fellow reassured us, 'it'll only be a nip and it'll all be over.' Our parents nodded their assent.

'It's Mr Abdul Al-Adeem, the ziarchi.' This was the name for the circumciser, every little boy's nightmare.

'He's our friend,' I urged Zaid, who was kicking his legs up and down on the bed and had to be held down.

I welcomed the blade of the circumciser. In my innocence, I believed that he was there to correct the anomaly I felt in

19

my body, the mistake nature had dealt me in giving me a little willy instead of the little flower I thought girls are meant to have. Resignedly, I closed my eyes, gritted my teeth hard and clenched the sheets with my hands. At the doctor's touch I doubled up.

'Is it done? Is it done?' I cried.

'I haven't started yet. Be patient,' he replied sternly, taking my limp organ into his hand.

With consummate skill he removed our foreskins as if he was peeling an orange, initiating a stream of hot blood, which he quickly stanched. Not to say that it didn't hurt. It stung like mad; it was excruciating. For several days thereafter, I was possessed of the irrepressible belief that the removal of the bandages would reveal a metamorphosis in those parts deemed so definitive in the ascription of one's gender. Of course, I was soon to be sadly disabused and disappointed, to say the least.

In contrast, Zaid harried me with fears that his little winkle might have disappeared, and closely examined the offended area until reassured that all was as it should be. But I felt at odds with the other boys who inhabited the suburb. Not without a burgeoning sense of guilt and shame would I happily forfeit the droll escapades of cowboys and Indians, to sneak into my mother's bedroom, regaling my imagination in an Aladdin's Cave of high heels, perfumes, and makeup that could transform one's appearance as if by magic; and beautiful, ornate clothes that hugged one's body in a soft, knowing embrace, as if they sought to confide a surreptitious whisper, 'we belong to you.' With what glorious alacrity I would lose myself in dream images as I modelled these garments before a full-length mirror! No, I was not a boy like other boys. Even then, a latent dysphoria was bubbling up in my childish breast. A voice at the foot of the stairs would then shake me free of my ambivalent reveries, and I would feverishly disrobe. One day, when my father was reading a newspaper, I naively asked him if I was a girl. Just like that, with consummate naivety, the words emerged as if involuntarily. He wasn't angry or dismissive, but neither did he laugh at me. He simply explained that biologically (referring to that organ again!) I was most certainly a boy.

4

A parallel community was that of the Al-Shacker, who lived at the edge of the suburb in mud huts. They had settled on the land many generations earlier and, in years to come, would themselves inhabit the villas. But that would be in the future. At that time, the area of the suburb they occupied was divided into a network of mud-built houses, each comprising an outer perimeter cut in two and entered through a gate. On one side of the division, which was unroofed, one would usually find a couple of chickens, perhaps even a goat or two, shielding themselves from the sun under the branches of a tree. Heaped against the walls were farming implements and old wicker baskets; at harvest time, these enclaves would be brimming with fresh fruit. Any protuberance, dowel, spike or peg served as a hanger for a sack, made from a goat's stomach, and filled with souring milk in process of transforming into cheese. On the other side of the division were the living quarters, which were again divided into two. The larger segment housed the livestock; the smaller, the family, sometimes consisting of as many as eight members. A couple of small orifices were the only means by which light entered and cooking fumes departed.

For water for washing and drinking, the peasants relied on a standpipe erected by the government on the outer-reaches of the suburb. The standpipe, set in a large circular slab of cement, was a popular meeting place for the women. Their black abiyas gave them the appearance of a gathering of rooks. A typical conversation might run something like this:

'Hey, Salha, is it true Abbas is thinking of getting another wife? He's always hanging around Zakiyah, helping her with her firewood. Whenever she's about he goes all silly and doesn't know what to say!'

'That's what you think Fatima, but I know something else!'

'Fatima's got her eyes on Abbas!' they all cried. A raucous volley of laughter ensued.

'If you come anywhere near Abbas . . .' Salha threatened, a huge cooking pot in her arms, which until then she had been lovingly cleaning with a handful of dirt, '. . . you'll get this round your head!'

'Don't get so worked up, Salha.'

Zakiyah smiled; she knew she was secure in Abbas's affections. A silence followed.

'Nadima dear, you're young, fetch that bucket for me, will you?'

'Fetch it yourself grandmother.'

'Show some respect for your elders, you scamp!'

'Get off with you, grandmother!' Nadima laughingly replied.

'Talking about respect . . .' Fatima piped up '. . . what do you make of these women walking about without abiyas? It's disgraceful, showing themselves off like that! There's no religion anymore!'

'I don't know Fatima, they're city people, and their men folk allow them to get away with anything, not like our lot!'

While the women were collecting water, the men laboured on their farms. Without modern implements, they had to rely on oxen, donkeys and the strength of their backs to till the fields. It was a livelihood they grew up with and accepted unquestioningly as their lot in life. Even before they could stand on their feet, the children, both male and female, were taken to the fields. The women cared for them in bamboo shelters set up along the Tigris. As soon as they were physically able, they were employed in picking ochre and courgettes; weaving baskets; or carrying loads of vegetables across the fields, which they heaved onto the back of rickety carts. When they were strong enough, the men were taught how to yoke the oxen, and apply a shovel to the resisting earth.

The day began at sunrise. From out their mud huts, the peasants met on the dirt track, with picks, hoes, and shovels slung over their shoulders. The elders headed off in front, with the little ones dawdling behind. Half an hour later, the track was again silent. At sunset the same scene was played out in reverse, only now the workers, especially the younger ones, appeared much in need of rest.

There was little interaction between the two communities. Not that there was any animosity between them; only, their respective lifestyles intercepted one another at very few points. The teachers and their families granted the villagers the respect due to indigenous inhabitants. At the same time, they saw their lifestyle as profoundly atavistic, reminiscent of a more primitive, tribal period. Sometimes, this gave rise to expressed feelings of superiority, especially among the younger members of the new community. Dressed in their smart outfits, with books clasped under their arms, they ridiculed the young peasants' clothes and rustic manners. When the peasant children sought to join in the games of the teachers' and ex pats' children, they would be rebuffed and mocked.

24

'Look at his torn dishdasha! Uh! And there's a bogey hanging out of his nose!'

Their fathers sought to moderate their ridicule, for stop it they could not. Any of those whom were members of our little gang, if caught playing with one of the peasant children, was ostracised from the group until he promised never to play with them again.

My parents' attitude, however, was not so prejudicial. Mother often spoke with the peasants' wives, who were fascinated by her and intrigued by her honest endeavour to learn their language and culture. She was their very own Mrs Bell. One lady, who regularly knocked on our door, selling vegetables and dairy products, took a particular interest in her. She frequently visited us, and I'm sure that eventually the sale of groceries became only a pretext for speaking to my mother. Her name was Salha. She was a tall woman and, from what one could descry from beneath her abiya, she possessed a fine figure. Below her ample, raven eyebrows, she had large, brown, liquid eyes, whose blackness gave the impression of the illimitable. A finely chiselled nose, with only minor imperfections, perhaps indicated some a more refined ancestry; her thick lips, ruder peasant elements. Clearly, she had once been a very fine-looking woman, but now she was beginning to fade.

'I came to the village many years ago . . .' she explained to my mother '. . . and now my husband, Abbas, thinks I'm too old for him. He talks of marrying someone younger. The other women whisper behind my back, but I don't let it bother me. Oh! It's a hard lot for us women, and we all have to face rejection as we get older.'

Mother frequently sought to console her with assurances that the lot of women was indeed a hard one throughout the world. It was a man's world in the nineteen-sixties. However, the culture of the West was beginning to respond to the growing hopes and aspirations of a new generation, reflected in new, vibrant music and the proliferation of liberal ideas. This fascinated Salha, who exhaled a deep sign when my mother conveyed these things to her. She felt very sorry for her, and assisted her in the only way she could envisage, by purchasing whatever we could consume or give away.

When my father saw the huge pile of vegetables, eggs and milk bought from Salha, he would cry:

'How are we going to eat all that? There's only four of us!'

'We'll give it to the neighbours,' my mother explained.

'But, what's the point of that?' he queried.

'The point is that she's a poor woman and needs our help. . .' and, with a concerned expression on her face, she'd continue, '. . . there's so much sadness in her eyes. You know, I think she's having another child.'

Father would retort, 'how many children do they want? Hasn't she already got three or four?'

'I think she's doing it for her husband's sake. She wants to show him that she's still fertile enough to bear children. You've seen her trying to compete with the younger women, carrying larger loads on her head?'

'How should I know?' father interjected, 'I've better things to do than observe the peasants? You can't help everyone!'

'But that doesn't mean we should help no one!' she retorted.

'Still. . .' father submitted jocularly, '. . . that doesn't explain how we're going to eat all that fruit!'

Sure enough, Salha's efforts to retain the unique affection of her husband proved futile in face of Abbas's desire for a younger woman. Some months after the conversation just related, the family was awoken from their siesta late in the afternoon by the booming of a hollow drum. Zaid and I threw the door open and ran into the garden. Mother was

26

busy cooking, so she couldn't come. Filing along the dirt track was a column of peasants, headed by a middle-aged man with a drum strapped about his shoulders. Behind him, two or three fellows piped away on flutes. They held themselves upright, strutting self-assuredly, and winked at the young peasant women who danced alongside the procession. Gipsies, dressed in richly adorned yellow, blue and pink dresses gyrated frenetically, swishing their fine black hair, which reached to their waists. Close on their heels a group of men, of all ages, fired guns into the sky. Some had old rifles, others carried heavy Kalashnikovs; still others carried antique revolvers. Following thereon was the cause of all this revelry: perched high upon the back of a pickup truck, was Zakiyah, Abbas's new bride. She was a young cousin of Abbas, who came to the village after her rebel husband was shot and killed during the revolution. She had a son of the same age as Salha's boy. Abbas thought he would be useful as an extra helping hand on his farm. Her betrothed was awaiting Zakiyah at his mud hut, from the yard of which the fragrance of spitted lamb, bubbling rice, and gurgling stew, wafted down the dirt track. Seats were ranged about for the men folk to recline; the women would have to squeeze inside the mud hut to celebrate, along with the bride. With the onset of night, the revelry reached a crescendo and the celebrants would escort the newlyweds, amidst much cheering, to the bridal chamber.

Contrasting with her husband's jubilation and that of the community, Salha glanced resignedly at the ground. She gathered up her progeny about her, holding her infant in her arms. Among them, a boy, perhaps about my age, stood out from his siblings by the haughty, insolent expression he adopted. He wore a brown dishdasha ornamented with gold-coloured filigree. No doubt, it was his best outfit, for he avoided the jostling of the other peasant boys, as they

27

scurried around to collect the scorching bullet cases as they fell from the men's guns, and repelled their invitations to play with a precocious disdain. His skin was somewhat lighter than that of his fellows. Thick waves of dark-brown hair fell in curves, framing his somewhat plump face like that of a cherub; he had a tiny aquiline nose, large ingenuous eyes, and teeth as white as the warm cow's milk that Salha brought to our door. I followed his movements. He looked at me, a gentle smile passing over his lips. Involuntarily, I returned his smile. He stopped for a moment. I felt he wanted to say something, but he remained silent. The procession moved on, carrying him along in its crush. Again, he glanced back at me, the same smile reposing upon his lips, and that was the first time I saw Salha's son, Mohammed.

5

Both communities were to be changed forever with the arrival of Saddam's Ba'thist revolution. I remember the day before the revolution of 17 July 1968. On that day, my mother and father, my brother and I, together with auntie Aminah's three children and her husband, Adel, drove out to Ctesiphon late in the afternoon for a picnic. I won't say that it was a glorious day, for at 33° north of the equator, every day is glorious in Iraq but for the extreme heat. And, weather apart, no clouds drifted over our horizon. We set up our picnic rug upon a small rocky promontory over-looking the Arch. Beneath the delicate shade of the date palms, a soft, halcyon breeze lightly tickled the back of my neck. The rich bounty of the palm lay forlorn about us, cast prodigally upon the dusty ground.

Father had never been so full of life. He loved these excursions and appeared exhilarated by the illimitable. The splendid, convex, canopy of the sky; the tawny, rippling crust of the desert, filled him with a sense of destiny, of that feeling of eternity which man finds within himself and sees reflected in the vast edifices of nature. All the children sat upon the rug, while our mothers relayed back and forth to the car, each time returning, arms laden with the fruits of their culinary expertise. Disagreeing with Adel's politics, father turned to my mother in an attempt to change the subject.

'Let me help you,' he offered.

'No, I'm nearly done,' she replied.

Anyhow, she knew it was pointless asking father to help her with anything of a practical nature. He would only end up spilling or dropping something, and then the picnic would be ruined. The poet, the ideologue, though embracing the whole world in his utterances, will often lose his footing in the kitchen.

'Why don't you children have a stroll around?' mother suggested, '. . . come back in half an hour and everything will be ready.'

With a begrudging and hard-done-by expression, Zaid and the other children lifted themselves from the ground and marched off in the direction of the Arch, where a group of people were taking photographs of one another. I remained seated.

'Don't you want to go along too?' mother queried.

I wanted to listen to my father, who was preparing himself for one of his impromptu recitations:

> Clear jar wine,
> Black night sun,
> Tear on the eyelid,
> Paradise wine!
> I saw a savage.
> He came from a village.
> With only one blow
> He broke open the jar.
> Then the wine sprang
> Just before our faces . . .

*

It as Abu Nuwas. An old Babylonian by birth, my father had the blood of libertines coursing through his veins. From the rocky perch where he stood, father spread out his arms, the placid breeze gently picking up wanton strands of hair that played lightly about his prematurely balding crown. His face was angled heroically towards the sky; his eyes broadly gazing. Mother smiled to herself. He was not like other men, she said. Deeply serious when it came to the overarching problems of life, a spiced levity pervaded all his utterances and actions, as if it were his part always to play the jester.

> For young boys, the girls I've left behind
> And for old wine set clear water out of mind.
> Far from the straight road. . .

At the same time, in Baghdad, a secret meeting was taking place in the house of the Party's Secretary General, comrade Al-Bakr. The entire leadership of the underground Bath Party were in attendance. At 3.00am of the morning of 17 July 1968, those comrades assigned to execute the armed uprising made a surprise attack on the tank regiment of the Presidential Guard and took control of it. They encircled the presidential palace, making short work of sealing off all exits. Simultaneously, President Aref was being contacted by telephone from the Guard Headquarters; he was asked to surrender, in return for safe conduct out of Iraq. Initially he refused but, when they fired directly on the palace, and he found himself completely cut off, he submitted. Immediately he was taken from the palace and sent abroad. At zero hour of the revolution, the Tenth Armoured Brigade started out for Baghdad, and camped in Abu Grabe.

31

6

The following morning, we were awoken by an insistent knocking at the door. Father arose from his bed.

'Whoever's that at this time?'

The knocking continued uninterruptedly.

'Hold on! I'm coming!'

It was a neighbour. The dirt track was alive with conversation and shouting, both from peasants and teachers.

'Put the television on, Kamal,' a voice urged, 'something's happening.'

The old valves took a moment to heat up. It was the new government's 'Communiqué No. 1.'

Iraqis are very fond of political dialogue. Wherever they might choose to domicile, even overseas, thousands of miles from the homeland, they will always find a café where they can gather together and sip tea endlessly while discussing the political problems of the day. But when it comes to action, they would rather choose to demur and remain in their comfortable seats. For the Iraqis are, as far as human beings can be, a peaceful people; a simple, yet highly sophisticated, nation whom find joy and meaning in those elementary aspects of life, that are often taken for granted by those who do not observe the hand of Allah in all times and seasons, in good luck as in bad. A tacit fatalism informs their lives. They say in-shallah or 'God willing' in recognition of this. Herein lies that Iraqi genius, the unique intermingling of the erudite and practical. They are a robust people, disposed to endure much to hold on to normality.

The family tensely united around our black-and-white television encased in a huge mahogany surround. The sound of military music was the first thing we were aware of; then the voice of a commentator. Military units, the robust voice informed us, had been mobilised by the Ba'thist Party, and taken control of the National Iraqi Television Centre. An elderly general, known to the older generation as Ahmed Hassan Al-Bakr, a man in his mid-fifties with a bald head, declared jubilantly that the Ba'thist Socialist Revolution had finally begun.

'The oppression of the poor by the rich. . .' he avowed, '. . . was finally over! Too long had Iraq been the servant of vested interests, shamefully abused by those in power! Sucked dry of the oil which coursed through the country's veins, by imperialistic aspirations! No longer could this be allowed to go on. Every citizen must put hand to plough, must resist the reactionary forces that would seek to re-establish the old, moribund order, even if this cost them their last drop of life-blood. Traitors of the Arab nation, both nationals and Jews, would be dealt with mercilessly. Only then will Iraq be cleansed!'

Such, in essence, was the harangue of our new president.

Father remained silent, anxiously hanging on the general's words.

'What's going on?' Zaid broke in, his forehead crisscrossed with the tracks of deliberation.

I glanced momentarily towards mother, so as to try to fathom some information from her expression. But my mother didn't want to worry us.

33

'Nothing's going to happen. Don't worry,' she uttered in hushed tones. For all her efforts to appear unmoved, her eyes told another story.

Looming ominously in the background of the screen, as if providing a sinister commentary to Hassan Al-Bakr's words, a man of about thirty, with piercing eyes, cast a menacing glance that no doubt unsettled all who viewed the broadcast.

'I know that man!' father broke in, 'that's Saddam Hussein.'

The president, whose countenance appeared positively genial beside that of the younger man, stepped aside so that his deputy could say a few words. This was a man with political prowess, sure of himself, steeped in intrigue – a true Machiavellian. One could tell from his thick accent that haled from Tikrit, a village in the north of Iraq, where, as part of the Al-Khatab clan, he had expressed an early predilection for violence, and gained the adulation of his peers by shooting a teacher who had thrashed him at school.

I desperately wanted to know more of this man, there was something so sinister about his eyes. The mere sight of him made my stomach knot with anxiety. Surely, I was old enough to be told the truth?

'Father, who is this Saddam fellow?'

Father shook his head from side to side, slowly and deliberately.

'Let me hear what he's got to say. You'll know him soon enough . . . Al Bakr's already in his pocket.'

The demagogue stepped forward. Drawing on the untutored people's feelings of resentment against their social superiors, he hurled the weight of his harangue onto the putative injustice suffered by the common man, the farmer, the peasant. When he came to speak of those responsible for what he considered the present deplorable state of affairs, Saddam's features were infused with profound passion.

'The traitors. . .' he urged '. . . will not slip through our fingers. You, the people of Iraq, deserve to be freed from those oppressing you; who are using the country's wealth for their own betterment.'

Altering his demeanour to fit the case, he implored the people:

'Join me, comrades, in cleansing the country of this pestilential influence. Spare no one, even if he be your friend; do not fear the rebuke of your fellows; for your only true friend is Iraq, the country that reared you, that fed you, that invites you to a glorious future under Ba'thist leadership!'

Shouts of applause rang out from the television as Saddam handed the podium once again to the general.

Father fell back in his chair. He asked mother, who remained standing, to switch the television off.

'Haven't we been through enough already?' he queried, as if in soliloquy, a deeply serious expression on his face. I was frightened; Zaid's fearful features reflected kindred sentiments.

'You know Saddam, Pamela? He's the one. . .'

'Yes,' she cut in, 'the one who attempted to assassinate General Qassim in 1963.'

She was now visibly shaken and foresaw what this would mean for Iraq's middle class, for its teachers and professionals and all the Westerners who live there. She knew little of Saddam, but that little was sufficient to inform her that Iraq was now becoming a dangerous place under his dictatorship.

7

Over the following three days a curfew was introduced. Occasionally, there were knocks at our front door: young revolutionary recruits, military men demanding our papers in their search for those noted on their list of dissenters. None of the school teachers were arrested, but the troops' arbitrary way of executing their commands (a slip of the tongue could get a person into deep trouble) made their presence terrifying. I feared that father would say something and get himself arrested. He was often too outspoken for his own good.

'How mysterious is life!' I uttered, 'only two days ago we were sitting out in the sun, laughing, innocent of what was to come. And today we cannot even leave our house for fear of being shot!'

Over the next couple of weeks, the work of locating and arresting those suspected of treason in one form or another would be completed. Some were hunted down trying to abscond over the border and slaughtered in their tracks; others, high-ranking officers from the previous regime, were ousted or eliminated; those accused of spying were arrested or gave themselves up voluntarily in the hope of saving their loved ones from persecution; others, conversely, were thrust forth by their parents and siblings, lest they cast suspicion on themselves by harbouring a traitor. Within two or three weeks of the curfew, the entire process of arrest, conviction and judgement had been completed.

The resultant 'trial' was broadcast on television. Squeezed tightly together on rigid wooden benches, perhaps thirty men to a row, five rows in depth, a mass of shaved heads were seated, thoroughly dehumanised. From a dais opposite, surrounded by a group of military men, a stolid, emotionless judge called out the names of the prosecuted one by one, each followed by the monotonous refrain 'death by hanging.' Embezzlement, spying, Zionism, opposition to the revolution – whatever the conviction, the same sentence awaited everyone. Cries of innocence, pleas to Allah, were met with by a blow to the body or head. Some there were that sat without stirring, apparently resigned to their fate. Their eyes stared vacantly into the distance, as they were manhandled and buffeted by guards and fellow-prisoners. Confused petitions to Allah, desperate cries for justice, for the opportunity of saying one last word to their loved ones, for mercy, arose from the hall. In noble contrast, a few stalwart individuals stood immovable, displaying profound courage before their accusers.

The room slowly emptied as the prisoners filed out, dragged, pushed, beaten from behind, accompanied by booming military music. Party members then appeared, praising the revolution and encouraging everyone to attend Liberation Square the following day, where 'justice' was to be carried out. As patriots and citizens of the new regime, it was their duty to attend. Again, Saddam appeared:

'Comrades,' he began, 'the revolution is for the masses, and the revolutionary masses are demanding a free Iraq from western imperialism, petty imperialist and Zionist agents, to achieve political independence. Free Iraq is to liquidate completely all foreign intelligence networks and agents. They have been arrested and tried. Our fight against the imperialist, Zionist enemy has been won. The public hanging of spies is a national demonstration and an overt, tangible reassurance of the liberation of the national will from its fetters! Our aim is to educate the masses, particularly the young, in the patriotic culture and to make them immune from any influence of foreign culture. These foreign cultural trends are incompatible with the mass's demands for Arab National Socialism. This important issue was completely disregarded by former regimes.'

On the morning of the hangings I awoke early. I couldn't sleep well; it was as if all that suffering had somehow swept from the capital and across the countryside, and now penetrated my mind. But for all the suffering that would follow that day – and let anyone who possesses limitless optimism in humankind only look on with me for a moment to be disabused of his faith – I still could not help dwelling on how all this would affect our family.

I had slept on the roof that night, as I usually did in summer. Just then the sun was commencing its effortless course. From the ruddy crest of its globe, crimson rays shot forth, flooding the sky with an ominous, bloody tint, that hinted at the sanguinary proceedings that would mark that day forever. In the distance, I could make out the grey spread of Baghdad's outskirts. So silent it appeared, yet so unutterably shrill were the cries that, even now, must be rising up from its heart!

By my reckoning it must have been about six-thirty when a disturbance started to arise in the village. Small clusters of peasants began to form along the dirt track, carrying hoes, shovels and pitchforks; some, with the butt cradled in their hand, laid them over their shoulder, as if holding a rifle; some wielded them by their side like javelins; others thrust them out in front, as if wishing to impale an enemy with a bayonet. From the terminus of the track, their dishdashas appeared a patchwork of greys, browns, and tarnished russet; their sandaled feet thudded on the ground, leaving a light cloud of dust behind them. Intermittently they would draw to a halt, whilst one of their number stood upon the tips of his toes, gesturing wildly, clearly seeking to infuse his fellows with boldness. The mob responded with voluble cries, hoarse shouts, and bellowed with as great a rigour as their vigorous lungs could muster. They waved the tokens of their profession above their heads, shaking them menacingly up and down. Both old and young attended; young boys, probably no older than three years of age, dragged large glittering scythes along the ground that caught up the rays of the adolescent sun in their sharp, curved blades. Old grey-bearded men, who rarely left the refuge of their homes, urged on their tired, resistant, frames, some doubled over with age. It was enough for them just to drag themselves along: they carried nothing, and only greeted the chants with a strained yet visible, smile.

A volley of gunshots reverberated. Spontaneously, I ducked my head, albeit not losing sight of the crowd for a moment. All these people frightened me. It was as if they had broken from their chains, which they now took up in anger to break down any resistance. With their approach, I could make out a few words from their continuous cries. The names of 'Saddam,' 'Al-Bakr,' 'Ba'thist', 'Arab unity' and 'socialism' featured in conjunction with 'resurrection'; so too the words 'peasant' and 'working man' echoed like a refrain. From the other end of the track, a similar grouping issued. They approached one another and finally coalesced outside what appeared to be the house of Abbas. Repeatedly they demanded an address from him, and took a few steps back, leaving an opening in their midst, an impromptu stage from where Abbas would speak. All cheered as he took up his position on a broken wickerwork trunk. The old fellow had never appeared with such consummate aplomb and assumed dignity. He puffed himself up like a peacock, dazzling the crowd with a volley of words.

'Comrades, comrades, our time has finally come – Iraq's time has come! No longer are we going to be governed by those cronies who've sought to tyrannise over us with their western views. Now Iraq is to be ruled by the peasants – real Iraqis, labourers of the earth!'

The crowd roared with approval, and Abbas recommenced his speech.

I didn't listen to any more, but hastened downstairs to tell my parents what was going on. On the first floor of the villa I banged on my parents' door – but there was no response; then onto Zaid's room – again no response. I set off down the next flight of stairs, leading to the ground floor, and made for the kitchen, where I thought I'd find everyone at breakfast, albeit a little earlier than usual. The samovar boiled away idly, hissing and whistling, as if to amuse itself. The table was half set. Leaving the kitchen behind me, I dashed into the dining room, the living room, even my father's study. But I found no one. Returning to the hallway, I noticed the front door had been left ajar. Images of horror passed before my mind. I imagined father being manhandled by a mob of angry peasants, my mother pleading for his release; Zaid trailing behind in desperate impotence. But then I opened the door.

At the foot of the garden, which meets the dirt track, father was engaged in conversation with Salem Tahir; mother - Zaid close beside her – spoke quietly with some of the neighbouring women. Many of the teachers had emerged from their homes and onto the dirt-track; they

40

gathered in small groups, wondering what would happen next. In the crowd's vanguard was a pickup truck. Two or three peasants stood upright at one end of it, the other end loaded with water melons.

'Long live Saddam and Al-Bakr; long live the Ba'th Party! Long live Saddam!'

Behind them another pickup truck, followed by another, filed along in parade-like fashion, flanked by peasants on foot.

'Long live Saddam! Long live Al-Bakr! Long live the Ba'th Party! Our life and blood we sacrifice for you Saddam!'

By now the bulk of the procession was passing our villa. Some of the peasants shot us threatening glances; most, however, habituated to displaying deference to the teachers and their families, looked to the ground or straight ahead as they passed us. Abbas walked proudly, assuming a serious air, no doubt believing that if he joined in his fellows' chorus, his demeanour would lose its gravity. And Mohammed was there too. He trudged resignedly along with his brothers, beside his father. Beyond the village, the peasants were met by the employees of the Iraqi Pepsi factory, the cement works, and the Farida beer factory. Together, they marched to the main road, where they were met by pick-up trucks and set off for Baghdad. The hangings would take place that afternoon.

8

Iraq's two main cities – Baghdad and Basra – were to see similar atrocities that day. The site chosen for the Baghdad hangings was Liberation Square, a rare piece of grim irony that a square commemorating the inauguration of Iraq's Republic should be the stage for the new party's first signal act of tyranny. Contrary to its name, the square is in fact a circle, a large roundabout flanked by the National Liberation Monument and several large, impressive buildings. Delicately tended flowerbeds ornament its inner circumference.

All were expected to attend this grisly event; it was in their interest to do so – they might otherwise be suspected of dissent. Thus, shortly after the peasants' and factory workers' departure, my father, mother, Zaid and I set off in the car along the east of the Tigris, towards the Rasafa part of the city. Father had warned us not to look at the hangings, but to keep our eyes averted. Such images, he maintained, could never be erased from the memory. The roads were very congested; so too every thoroughfare and byway overflowed with pedestrians. And rather than the solemn, funereal aspect that stamped the faces of our party, we saw much jubilation and evident revelry in those who came to watch the proceedings. This macabre dance of death appalled me.

'How can they act like that?' I asked father.

'They're just frightened,' he assured me.

From his expression, he didn't seem to be particularly convinced.

'Isn't it enough that they're here,' interjected mother, 'do they have to sing and dance as well?'

'There's much that remains inaccessible to our eyes,' affirmed father, 'and, probably, these same people could not themselves explain their actions. What goes on deep inside a person's head often eludes us.'

I wound down the window. Disjointed fragments of anti-Zionist slogans, Ba'thist songs, and the general din of celebration could be heard.

'Shut the window, Sami.'

Father only used this tone when he would brook no opposition, so I closed the window without comment. We had to leave the car some distance from the square. All the roads were jammed up and impenetrable. For a while we thought it might be wise just to remain in the car for a few hours and then drive home. But we knew that any of those passing by might be Ba'thist agents, who would be only too happy to prove their dedication by hauling in a few extra traitors.

From the car we stepped into the bustle and were immediately engulfed in the flood of people flowing from numerous tributaries, which possessed an overwhelming power that caught up anything that entered its path and thrust it forth to where it reached it terminus. It was estimated that between two-hundred-thousand and half-a-million souls had that day marched on the capital. For a moment I was separated from my parents and Zaid; we were

43

all carried off into different directions. I no longer felt at home amongst these people – it was as if I had been living all these years in error amongst strangers. And, try as I might, I could not believe that what I saw were the actions of frightened people; rather, this was a side of human nature that had until then remained concealed from me; a potential ready to actualise itself when conditions were favourable.

I was soon reunited with my parents and Zaid.

'We can't go on any further; we'll be crushed.' Father paused for breath.

'Let's just stay here – to hell with them and their hangings! Is this some kind of nightmare? No more; that's it! I'm not staying here a moment longer – let them do what they will.'

Seldom had I seen my father so determinately incensed. Clearly, he was having difficulty reigning in the righteous indignation that seethed inside him.

'Don't let your anger get the better of you, Kamal. If we don't stay here we could end up with those poor souls over there,' mother uttered, pointing in the direction of Liberation Square.

Beyond the flood of heads that undulated between us and the square, the hanging had already got underway. Arranged equidistantly around the periphery of the huge, concrete island that forms the square, an army of makeshift gibbets – little more that posts – had been erected amidst the flower beds. Many of these gibbets were already occupied by their ghastly tenants. There was too much work here for a single executioner, so the work had been distributed between a squadron of hangmen who, with great speed and dexterity, threw a noose around the necks of the condemned and shoved their footing aside. With the earthbound plunge of each victim, there were cries from the crowd:

'Death to the Zionists, imperialist agents!'

'Long live the Ba'th Party!'

'Victory to the revolution!'

Hands tide stiffly around their backs, those hanged writhed violently for some time, gasping for air. The drop was not sufficient to break their necks, so they remained twitching and jerking for some time before the welcome end came. The only sign of mercy (if such a word has any place here) was the small black, cloth bag that was hastily thrown over their heads – perhaps the ghastly sight of purpling tongues half-bitten through and bloodshot eyes bulging from their sockets would have shaken the crowd out of its hysterical somnolence and brought before its eyes the true import of what was taking place.

Contrary to father's advice, there was something in me that made me look on this spectacle, some perverse imp that urged me on. Zaid too looked on. His features were pale and aghast, yet deeply intent. If any image remains to this day indelibly branded on my memory, it is the sight of the victims' necks slowly extending as they were pulled earthward by the weight of their bodies. Later I heard that the heads of some of those condemned had actually been ripped off when their elasticity came to an end – but I praise the mercy of Allah that I didn't have to bear witness to such a hideous sight.

We remained in our position for two, or maybe three, hours. Father was visibly sickened, and looked defiantly towards the ground. Mother's eyes were vacant; she was deep in introspection. It was a scorching day, and those standing, without shade, around the square's periphery, were starting to give way to the heat. Seeing the opportunity, a few groups and individuals scattered into the surrounding streets and made their way home. The majority felt obliged to see the affair through to the end. And when the end finally came, and the immolation was complete, the crowd slowly, intermittently, dispersed from the scene.

9

For all his faults, Saddam also did some good in modernising Iraq, much as Adolf Hitler won early praise for galvanising German industry, ending mass unemployment and building autobahns. Saddam established and controlled the 'National Campaign for the Eradication of Illiteracy.' Largely under his auspices, the government established universal free schooling up to the highest educational levels; and hundreds of thousands learned to read in the years following the initiation of the program. The government also granted free hospitalisation to all, and gave subsidies to farmers. Indeed, Iraq created one of the most modernised public-health systems in the Middle East, earning Saddam an award from the United Nations Educational, Scientific and Cultural Organization (UNESCO). A propaganda machine was instrumental in many village youths ceasing to work on their parent's farms and instead enrolling in city schools. Saddam also embarked on a secularisation programme, and in 1968 the Baghdad School for Music and Ballet was established. The Bolshoi Ballet Company was invited to perform shows in Baghdad and to teach ballet to Iraq's children.

The trauma I suffered witnessing those atrocities remained buried in the back of my mind. I again started looking inward and was unable to escape the anxiety engendered by my realisation that I had been born in the wrong sex, and that there was nothing that could be done about it. At that time, no one in Iraq ever heard of treatment for transgendered children, never mind sending them for such treatment!

My parents started to notice things about me that did not conform to the expected behaviour of a young lad, which distinguished me from my brother. Among other things, I put up a stern and indomitable resistance to the barber's scissors, preferring to maintain a female style (or, at least, one not overtly male). Following a visit to a ballet performed by a Russian troupe at the newly-built National Theatre in Baghdad, I gained much pleasure mimicking the pirouettes of the dancers. My mother encouraged me in this endeavour and purchased a pair of ballet shoes for me. Seeing how agile I was in my gyrations – particularly on the polished marble floors – and the visible demonstration of a real potential, she sought to convince my father to enrol me in a newly-founded ballet school for children.

Nevertheless, she expressed some disapproval when I carried my forays onto the dining room table, at which time she would enrol my father in a joint effort to bring me down to safety. Perhaps my mother underestimated the conflict that the nurturing of my interest would cause; particularly the strength of Eastern mores and values, a force sufficiently potent to thrust me into harm's way. She thought it sufficient to confide her predicament to her inner circle of expatriates and school teachers, alongside whom she taught English. Looking back, I believe that she did not see the gravity of the issue. Neither perhaps did I. She thought it was just a matter of socialisation, that there was not enough masculine influence in my life; and that it would ultimately, 'just pass.' Similarly, my father, being of a somewhat idealistic nature, also appeared to be content to let things run their course. He never said anything to me and essentially let my mother deal with the situation. When I consider Iraq in the 1960s and 1970s, I am struck by the ease with which he let things run on. Not being brought up in the Middle East, my mother's intervention was perhaps more understandable. But in this my father appeared terribly progressive. Most fathers would not have done the same in his situation, and would have instituted the harshest measures in 'correcting' the issue. We are led to believe that these things create fireworks in their inception; but for me it was more like a slow, stealthy progress that didn't give rise to anything so explosive.

Ultimately, as a result of my mother's discussions with her friends, it was deemed fitting that I spend the school holidays in company of a group of boisterous, young lads, a gang, in fact, of tearaways. This, of course, did not appeal to me in the least. But with this decision clearly impressed upon me, I resolved to cease entering my mother's bedroom and embarking on the dreams it contained. I knew that this had to be overcome. Thenceforth, I tried with great determination to fit in with the other boys.

'Sami, are you coming out?'

I jumped up from my chair, where Zaid, my parents and I were having dinner, and ran to the door. The 'gang' had arrived.

'I'm coming!' I cried.

'Not until you've finished eating,' father interjected from the dining room.

'We'll meet you outside Al-Shaklee's place. Don't be long!'

Because our parents shared similar backgrounds and profession, to my great surprise, we soon became inseparable.

The gang was headed by a boy named Hilal. His father, who was known as Abu Hilal, was a retired army colonel from the era of the monarchy, one of those colonial types that have since become an extinct species. He swore by a cold washdown every morning, and spent an hour before the mirror, taking exquisite care that his moustaches were even on both sides and displayed uniform curvature. Abu Hilal dressed in the style of a 'great white hunter,' and bore himself as upright as a post, which became increasingly difficult as his ageing frame resisted. Twice daily, as regular as clockwork, he bounded from his front door, accompanied by his well-groomed dachshund, whose tiny legs had great difficulty keeping up with the colonel's brisk pace. The old fellow strutted along as if on a parade ground. With nose inclined toward the sky, his large, even steps carried him from the Tigris to the peasants' village and back again, his poor companion's tongue hanging limply from its greying muzzle.

His firstborn had adopted some of his father's military bearing. Young Hilal marched like his father and, despite his years, sought to duplicate a gravity more suited to a retired military man. Khalid, the younger of the two, was not assertive like his brother, but claimed to be subject to interminable boredom. Wherever he was, whatever he was doing, nothing could sate his droll plea:

'I'm bored.'

Make any suggestion you will, it would always be met by the same refrain. Suggest playing football, he'd reply:

'That's boring.'

Suggest a swim in the Tigris, he'd reply:

'No, we did that yesterday. Anyway, it's boring.'

Propose a bicycle ride, he'd reply:

'I can't be bothered, it's too boring.'

At a time when most children find joy in exploring a new world, he seemed utterly inconsolable. That was Khalid.

Besides having a waist the width of a fuse wire, and arms that hung from his emaciated shoulders like a couple of pipe cleaners, very little can be said of Majid. A short lad, he had a very distinguished shock of dark, wiry hair which, to his detriment, served only to highlight his narrow and elongated face. He spoke little and fell in with any suggestions, even the most ridiculous. He was like an old broom or shovel, waiting to be put to use. What was going on in his mind was solely his own affair, for we never really knew anything about him. We believed he was too thin to have a personality, and were too young to suspect that within that narrow, fluffy head, it was the eager cogitations of his brain that was drawing all the sustenance from his body.

In Thameer and his brother, however, there was enough flesh to construct five Majids. They were the odd members as being new money with a humble background. They were the children of a burly and coarse blacksmith. Their father infiltrated the teachers' community by purchasing a freehold from an aged geography teacher who had never left Baghdad and was horrified at the thought of moving outside the capital. Henceforth, his children were doomed to a youth of fabrication. They felt ashamed of their father's profession and sought to conceal their ignominy by asserting that their father had been a prize wrestler, who was allotted a villa for his services to international sport. The brothers also tried to pass themselves off as budding wrestlers and strutted around like cocks-of-the-roost, throwing their flabby chests out and contorting their features to look mean. Because of all the weight they carried, they sweated copiously, which caused their hair to stick to their foreheads, and their tight-fitting clothes to give off a pungent, malodorous odour. Under their rolls of fat, the brothers were more or less indistinguishable, and that is why we treated them collectively as 'Thameer and his brother.' To this day I do not know the name of the 'brother.' Probably none of us do. The rest of the gang didn't really believe their stories, but we let them tag along under the illusion that they could provide the muscle if we ever got into a sticky situation; not that we needed muscle, but our exposure to western movies made us believe that every gang needed muscle and could not be a gang without muscle.

The final member of the gang, excepting myself, was my brother, Zaid. In every respect, both physically and mentally, he was my opposite. He was short and stocky; I was tall and thin; he was difficult to motivate, and clung tenaciously to a course of action once adopted; I was easily excitable, and dropped any pursuit as quickly as I had taken it up; he showed an early aptitude for the sciences, I for art. Those who've had any dealings with the natives of our illustrious country will perhaps have noticed that, if ever there is a problem requiring a solution, everyone present, notwithstanding how qualified he is to help, will offer advice which they deem to be the best possible. In Zaid this characteristic had developed well beyond the scope expected in someone so young. Whatever we decided to do, he always felt it necessary to give his advice on how it was to be done and whether it was the done thing to do.

When I caught up with them, the gang was waiting outside Al-Shaklee's shop, a converted garage, known somewhat generously as 'Dukaan Al-Shaklee.' When Al-Shaklee heard that a new suburb was being developed in Al-Za'franiya, his ambitions unfortunately overstepped his ability. He dreamed of becoming the proprietor of a large store, an outlet so capacious that no customer would leave without having found the item he desired. He conjured up images of huge, unending rows of tins and packets, cartons and boxes. It made his mouth water. No one would be able to live without him. When he found that his dreams were no

51

more than dreams; that he was equally poor whether in city or suburb; that his hopes would have to confine themselves to a cobweb-filled garage with very few customers, he ultimately became a very bitter man.

Since I was something of a newcomer, the gang wanted to initiate me in act of supreme daring-do, at the expense of Al-Shaklee. They, however, would remain at a safe distance. I crept into the shady opening. All was silent, except for the buzzing of flies.

'Uncle, are you here?' I tapped a ten fils coin on a little glass counter, from beneath which sat some rather unappetising cuts of meat, decorated with overripe tomatoes.

'Uncle, are you there?' I repeated 'I want to buy some things.'

I was frightened and walked slowly backwards so as to leave. And then the old fellow appeared.

'Yes, what do you want? I'm not having you wasting my time!' Al-Shaklee grumbled.

He was a man of medium height; his head was balding; his face bristling. Perched upon his upper lip, as if it were about to pounce, a massive unwieldy silver-grey moustache reclined.

'What do you want?' he again grumbled, giving me a suspicious look.

'Some things,' I muttered, seeking for a piece of paper in my pocket.

'Go on then.'

'Eh . . .' I mumbled.

Pretending to read from a discoloured slip of paper, I enumerated a list of items, which he patiently gathered up on the counter:

'Six eggs. . . mango chutney. . . tahina, date syrup, pickled gherkins. . .' and so on and so forth.

The process could not have taken any less than ten minutes.

'OK, that'll be two dinars and sixteen fils.'

'Will this be enough?' I uttered, holding out my ten fils coin.

'Now, what's your game, you rascal?' His features turned red.

'You urchin, I'll give your backside a good thrashing for you.'

I shot out of the door, Al-Shaklee in hot pursuit, shaking his fist. He didn't follow me far, however, as he was worried that he might miss a customer. Outside, the rest of the gang was not to be seen; they'd left me to it.

'Come here. I'll tan you're hide, you rascal! Come here!'

My little legs took me as fast as they could. I didn't look back until the bluster of the surly shopkeeper's voice became inaudible.

I caught up with the gang at the site where a new villa was being built. They sat on a pile of building blocks, laughing uproariously at my misfortune. I was so out of breath that I could hardly find enough wind to launch my protestations.

'I'm never doing that again! If he'd caught me, I'd have been done for!'

'It's Zaid's turn next time!' Hilal shouted.

Still sulking, I responded: 'I'm not playing if you do that again.'

'Hey! What time's it?' Khalid queried '. . . isn't the mosquito man coming soon?'

'Yeh. . .' the fat brothers chimed in.

And sure enough, we could vaguely discern a muted chugging in the distance. Until recently the government had been content to let the mosquitoes bite the native inhabitants to their hearts' content. With the coming of the teachers, however, something had to be done. The government appointed one Salem Tahir to the position of mukhtar or mayor of the district, and he immediately set to eradicating the mosquito problem. Five years later, the mosquito population had proliferated a hundredfold and Salem Tahir could do nothing but scratch his large, round, bald head.

'What can I do?' he mumbled resignedly, '. . . the little blighters will breed.'

Nevertheless, he was immensely proud of what he referred to as his 'mobile mosquito unit' which, ultimately, was nothing more than a broken-down pick-up truck with a device for spraying repellent attached to the rear. It was this device that attracted us children. It looked like a large floppy elephant's trunk swinging about randomly, spewing out a dense, pestilential white cloud.

'It's coming! Quick, hide!'

We darted behind a heap of building sand at the edge of the dirt track, the brothers Thameer being the last to secrete themselves. Waiting silently, we suppressed our giggles until we could have burst.

'He's getting nearer.'

'He'll go past.'

'Not yet, not yet.'

'Ready, get ready. . . now!'

We sprung from behind the sand and ran out into the road, extending our arms and buzzing like mosquitoes, weaving in and out of the cloud of pesticide. We circled the vehicle, waving our arms up and down, our buzzing now giving way to laughter. The driver wound down his window and thrust his head out.

'You boys, that stuff's poisonous! Get out of it! Clear off!'

The vehicle came to a sharp halt, and we scattered in all directions. In this manner would the gang employ its time in mischievous escapades and adept feats of the most cunning invention.

But as it has been sagely said, 'drive out nature with a pitchfork, and she returns.' My interest in the gang activities faded as quickly as they began, terminating along with the summer holidays and the commencement of the school term. Unable to suppress that voice within that told me I was not a boy, I resumed my interest in ballet practice and the yielding caresses of female attire. These were lonely, solitary pursuits, but in this way they enabled me to develop my imagination and to dream warming dreams of being a little girl. No longer was I Sami, but in this ideal world I became Susan, throwing off my male persona along with my male garb. Once I had applied, albeit somewhat clumsily, the makeup I found in my mother's dressing table, the illusion that was also reality, was complete.

One afternoon, departing from a foray into this ideal world, I ventured alone through the exit of the villa that abutted on the dirt track and irregular mud huts. While I had previously been very circumspect in replacing my mother's things to their original order and position, repetition ultimately blunted this caution, and one day I failed to remove the traces of makeup I wore. The satisfaction, or partial completeness, it made me feel was something I did not so easily part with. In a sense, I wanted (or rather, needed) to liberate Susan from the confined world of the closet, and bring her out into the open. Thus, I set off along the dirt track, and noticed that one of the ranch doors was ajar. The hut was nestled beneath a walnut tree. From within its tangled branches, a young boy, overflowing with life, cried:

'Hey, girl, I bet you can't climb this tree!'

Nothing could have made me happier than being called a girl.

'Where are you?' I shouted, casting my eyes upwards and wincing, to avoid the glittering shafts of light that shot through the broken apertures.

'I'm here, right above you!'

Above, nestled as comfortably in the tree as a bird in its nest, was Mohammed, Salha's boy.

'You can see the roofs of all the villas from up here,' he bellowed, adding, 'What's your name?'

I replied laconically and with great satisfaction, 'Susan.'

'You're the English woman's daughter!'

I clung eagerly to the trunk of the tree, and in a few moments ascended into the hoary entwines, a flurry of leaves coursing gently to the earth.

'What a good hiding place!' I shouted.

We both giggled. Mohammed was reclining with perfect composure upon a rough plank of wood set between two knobbly branches.

'Sit here,' he urged, 'there's plenty of room . . . You're not a bad climber for a girl!'

We both giggled.

He reached out his hand, which was hard and calloused, and drew me towards him. 'Look,' he urged, pointing out all the landmarks: an old watermill on the bank of the Tigris; the position of my parents' villa, etc., etc.

It was great fun, and I wanted it to continue all day, but my parents kept a tight rein on me and my absence would cause concern. Mohammed sought to detain me longer, attempting to reassure me with claims that his absence would certainly be noticed, having already sneaked off from working in the fields, which he hated. Conceding to my decision to go, he implored me to return to the village to play the following day, but I explained that I was starting a new school and was not at liberty to do what I wanted.

'Oh,' he mused, 'it must be great going to school. My father makes me work all day!'

With the approach of his father, Mohammed's expression changed, and he assumed a serious aspect.

'Quick, let's get down,' he urged, 'or I'll get in trouble.'

He shimmied down the tree, while I followed close behind.

'You'd better go, Susan. Maybe we can be friends?' he concluded, a momentary smile igniting his features.

I ran out into the track and shortly passed by Mohammed's father. He cast a scowling glance at me; his eyes were steely; his pace full of the sinewy dexterity of the vigorous peasant. I did not like that man and experienced a foreboding that he would cause me trouble in the future.

10

Salha held on tightly to Mohammed's hand, not for the boy's comfort, but for her own. He was seven years old now, a precocious lad, and stood on his own feet as if he were a grown man in miniature.

'I've paid dearly for you, my son. I wouldn't have done so had I not been convinced by your determination.'

'I want to go to school, to learn things like other boys.'

She looked down at Mohammed, a fleeting smile passing over her lips.

Since her husband's marriage to Zakiyah, Salha had been edged onto the side-line of Abbas's affections. No longer did she share his bed; seldom (although it had always been rare) did he deign to address any endearments to her. But in her son, she had found a substitute for her unreciprocated love. She was proud of Mohammed's aspirations, and was convinced that he would make something of himself one day. She understood, perhaps better than anyone else, what it was to stand apart while others clung tenaciously to one another, shielded by an impenetrable wall of what was expected of a person. Her mother died in childbirth, leaving Salha at the mercy of a brutal father who treated her like a common servant. He blamed her for his wife's death, which he bemoaned and lamented continuously, and never let Salha forget that her life had cost the life of her mother. She would have hated him had she not believed that what he said was true. In her pain she saw the just recompense for her crime. When her father died one night in his bed, she wept violently and took upon herself the weight of both her parents' demise. If she hadn't killed her mother, young Salha reasoned, her father would not have died of a broken heart. She was six at the time, and was taken in by Abbas's cousin's family, where she immured herself in housework, and meekly followed their orders. They, in turn, were good to her, and recognised in Salha a noble spirit and calm fortitude seldom found among her peers. She grew to be very pretty and became the sweetheart of all the peasants who worked the soil. Gallantly she spurned their overtures, though couched in terms designed to make a young girl's heart tremble with joy. At fourteen, her guardians decided that the girl would be an ideal match for their cousin, Abbas, himself a young lad. Salha wanted none of it, but seeing little option, obeyed and took up her place beside Abbas in Al-Za'franiya.

Salha looked fondly at her son as they approached the villa.

'The English lady, Um Sami,' as she called my mother, 'will be able to help. She's a nice lady. I visit her often.'

'Yes, she's got a daughter called Susan,' the little fellow interjected.

'No, she's got two sons! She doesn't have a daughter!'

Closing the iron gate behind them, they made their way hesitantly up the drive. Salha took the lead, while Mohammed followed closely behind. From the kitchen window, my mother, who was clearing up the lunch things, saw the black silhouette of Salha's abiya approaching. She quickly untied her apron and went to the door, which she opened before the peasant woman had opportunity to knock.

'I'm sorry to intrude upon you, Um Sami. I've brought my son, Mohammed, with me.'

Her large, ingenuous eyes inclined toward her son. His arms hung limply at his side like a wax figure, his head directed toward his feet.

'My son Mohammed,' Salha repeated, urging the boy to acknowledge my mother's friendly smile.

'You're the only person I felt I could speak to,' she continued.

'Why don't you come in?' mother urged, 'you're our friend, and I'll help you if I can.'

'Oh, I couldn't do that Um Sami, it's enough that I'm disturbing you.'

'Really,' she continued, 'you would be doing me a great injustice if you refused to come in.' 'Oh no Um Sami, I would be disturbing you.'

Salha appeared adamant, and Mohammed remained immovably glued to the spot.

I left my room when I heard them talking.

'Mohammed!' I cried.

'You know Mohammed?' my mother asked me.

'He's my friend. Can we go and play together in the garden?'

As if awoken from slumber, Mohammed's features once again quickened. He smiled that same impish smile that day when we climbed the tree.

I grabbed him by the arm and whispered:

'Don't tell anyone about Susan!'

Together we ran through the house and out the back door. Outside I tried to explain the whole story of my predicament. He was rather confused (as indeed I was), but nevertheless accepted the situation with the innocence and alacrity characteristic to childhood.

Mother looked knowingly at Salha.

'Let us follow the children's example. Come on, we'll talk in the kitchen. The samovar's on the boil.'

'Truth be told, when I first saw you,' mother began, 'I thought you were bringing me some dairies!'

'Oh, not today, Um Sami, it's my son I've come about.'

Salha sipped her tea diffidently until it was all gone. She wanted to begin, but didn't know where to start.

'More tea?'

'Oh no, Um Sami, there's plenty enough for me here. I don't drink much tea.'

'Will you have some kletcha then? They're freshly baked.'

'Oh no Um Sami,' she repeated politely, almost obsequiously, 'I've just eaten. I don't eat much. I eat like a bird.'

My mother replaced the plate of kletcha on the table.

'So, you've come about Mohammed?'

'That's right,' she finally began, as if by way of apology, 'we're humble people, and have no presumption as to offend you foreign people. We can never be like you and wouldn't be so foolish as to think so. It's just . . . well, Mohammed's not getting on with working on the farm. He's taken it into his head that he wants to learn to go to school with Sami.'

Mother smiled with delight.

'But that's wonderful, Salha. All children should go to school.'

She paused a moment.

'But Sami goes to a special school for ballet.'

'Will they teach him how to read and write?' asked Salha.

'Well, yes they do – in addition to ballet.'

Salha did not know what ballet was, but gladly went along with mother, agreeing that ballet would be really good.

'You're a godsend, Um Sami.'

'But they'll have to test his agility and coordination first.'

Without hesitation, Salha replied:

'Yes, he's really good at that.'

Mother got up from her seat.

'I'm so glad you came to see me. It's commendable that you should wish the best for your son.'

'So, you're able to help me Um Sami?'

'If you feel this strongly, I'm sure I can even take him there and back every day.'

Salha arose excitedly from her chair and threw her arms around my mother.

'Thank you, thank you, Um Sami.'

Then, realising she had perhaps taken a liberty, interjected:

'Oh, I'm so sorry Um Sami, I forgot myself.'

'You're welcome Salha, leave everything to me.'

11

An uneven row of canopies, constructed of palm fronds and roughly hacked branches, lay alongside the Tigris. They abutted one another, forging an unbroken chain that reached as far as the eye could see. At midday, the peasants would trudge across the upturned soil, some with bare calloused feet, others with improvised sandals, and settle beneath the shade, where they would find the womenfolk preparing a meal of stew and rice. The youngsters, full of unflagging energy, would throw off their dishdashas and bound into the Tigris, uttering cries of delight as the water embraced their heated limbs. Beneath one such canopy, a sober discussion was taking place.

'Brothers, I don't know what to do with him.'

Abbas, Mohammed's father, shovelled a handful of rice into his mouth, from which stray grains fell like a hailstorm. His interlocutors looked on silently, as Abbas's steely eyes surveyed them, awaiting a response. No one could say that he was Abbas's friend. Certainly, they respected him, and faithfully committed any problems they might have to his judgement. But he was not a man one would want to get close to. He was very irascible and haughty, and there was not a single peasant who could recall him having uttered a light-hearted word. His father had taught him that the best way to bring his wife and children in line was to beat them, and he followed his father's prescription to a word.

'Well, no one got anything to say?'

He took a bite from a charred piece of khubz, and once again begun:

'My son now wants to go to school like the city children with that little pansy boy, instead of helping his father in the field. Have I wasted seven years of my life bringing up a lad that'll do nothing but sit around, consuming the fruits of my sweat? Is he never going to repay me for these years I've looked after him?'

He surveyed those present, as if awaiting some visible sign of approval.

'Whatever task I give him, he messes it up, whether on purpose or because his dull-witted, I don't know. Connect the irrigation, he floods the field; tend the animals, he over-feeds them. Whatever he tries turns out badly. Things didn't use to be like this. A father's word was final. I'm too soft.'

'I'd give the lad a good thrashing if I were you, scare the life out of him.'

'Oh, haven't I already tried, Yusuf! That was the first thing I did. He's so headstrong, my right arm makes about as much impact as a handful of sand cast into the desert.'

Yusuf looked on blankly, a half-filled stikan perched nimbly between his index finger and thumb.

A wiry old man, hard of hearing, with sunken, bristly cheeks and tiny bird-like eyes, straightened the band around his yashmak:

'Send him over to me. My boy got lazy once. I soon broke him of his habits. He's my best worker now, the pride of the family.'

'Hadji Rasheed, I thank you for your suggestion, but we'll not sort the lad out by those means now.'

He paused a moment, shovelling another handful of rice into his mouth.

'You know, he's taken refuge with his mother, and she only encourages his whims. Now I've got the pair of them on my back.'

'You let those women rule your life,' Raheem volunteered, a brawny labourer with a curly jet-black beard, 'time was when my wife started getting slack, a little too free with her conversation, started yapping at me every time I didn't give in to her whims. Enough is enough, I thought one day, and gave her a right good clobber! She's as good as gold now.'

The men nodded and laughed.

'It's those city people who're to blame. I knew they were a bad lot when they began to move in. There's no religion in them. They think our ways are primitive, yet they expect to eat what we've broken our backs to produce.'

'That's the modern way,' Yusuf broke in, 'they're all behaving like that nowadays. I'd hoped we'd get more respect when they got rid of the king and those other parasites. But the government doesn't know what it's about. Never you mind though, our time will come brothers, our time will come.'

Abbas's eyes glinted, as if transported into his own proper element:

'I'll tell you one thing, when that day comes, you'll see a few changes around here. Those upstarts will pay for ruining my child. I'll personally take care of that. I'm not fooled by their empty pleasantries. Don't you ever forget who you are – Yusuf, Rasheed, Muntaha – don't ever forget we're sons of the soil and honest farmers. Praise Allah and His Prophet! Let us never throw out shovels aside to eke out a life of idle talk!'

Not one of the group understood that Mohammed was not to attend an ordinary school but, in fact, was to enrol in no less than the Baghdad school of Music and Ballet.

12

The summer holiday finally ended, and the new school term began. I was still getting dressed when Mohammed arrived at my house. We were to catch the school bus together which, from Al-Za'franiya, would take about thirty minutes to reach the vast sandstone edifice of our school in Karrada. Mother called up to me – I was always late when it came to keeping time – to say that Mohammed had arrived.

'Come on Sami, you'll miss the bus.'

I was proud of my uniform – my parents purchased it in Beirut during the holiday – and strutted down the stairs like a little gentleman. I imagined what a fine figure I'd cut in my new clothes. But when I saw Mohammed I felt almost ashamed of my opulence. If he had set out to provoke the other boys, he couldn't have arrived at a more effective means. He wore an enormous pair of faded balloon-like trousers, redolent of a bygone era, hitched up with braces; and a white shirt discoloured by so many different stains that they gave a detailed resume of its previous owner's eating habits. The wily old market-seller that sold the garments to Salha had assured her that with a little taking-in the trousers would fit like a glove; that the rip across the knee would be barely perceptible once it had been stitched together; and that the stains on the shirt would only be visible in direct sunlight. She accepted the fellow's assurances, following his recommendations to the letter. After all, he only wanted a quarter of a dinar, a bargain by anyone's standards!

It is often said that no one can be crueller than children, and as soon as we took our seats on the school bus, jokes on the expense of my friend started.

'Hey, Sami! Tell your friend that we're going to school of ballet and not the school of gypsy dancing.'

Coarse laughter resounded through the bus. I felt that I had to cause a scene to make them desist, but seeing Mohammed frozen on his seat, and gazing from the window without saying a word, I understood that the poor boy did not want the attention such a scene would have caused, so I sat down quietly beside him.

From the first day, Mohammed remained glued to me, seeking to duplicate whatever I did. But soon he surprised us all. One day, as the teacher sat at the piano (as she was accustomed to do), she asked him to perform a solo movement to her accompaniment. Despite being afraid of being ridiculed by the class, he moved with such natural elegance and coordination that it left us all breathless. I vaguely recognised the same dexterity with which he had earlier ambled lightly from the tree.

Whatever dance technique the teacher demonstrated, Mohammed somehow picked it up without apparent effort. He would display a perfect poise that rivalled that of our teacher. Those who had previously ridiculed him now began to reconsider whom it was that warranted mocking. Not a few scoffers – admitted to the school as a result of their parents' influence rather than for personal merit – failed in their attempts to replicate the poise displayed by Mohammed. They were like wooden figures in comparison. Confronted with the teacher's frustration, they quickly understood what it meant to wish to sink into oblivion. There was no shortage of long faces; and I'm sure Mohammed had to supress a mischievous smile in response to his obvious triumph.

Despite never having attended school previously, Mohammed did realise that the curriculum didn't usually involve dance. When challenged by his query, I said that my mother had explained this to his mother when making arrangements, and that she'd been encouraged by Salha's endorsements of Mohammed's dancing skills.

'She said you were really good at ballet,' I commented, 'and she certainly didn't mislead her!'

Mohammed saw the humorous side of things, albeit a note of apprehension accompanied his laughter.

'I did enjoy the dancing – and it appears that I am good at it – but you mustn't let on to anyone what kind of school it is.'

I assured him of my silence; and confirmed that my mother would observe a similar reticence.

Mohammed exceeded all our expectations, both in dance and in more mundane subjects. Sponsored by my mother, the school compounded its appreciation by permanently enrolling him and meeting all associated expenses. In response to those few who continued to taunt him with offensive remarks, about his appearance and origin, he exhibited a truly admirable tolerance; and with a robust composure deflected what to others might have been deeply hurtful. Nor was his ability restricted to dance – rather, he excelled in all his studies, surpassing his classmates as if he was an adult among children. Knowing he was a very able student buoyed him up into an atmosphere where rancour could not enter. Inevitably, there were many who would have valued Mohammed's friendship, but he was one of those who sustain only a single friendship throughout life, adding in intensity what would otherwise have been dissipated in extensity. Thus, it was for me that he reserved his especial affection. We ultimately became inseparable, and his presence at our villa was such that only his absence was noticed.

My mother, in turn, felt truly vindicated. If ever there was an irrefutable argument for the education of the peasants, that argument stood before her in flesh and blood – Mohammed. Of course, Hilal and his parents would not accept any of this. The lad's achievement had been the result of certain liberal elements in the profession who desired to unseat the old monarchists by showing that privilege had no bearing on ability, and that peasants could outwit the wealthy few. My mother saw no reason to explain the nature of the school and Mohammed's talent for dance to his parents. She feared they would deprive him of what he really wanted; all they knew was that my mother was taking care of his education, almost like adopting him.

Abbas, being a stubborn fellow, remained adamant that his views were correct and, if only for appearance, continued to harbour enmity against those who had engineered Mohammed's schooling. With habituation dissimulation resolved itself into reality, and what was only a mechanism to retain the appearance of infallibility became second nature. He really did believe that the teachers had done him a bad turn and, what could not be gainsaid, he remained short of one field hand. He continued to view the city-dwellers with suspicion; their western-style life as irreligious. For many peasants, the Agrarian Reform had given them the first taste of owning their own land, an opportunity never dreamt of in the days of the feudal sheikhs. To make it work, every peasant's labour had to be utilised, and none forfeited to the increasingly voracious appetite of the city. Many resisted the drive to oust illiteracy, which to them appeared a waste of time and a loss of much-needed labour.

Thus, Abbas conceived Mohammed's desire to enrol in a city school – one, moreover, that catered primarily for middle-class children – as the first sign of erosion of their way of life; it was like a cliff face being whittled away by the imperceptible, yet indomitable, onset of the flirtatious sea. Indeed, both his family and the other villagers had shown a change of attitude toward Mohammed. They mocked him, accounting his fondness for learning evidence of effeminacy, and a lack of manliness. If they knew that, in addition, he was now becoming a rather talented dancer they would've probably killed him. He would be deemed a 'Nestlé child,' that is, one raised on manufactured babies' milk, rather than the wholesome influence of the breast. This was tantamount to being called a 'sissy.' The soil was too tough for him, they said.

His fate, as was to be expected, was attributed to the baneful influence of the city folk. He was the first victim of a way of life to which they'd all succumb if they sat idly by and let themselves be taken in. Had it not been for Salha's interference, Abbas would have simply shrugged off the lad's importunities until he gave up his silly ideas. The other villagers, in turn, couldn't understand Abbas's indulging his wife's whims, and thought the old man had finally lost his senses. When he learnt of their snickering, he bore it with suppressed indignation. His time would come; but, for now, he would no longer regard Mohammed with paternal affection. After all, Abbas had a stepson in Ahmed, Zakiyah's son. He wouldn't let him down.

Mohammed was surprisingly unaffected by any of this. His equanimity seemed to me to sit strangely with his sensitive nature. A boy so attentive to the world must, I thought, have felt keenly the displeasure of those around him. But this was not the case; at least such was not apparent to me. Maybe the life he led had hardened him to circumstances that would have upset any other child. Perhaps he had grown accustomed to Abbas's incessant fault-finding, and this had worn away the sharp edges of his nature that catch upon discord.

Mohammed loved to dance. He would practice at my parents' villa tirelessly for five or six hours a day, rivalling both my interest and ability. Contrary to what would be assumed by the community in which he lived, his love of dancing did not imply that he was gay or effeminate in any way. This would cause his whole tribe to be shamed, and potentially cost him his life.

My situation was different. Secretly, if it were possible, I would have liked to attend girl-only classes and compete as a female dancer; albeit I made continuous efforts to purge my mind of this desire, that could do nothing but cause me anxiety and distress.

13

Mohammed was a frequent visitor at my parents' house. There was something fresh, spontaneous and unsophisticated in his behaviour that greatly endeared me to him and set my heart against the gang's monotonous pranks. He opened up to me some portion of myself that had hitherto remained dormant. In him I found a playfulness unencumbered by artifice, a child of the imagination; a reflection of my own disposition, one often fraught with fantasy and vision. Where other children require external stimuli to move them to action, we adorned the world with our thoughts and illusions. Where a wasteland once stood, we set up a kingdom rich in distraction. He introduced me to all his camps and hide-outs where, he said, undisturbed, he would sit for hours and lose himself in daydreams. In such isolated places – some rural setting or other – we fulfilled our love of dance, moving in response to music playing from a cassette player. Frequently, I would adopt a female persona, which he accepted without question. We would dance a pas de deux, and I would gaze into his eyes, deeply impressed by his passion and talent.

The place we liked best was an old watermill. No one else but he, I was assured, frequented the place. Though long-abandoned, the pales that turned upon the revolving wheel continued their onward progression without heed to their wasted labour. A repetitive cranking – crank, boom boom, crank, boom boom – followed the movement of its rusty mechanism, producing an eerie accompaniment to the deathly silence that pervaded this part of the Tigris's weary flow. Within the dusty ground floor of this clay mono-lith, a large iron wheel drew a belt that produced a persistent whirring sound. It rotated at a speed tenfold that of the waterwheel that drove it, occasionally dragging as the wheel strove against the oncoming tide. Close on, a ladder with many of its runs missing, was propped against an opening high up in the ceiling, an attic, from where a magnificent view of the surrounding landscape could be descried.

I had known of this old watermill for a long time, but my father always warned me against venturing here.

'It's dangerous,' he would urge, 'that's why they closed it down.'

I was satisfied with his admonition and, so too, it seemed, were the rest of the gang, whom had received a similar warning from their fathers. It was only at Mohammed's entreaty that I dared set foot there – and much courage and determination was needed before I would ascend that rickety ladder.

'What if it breaks when we're in the attic? We'd never be able to get down!'

'Don't worry Sami,' Mohammed would reply, 'it won't break.'

I accepted his words as if I were listening to an adult; for whatever he said had a gilding of authority that gave me unshakable faith in the infallibility of his utterances.

Soon, he transformed my fear into love. I learnt to cherish the watermill, and delighted in its clangour, its hoary age, and all its little rustic features that ignite a child's imagina-tion. It was from the little attic that I discovered a deep and lasting love for the grandeur of the rolling Tigris, a love introduced to me by Mohammed, which bound us together in wonderment. From the little aperture that opened onto the sky, we sat, close beside one another, lost in reverie until reality bore upon us, and the setting sun threw its fading shafts directly into the opening.

Falling backwards onto the rough, splintered planks that formed the platform of the landing, we let our gaze penetrate the openings broken into the roof, observing the changing hue of the sky as day was eclipsed by night. We lay in a straight line, our heads touching one another.

'Mohammed,' I asked one day, 'why don't you have any friends in the village? I've never seen you with anyone.'

'I don't like the other boys, and they don't like me. For a time, they seemed to be offended by my indifference, and set about picking on me. But I always got the better of them. Now they leave me alone, and just ignore me.'

He paused for a moment, then continued:

'You've got friends, haven't you? I mean, besides me?'

I sat up. The hard planks were giving me a back ache.

'Well, I'm part of a gang (if that's what you call it!), just a few boys messing about. I don't really hang around with them anymore. It all gets so boring.'

I wanted to describe the new feelings I had experienced since we met, but I couldn't find the words.

'I could go on sitting here forever, you know, and not get bored.'

I looked out of the opening, the purple sky falling in sheaths upon the darkening horizon.

'It's so lovely, and I never saw any of this until now!'

'I've been coming here since I can remember. . .' Mohamed responded, sweeping a rebellious curl from his forehead, '. . . and I shall come here always.'

'So will I, so will I Mohammed!'

74

The gang didn't share my enthusiasm for Mohammed. At best, most of them were indifferent towards him; others made insensitive remarks; only Hilal, however, made it his business to criticise the lad whenever opportunity arose. Had he been older, perhaps he might have learnt how hurtful some of his remarks were and learnt some restraint. As it was, he took an instant dislike to the boy, which issued in such comments as:

'He shouldn't be allowed in your house; he belongs in mud huts, where he sleeps with animals.'

'He's stupid, he should be working in the fields.'

Often, I reproached him for his nasty comments, for it was only I who knew Mohammed, and I could not conceive, even at that young age, why some people should be treated so unjustly because of their origin. I had yet to learn from the world that to be different is to forfeit one's dignity. Sometimes I despaired of Hilal's behaviour and the two of us came to blows. None of the group supported me; but, then again, neither did they support Hilal. Here was a lesson to be learnt: when people are demanded to take a stand morally, they would often rather remain silent than fight for what is right, and stand out from the multitude.

My mother, conversely, felt great warmth towards Mohammed, and looked upon him as almost her own son. She wanted everyone to be given a chance in life to reach their potential, and saw in the young fellow an image of what would be the norm one day. After all, she was first person to give him a chance and take him under her wing. Even in England when she was educated in the 1940s, women suffered the same discrimination as the peasants were then suffering; people believed that a woman's sole concern was to bear children, feed her husband, and clean the house.

Father was friendly towards Mohammed, but was more cynical than my mother about the future. He felt that the secret of his dance education could not be maintained for long and that trouble was just around the corner.

'Give it time. . .,' mother would retort, '. . . and we'll see.'

'Don't get ahead of yourself, Pamela. You don't know how narrowminded this culture can be.'

But she remained optimistic:

'You'll see Kamal. I'm right. Iraq is changing.'

'You're too idealistic,' father replied, 'Iraq's like a tottering giant. Who knows where it'll fall next time? All our dreams are in the hands of a man who is willing to sacrifice this country for his own crazy ideas.'

14

Iraq was undergoing a shift in the relative position of the middle classes, professions and the peasant population. Hitherto, the professions had occupied a privileged position, and it was in reference to their betterment that many political initiatives were ratified. Of course, since the overthrow of the monarchy under the Agrarian Reform, land was distributed among the peasants, who were accordingly transformed from serfs into landowners. But for many this was not enough. The peasants still had to struggle to scrape together a living and, moreover, it was damn hard work. Thus, the ten years that followed saw an exodus of peasants from the countryside into the city, who took up work as labourers, drivers and other low-paid, often menial, jobs. It was not possible for them to find affordable accommodation on their meagre salaries, so they erected shanties, makeshift constructions that soon engulfed the outskirts of Baghdad and became one of the chief eyesores that Saddam would later eradicate, replacing them with new apartment blocks. This was just one of a number of changes implemented by Saddam (although Al-Bakr held the nominal presidency) that would directly favour those who, like himself, were from a peasant background. Immediately upon the Ba'thist's accession to power, he organised the workers into unions and trades, with compulsory membership and appointed foremen; for the peasant youth, he introduced curricula that would directly indoctrinate the new generation in the principles of Ba'thist ideology, and replaced much of the existing time-table with elements supportive of this ideology.

Abbas was appointed representative of the peasant farming community. He was responsible for submitting any grievances to the higher authorities, thereby gaining him an unprecedented ascendancy over the community of Al-Za'franiya. He kept a very close eye on things, making it his business to uncover any suspected communist, monarchist or other dissident convictions among the populace. For this purpose, he instructed every peasant to report to him even the slightest hint of anything untoward arising. Each week he gave highly edifying addresses to his comrades in the newly constructed cement building designated for the purpose. In this he found great satisfaction.

Father was a teacher in a local secondary school. This enabled him to observe, from within at it were, the many changes that affected the new teaching methods. He saw how the history of the country, according to the newly written texts, had been rapidly replaced by a chronology that figured the past specifically in terms of a Ba'thist apotheosis; how scientific studies had been brought to the forefront and humanities pushed to the background; and the many technological breakthroughs historically attributed to western scientists, were foisted upon middle eastern invention. Thus, for example, it was urged that the Wright Brothers had their forerunners among the Iraqi's ancient forebears, who devised a crude mechanism for flying which never so much as got off the ground! The new regime desired to educate its youth in areas with a practical, utilitarian value, rather than an intellectual one. Salutes, repetitive military and party slogans, together with praise of senior Ba'thist members, were introduced at the opening and closing of every class and assembly; and, finally, father observed how the peasants, who attended his classes, up to now so well-behaved, had become somewhat undisciplined.

It was regarding this final point that we find the good teacher decrying one late afternoon.

'There's nothing you can do about it, Kamal,' mother urged, 'just try to ignore these things.'

Father, who set so high a value on the profession could only express his irritation:

'I don't think you understand what's going on here. You only have to teach the youngsters, and don't have to put up with what I do. How would you react if a student of yours brought a Kalashnikov into the classroom? It makes a person feel very uncomfortable.'

It was at that moment that a heavy knocking resounded from the front door. Father, as always, opened the door, and was confronted by Abbas's haughty demeanour.

'Good afternoon Abu Sami!'

'Good afternoon Abu Mohammed.'

'As you know,' the peasant began, 'the political situation has now changed, and this means things that were formally acceptable are no longer so.'

He paused for a moment and looked at father with an inquisitive expression.

'Didn't you write some book or other – the Golden. . . cup, wasn't it?'

'Chalice, the Golden Chalice,' father confirmed.

'That's it. Yes, I remember. . . you got into some trouble, some communist sentiments or other.'

'Please, Abu Mohammed, if you'd kindly get to the point. Is there a problem?'

'There's no problem. But, as a matter of fact, it's for your wellbeing that I called today. Maybe you've heard, but I've been given a political position in this suburb – a position I take very seriously – and I'm responsible for keeping an eye out for any dissident views that might arise. Not that I'm saying that you harbour such views. Anyway, I just wanted to let you know that your name cropped up and I thought I'd tell you – what with that Golden. . .'

'. . . Chalice,' father added.

'Yes, Golden Chalice.'

'I know what you're saying, Abu Mohammed. I was questioned about it in '63, when I enjoyed the hospitality of the Ba'thist's torture chambers,' the other concluded.

He then turned about and strode towards the dirt track, where he paused; there was something he had forgotten to say.

'Oh yes, please apologise to you wife, but Mohammed will not be attending school anymore. I've found him a place near us more suitable.'

Father slowly closed the door. He didn't know what to make of the peasant's conversation. When he related the details to mother, she was upset that her protégée had been snatched away, and admonished father not to be so open in his sentiments – perhaps it was time to conform, at least openly, and lay aside his pen.

15

News of Mohammed's changed circumstances greatly upset me. I was worried how this would affect our friendship; whether, indeed, I'd be able to see him again. The ruling party was now conducting a census of each household. His involvement in local leadership meant that Abbas was privy to everyone's domestic affairs, including details of school attendance. Soon he learnt of Mohammed's presence at the School for Ballet, making it his business to find out what ballet was. Zakiyah's teenage son, Ahmed, was summoned to rummage through Mohammed's school books that were concealed under his bed, thereby confirming his suspicions. He was mortified that it had taken a government census for him to be informed of his own domestic arrangements. I was sadly disabused of my belief that things would not be brought to a head so quickly when I found Mohammed's desk and locker empty upon my return to school.

For a while I lost interest in dance and my other studies, but soon I learned how to create a thick shield around myself, to deflect the assaults of fortune (this would be of service to me throughout life). The pain I felt within my heart meant that for some time I would have to perform mechanically what was demanded of me. Just as we habituated ourselves to those ghastly hangings – and there were more to follow – so too did Mohammed's absence fade like the print of an old newspaper, and become no more than a vaguely discernible image from the past. At least I felt such to be the case. There is a great fatality at work here – that voice within that screams for some kind of decisive reckoning in its interaction with the lurid events that pass before our eyes. But, however much we may try to sustain that initial wound, even if it hurts us to do so, nevertheless it ebbs away, and life returns to its former order. So, we try to sustain our sense of indignation, but it too dissipates, and soon the very events we so abhorred become detached from life, and are deposited in grey, lifeless concepts.

While the teachers felt that the ballet school had lost one of its finest talents, they quickly became lost in the whirlpool of life, and the developments that were sweeping across the country. So too did my parents, who became regular attendees of a very upmarket country club for ex-patriots, the middle classes, and wealthy merchants. Patrons could be found rubbing shoulders with senior Ba'thist members, in an atmosphere of modern music and cool drinks served at the poolside.

When I was in my early teens, it was at the club that my mother gave me my first taste of alcohol, an important rite of passage for a youngster. There we also met Louise, a pretty young English lady who, like my mother, had married an Iraqi. She worked at the British Embassy and became my mother's best friend. Together they shared reminiscences of the homeland, often finding a ready audience among those who believed that in the capital all men wore bowler hats, and that London was engulfed in smog.

The gang, who remained peripheral in my world, abandoned its childish escapades and developed into young men.

Thameer was tremendously proud of a little fluffy moustache he swept together from a few wispy hairs. Now he was a man – who would dispute otherwise? We became greatly enthusiastic about the fashions emerging from the West, and wore flared trousers, platform shoes, and grew our hair long. Western music also became our passion. We idolised the Beatles, Barry White, and Demis Roussos. One of our number obtained a poster of Brigit Bardot, circulating it among the group. They went crazy over it and competed in offering large sums of money for it. I don't know what I was supposed to feel, but this image of the scantily clad film star left me cold, albeit a little confused. I hated the unwelcome onset of puberty; I hated the changes that were taking place in my body, in manifold ways thrusting upon me a form and attributes I experienced as alien to me.

Throughout the period – it must have been nearly a decade – I saw little of Mohammed. This would always be a very fleeting glance, perhaps as he accompanied his father to the cement hall where he gave his weekly speech to the gathered peasants, or on his way to his new, 'more appropriate,' school early in the morning. I would have liked to speak with him, but it always seemed somehow difficult, as if there was some mental prohibition, or he was accompanied by someone.

Moreover, I didn't know what I'd say to him. Mohammed's features had visibly matured; he was, in fact, growing to be a very handsome young man. Nevertheless, he still wore a dishdasha around the village– the regular apparel of a peasant farmer– and seldom left his father's side, except when at school. On several occasions our eyes met, and as with our voices, so too our eyes didn't know what to say to one another. He looked at me diffidently, and I returned his glance with a barely imperceptible, yet warm, smile. This, in brief, is the situation as it stood at the close of 1976.

16

The following year, things were not so great at the villa. My mother's health was failing, and the doctors made a worrying diagnosis in relation to her liver. Our happy home, immaculately maintained and running as smooth as a machine, started to founder. One day I was sent to fetch auntie Aminah, who had previously offered to help out if things became too difficult for my mother.

It took me about fifteen minutes to walk to Aminah's house. Her villa lay at the far end of the suburb, near Al-Shaklee's shop. I explained the situation and how my mother's health had deteriorated.

'Oh, tell your mother that I'll be there within the hour! And how are you coping, son?'

'I'm doing fine, auntie Aminah,' I replied, offering a stock phrase that frequently conceals much unhappiness.

'Don't worry,' she reassured me, 'she'll be alright.'

With this she entered her house. She was always a positive and jovial woman, one of those very rare people that can truly be described as magnanimous; nothing upset her, and she was incapable of harbouring any rancour or ill will towards anyone. Just as I was about to depart, her door opened:

'Here's some baklava. Mind how you go.'

I took the plate of baklava, covered with a napkin, and returned home. It was the hottest time of day, so I decided to cut around the rear of the villas and past the peasants' village, where it was more shaded. It was usually very quiet at that time of day. Excepting the chirping of cicadas, the cooing of pigeons, and the sporadic bark of a distant stray dog, all was silent. I crossed over a patch of waste ground, slipped through a gap in a broken fence, and weaved my way through some discarded building materials. In front of me were the peasants' mud huts. I gathered up my pace, staying close beneath the shade of the date palms. I recognised that familiar ranch, adjacent to the dirt track, where I first met Mohammed. For many reasons, I had avoided the place up to now. I stopped and looked at the walnut tree. Overcome with emotion, I could not constrain the tears I felt accumulating within. How nice it would be to turn the clock back to that inimitable day, brief in memory, yet infused with so great a sentiment of the perfect. Everything seemed to be deteriorating.

When I arrived home, auntie Aminah was already there. Louise, who taught at the British Council, and two female friends of my mother, were also present. It had been decided that, within the next few days, my mother was going to travel to London for medical treatment. Louise, who was returning to England, was to accompany her. We would join her in due course. My father was unhappy with the arrangement, particularly with the implication that the Iraqi doctors were less qualified to treat her. Most importantly, while he was banned from travelling by the government, he would not be able to be with her. Confronted with this unfortunate turn of events, he retreated to his study where he sulked for a while. Shortly thereafter, I entered the study and found him sitting in the dark, gazing at a screen on which he watched National Geographic films.

An eight-millimetre projector blazoned images onto the far wall of Eskimos lumbering around in heavy furs, their beards festooned with icicles. Opposite the screen, his spectacles reflecting the images that passed before his eyes, my father balanced on the edge of an old threadbare chair, too timeworn to show its tattered upholstery elsewhere in the house.

'Father,' I whispered respectfully, 'are you alright?'

'One moment Sami, this is just finishing.'

He gently fingered the projector which kept catching and throwing the images out of time with the distorted English commentary.

'I'll just finish this,' he repeated.

I quietly sat down cross-legged on the floor and was quickly absorbed in the programme. While my thoughts kept revolving around the many problems that life was presenting me with, I made a conscious effort to lose myself in the alien world playing out before me. After all, this was how my father always coped when things became too difficult.

At that time, my father was an associate of the Royal Geographical Society. Every six months they sent him large cases containing reels of films shot in exotic places. Upon their arrival, my father scurried off into his study, hugging the precious cargo tightly to his chest. From that moment, until the last reel had run its circuitous course, he set up a bold resistance to the demands of the outside world. Ever since the society intimated that it was arranging an expedition to the Antarctic, my father's thoughts had migrated to that icy realm, where he envisaged himself mounted on a sledge shooting rapidly through the snow at the forward-thrust of a dozen bristling huskies. He imagined the little silver sleigh bells jingling furiously as it cut a silken channel in the snowy wilderness; the swishing of his leather whip, stiffened by the blow of icy winds; and the mighty blizzard, blanketing the sky with its icy mantle, shooting glistening darts at his frozen features.

During the next few days we were all busy preparing for my mother's departure to London. Knowing how incapable we were when it came to domestic issues, she sought to impress upon us a variety of instructions about how to prepare meals; what clothes we should wear for our respective roles – my father as a teacher, me as a student, etc. She was obviously frustrated, seeing that all her efforts would not save the household from chaos. The final night before her departure, she consoled father and I by making our favourite meal. She hugged us and sought to assure us that everything would be alright.

Following her departure, my father was like a lost sheep and withdrew into himself. When he was not teaching, he retreated to his study, sometimes even sleeping there. I think he felt a little guilty about his aloofness and decided that it was a good time (I had just completed my Baccalaureate exams and was waiting for the results) for my brother and I to visit our grandparents in the centre of Baghdad. They lived in the old city, near Al Rasheed Street.

Paradoxically, I think my father felt that we were slipping away from him – that we were going to leave both him and Iraq for good – and wanted to introduce us to what he considered the real Iraq, perhaps in the hope that a visit to old Baghdad might make us reconsider what we would be leaving behind. Elderly folk like my grandparents continued to embody the values of a bygone era, linking the slowly fading past with the brash new present. There we would be exposed to old Baghdadi culture and customs. But regardless of the future, I was keen to learn what I could from my grandparents, to sample old city life before it was gone forever. Father drove very fast all the way from the suburb to the centre of Baghdad, and we quickly entered Al-Rasheed Street, where Baghdad's main souk, Al-Shorja, was located.

The siesta had shortly passed, and the street was inundated with pedestrians. Amidst a cacophony of horns, the car crawled along between two impressive rows of colonnades. Delicate wood-carved façades leaned heavily onto the street, overlooking the hubbub with silent majesty. From out the alleyways meeting the street, young children, aged between five and eight, threw themselves in front of the cars, selling cigarettes, sunflower seeds and lottery tickets.

A rhythmical tapping indicated that the brass market, Souk Al-Safafeer, had arisen from its midday rest. Young men sold lebb-lebbi, (boiled chickpeas) from large portable cauldrons, singing:

'Lebb-lebbi, bee umak wishtry!' ('Chickpeas, buy them even if you have to sell your mother!').

Others shouted:

'Lexitic alkahraba' ('Ice-lollies made with electric').

Old women, their faces heavily channelled with age, sold fava beans on bread dipped in oil; others sold amba wa samoon (mango pickle in bread). A moist cloud of steam rushed in through the open window, followed by a small child's head:

'Chickpeas, would you like some chickpeas? Sir?'

'No thank you.'

My father slipped a coin into the boy's hand and wound up the window.

'Nothing ever changes here,' father lamented wistfully, 'these boys should be at school, not wasting their time selling rubbish.'

17

Al-Rasheed Street hadn't changed much since my grandfather set up his shop in the 1920s. Indeed, some might have ventured to assert that life at that period was much akin to the Golden Age of the legendary caliph of the Arabian Nights, Haroon Al-Rasheed, the eponymous hero of the street. Closely packed along the narrow, labyrinthine lanes that led off the famous thoroughfare, the houses had stood immovable for hundreds of years. Hand-carved shanasheel or ornate wooden verandas, projected overhead, whose cunningly wrought shutters allowed the occupants to look out without being observed. The houses were alike and followed the same pattern. From the lane, a massive door, striated with bands of iron, led into a courtyard bedecked with geometrical mosaic patterns. Soporific and tenderly cascading jets of crystalline water rose from a central fountain. At midday, when the sun threw its indolent shafts directly onto the surrounding streets, the courtyard remained sheltered, except for tiny filaments of light that penetrated the fronds of majestic palm trees set within its confines. The shadiest recesses of the sanctum were marked by the presence of hibs, or large clay jugs, used for cooling water.

In contrast to the vigorous discord that reverberated throughout Al-Rasheed Street, the houses reposed in relative quietude. The lane was too narrow to permit cars to pass and those foolish enough to make the attempt were derided angrily by the inhabitants, who feared damage to their properties. The silence was disturbed only by the distant tapping of a cobbler at the end of the lane; the slow repetitive grating of an occasional rusty trolley wheel; or the shrill exclamations of a few bedraggled children who strayed there. The roofs of these old houses, which reached three or four stories, were partitioned with corrugated iron panels, providing makeshift privacy for those wishing to sleep beneath the stars on hot summer nights. With night's impenetrable mantle thrown across the sun, the cloudless sky revealed a brilliant filigree of twinkling stars, set against the glorious backdrop of the Milky Way. Such was the popularity of sleeping under the heavens that slumber was often impossible amidst the snoring chorus of pot-bellied sleepers, subdued voices and the warbling arising from tightly-packed pigeon aviaries.

The mutayerchi or pigeon keepers were devoted to their head-bobbing friends. In the day time, swarms of the birds were released into the sky, somersaulting and swooping around their master's head, before losing themselves in the immense blue. At a whistle from their keeper, the birds would appear as a grey, white and red swarm congregating in the sky from all directions, descending in an eddy to their keeper's rooftop. Unfortunately, the mutayerchi were not popular, and to be known as a pigeon-keeper was sufficient to preclude a person from an honourable marriage. Everyone knew that his sweeping whistle was often a pretext for catching the attention of some young lady hanging her washing out on an adjacent rooftop. In these amorous interchanges, the pigeons obligingly bustled around their keeper, willing conspirators in their master's lewd business. Thus, the mutayerchi was synonymous with the lecher and second only to homosexuals in public opprobrium.

My grandfather was an elegantly turned out man, and very robust for his seventy years. He had a neat little white moustache and sparse grey hair, slicked down with olive oil. Upon his head sat a Baghdadi sidara, which distinguished the professional city dweller from provincials. He attributed his sprightliness to a regime of early rising and hearty breakfasting. Like many relatively wealthy Old Baghdadi families, my grandparents were both modern and conservative in their outlook. Granddad was a great believer in women's education, and beside my father his only son all of his seven daughters – the youngest, fourteen; the eldest, thirty-eight – were university educated and all ultimately became school teachers. They adored their father and openly fought with one another to anticipate his wishes. When he returned from the shop, the young ladies scurried around him, kissing his hands, offering him tasty things to eat, and gently easing a cushion behind his back when he sat down. Grandmother was a small, svelte lady with neatly arranged white hair. A quiet, yet contented woman, she spent much of her time in the kitchen, and busied herself caring for her offspring.

Nominally Muslim, the household had long since ceased to observe the ritualistic elements of Islam. Only my great-grandmother, whom we referred to endearingly as 'bibi-bubow' performed the five daily prayers expected of the faithful. She was a diminutive little soul of nearly ninety years, was blind, and subsisted on half a dozen dates and a bowl of yogurt daily, a regime to which she attributed her longevity. Before losing her eyesight, her sharp, feline eyes had viewed the centuries rolling into one another. She eagerly recalled the time when cars were introduced in Iraq.

The older generation – her parents – could not understand how such a conveyance could move by itself, and variously attributed its motion to horses secreted beneath the bonnet or the mischievous power of jins or spirits. Having witnessed almost the entire twentieth century, she often alluded bitterly to the British colonisation of Iraq in 1915-1920, and the plunder of Babylon by soldiers.

'If it weren't so heavy,' she claimed, 'they would have filched the Great Lion of Babylon – but that didn't stop them defacing it!'

She fondly related the appointment of the Ottoman Sultan Abdul Hameed as governor of Baghdad, and his first commission to eradicate the enormous population of flies that had descended on the city. This gave rise to the witty saying 'pashatna ji zahlan awal hookma al thiban!' ('Our governor's angry, he's executing the flies!').

18

At five in the morning grandfather roused me from my bed in the rough manner of someone for whom sunrise was the middle of the afternoon.

'Come on Sami, we're going to miss breakfast!'

Slowly, my mind integrated all the disparate sounds and images that fell upon my somnolent senses.

'A hearty breakfast will put you on your feet!' he urged.

'I'll be right down granddad, just give me a minute.'

When I reached the foot of the stairs, granddad was pacing back and forth, looking anxiously at his watch. Outside, only a few sprightly stragglers could be seen, listlessly pacing the empty lane; the occasional bark of a stray dog broke through the still air.

A taxi awaited us in Al-Rasheed Street, its engine throbbing in anticipation.

'Morning Hadji. To Qadhimiyah?' the unshaven driver asked grandfather.

'As always.'

The taxi began its journey through the backstreets of Baghdad.

'Young Sami will be joining me for breakfast this morning. He's helping me in the shop.'

'Good,' the driver replied, laconically.

We made quick progress, crossing the Iron Bridge in about fifteen minutes. Small clusters of workman began to emerge, increasing in number as we approached our destination. The sun started to lift its golden iridescent orb above the horizon, its rays igniting the Golden Minarets. The landscape blushed in its reflected hue.

'Come on, it's nearly six,' grandfather urged, anxiously glancing at his watch.

Stepping from the car, the three of us entered the restaurant, at once enveloping us in a thick, brawny steam. At the far end of the room sat a plump gentleman, the owner, his forehead beaded with sweat.

'Morning Hadji,' he cried.

'Good morning to you, Hadji Abid. The usual, please.'

'It'll be over right away.'

The aisles were blocked by customers reclining lazily in their chairs, with their feet outstretched. Orders were shouted in raucous voices in this men-only establishment, accompanied by a continuous racket of crockery knocking together and spoons clinking against tiny cups. The door swung on its aging hinges, admitting the devout who were returning from Morning Prayer, the cry of the muezzin following closely behind. We found a couple of seats.

On the table before us a plate slammed down with a heavy thud.

'Here's your patcha, Hadji.'

Beneath a welter of smoke was a sheep's head, boiled dry, with vacant apertures where eyes once resided; knobbly trotters; a stomach, interlaced with a network of arteries; the two hemispheres of a gelatinous brain; and a slab of tongue, somewhat akin to sandpaper in texture, all swimming in an oily liquid.

'Take some, Sami!'

Grandfather plunged his fingers into the sheep's head, tore off a hunk of flesh and wrapped it in sheath of khubz. A trickle of oil ran down his chin, which he swiftly mopped with a neatly folded napkin.

'Don't be afraid, Sami.'

Hesitantly I impaled a piece of tongue and put it on my plate.

'That's no good, Sami, take a piece of the head and a slice of brain. And the juice, dip your bread in the juice – that's the best bit!'

Grandfather's shop was located at Medaan, Al-Rasheed Street's main souk. At seven in the morning, it was much busier than the previous evening. Fouad, the junior, was crouching down on the pavement, removing the locks from a corrugated iron shutter. It rolled back with a metallic grating. He held the door open respectfully for grandfather, quickly nipping in front of me, no doubt to assert his authority. On both sides of the shop interior, from floor to ceiling, the walls were lined with glass display-cases, containing a vast assortment of neatly labelled tea caddies. Arranged in a pyramid was a pile of black weights and smaller brass ones nestled against a huge pair of heavy iron scales. The spacious counter separated the upper portion of the shop, behind which I was accustomed to sit on a high stool. Grandfather sat at a heavily-worn desk, behind a thin partition.

'Fouad, I want you to continue sorting those tea chests from India. They're taking up too much room in here. Put them in the store at the back.'

'What about Abu Ali's order?'

'Haven't you done that yet? Get to it young man, I don't pay you to watch the flies buzzing.'

'Yes sir, I'll get right to it.'

The junior's lumbering figure shuffled out through the back entrance.

'As for you Sami, get yourself to the chi-chee (tea seller). We'll have customers arriving soon.'

Only twenty minutes or so had passed since entering the shop, but outside, the pathway was by now barely navigable. Vapid and lifeless, the atmosphere portended a brutally hot day. Porters pushed heavy wooden trolleys in alternate directions, occasionally stopping to greet one another before continuing on their way. Two thickset men loaded rugs onto the roof of a car, unconcerned by the shouts and shrill beeping of horns emitted by impatient drivers waiting to pass. A group of traders, arms gesticulating wildly, discussed import prices of textile materials. And, scattered here and there, throngs of scruffy, forlorn children darted about, some hawking cheap products; some selling refreshments; others offering to black people's shoes. In front of the chi-chee's kiosk, old men sat at wooden tables, playing back-gammon and dominoes, whilst they puffed indolently on tired smoking pipes. They jealously guarded their seats and displayed a muted hostility to anyone who innocently encroaches on the group's space. I weaved my way through the close-packed seats, and found the proprietor buried in the shadow of a sun-bleached canopy, where a shiny chrome samovar seethed. A young lad, teacloth thrown over his shoulder, briskly rallied back and forth trays of tiny cups.

'Ah! It's Hadji's grandson. How are you?'

The proprietor recognised me, and deferentially took my order.

'There's no need to hang around, I'll send my boy over to the shop.'

Back at the shop, grandfather was engaged in conversation with an elderly merchant. He introduced me to his customer.

'This is my grandson, Sami. I don't know what I'd do without him.'

'Good morning sir,' I ventured, not knowing where to rest my glance.

'Good morning young man. My name's Taqi. I've known your grandfather since he was a young man about your age.'

The merchant leaned heavily onto the counter. He wore loose-fitting grey trousers, the enormous waist hitched up with braces. A roll of soft, ruddy flesh hung over his tightly buttoned collar, upon which his genial face reposed as on a cushion. His small arms flitted about energetically, providing a visual accompaniment to his utterances. I observed him closely, and he met my glances with an affable smile, which hung upon me somewhat longer than was comfortable. It made me feel odd, so I fumbled around with some pencils on the counter. While grandfather drew up a receipt, the merchant sauntered over to me, pulling up his trousers:

'You must come and help me one day at my shop. Everyone knows me. Just ask for Hadji Taqi.'

The aged merchant put his arm around my shoulder, letting his hand rest on the nape of my neck. He scrutinized my face with his narrow eyes.

'A fine lad, Hadji.'

His recommendation made me somehow uncomfortable. Grandfather detected my discomfort, particularly as he was aware of the rumours circulating about Taqi's interest in young men. With a timely interruption he asked me:

'Did you go to the chi-chee?'

'Yes, granddad.'

'He'll take all day,' and turning to Taqi, said, 'Come on, let's go and sit at the chi-chee's for a tea.'

'Get back to the counter then. I'll leave the shop in your hands!'

Grandfather and Taqi departed.

Perched upon my stool, I looked blankly at the display cabinets, and sniffed some tea samples that sat upon the counter. Fouad came in into the shop, sweating profusely, having dragged the heavy Indian tea crates to the storage. He gave me a sullen look and muttered a curse under his breath.

Business was slow at first, but soon the stream of customers increased until Fouad had to abandon his tea crates and start serving. He went about his task with an aptitude forged through habit; he knew where everything was kept and met my inquiries with open disdain and a show of despair, as if I was supposed to know intuitively where things were stored. Clearly, he did not appreciate my presence, but his respect for grandfather was sufficient to prevent him from being too difficult.

In the afternoon, my grandfather and Fouad went for their siesta. It was the quietest period of the day, and no one usually came into the shop. Other merchants invariably closed their doors, but grandfather never risked losing a customer. Once on my own, I would nip down from the stool and saunter around the shop, my hands behind my back, as if I were the proprietor. Then I would take a bag of marbles from my pocket and roll them listlessly against the counter; my interest spent, I began opening and closing the glass display cases, inhaling the fragrances that escaped from the caddies; and concluded my idling by piling the little brass weights into the scales. All means of entertainment exhausted, I returned to my stool and gave myself up to daydreaming, where I would be rudely awakened by grandfather.

'Wake up!'

A cigarette carton struck me on the head.

'Sorry, granddad, but we didn't have any customers.'

'But we might've done. Always be ready and attentive. Don't get lazy like your brother. He sits around all day doing nothing except teasing his aunties and scrounging food from your grandmother.'

He paused and looked kindly at me:

'Still, we'll make a merchant of you yet.'

Such were the days I spent in my grandfather's shops. We finished around seven in the evening, and I was so exhausted that I couldn't even think about eating. Zaid, on the other hand, wouldn't go to bed for love or money. He loved to listen to bibi-bubow's interminable tales of yesteryear.

19

In such manner the summer passed while waiting for news of my mother's treatment and for our travel documents to arrive. But soon there appeared a marked change in grandfather's mood. He became aloof and preoccupied, and displayed irritation and melancholy in his discussions with anyone who chanced to enter the shop. How things had changed in so short a time! The days at the shop became truly tiring, and I was heartily glad when it was time to go home at the end of the day. But even there, where raillery and laughter once resided, grandfather's sombre mood had affected everyone.

It seemed that all my aunts had contracted the same melancholy as that exhibited by my grandfather. Somehow, they looked at my brother and I differently, with tears in their eyes. My suspicions aroused by this behaviour, they confided that my mother had succumbed to her illness and died. Prior to this, they had some insane idea of wanting to protect me, at least for the time being, until they knew how to break the news. On top of that, the Iraqi government had instigated a blanket travel ban, and were suspicious of all Westerners or Iraqis that had intermarried, particularly those Westerners from the United Kingdom and the United States. In this political upheaval, it would not be wise for my father to bring attention to himself and alert the secret police, by applying for permission for my brother and I to leave Iraq. Anyway, there wasn't any particular urgency for us to travel, as our mother had now passed away.

My father was assisted in the funeral arrangements by some colleagues my mother had known when she lived in London. When things were concluded, my brother and I returned to the villa to stay. Needless to say, the old gaiety so apparently essential to his character was now gone. He was taking things very badly. He found some solace, however, in refining his grieving into poetry, upon which he would labour indefatigably. Unlike my brother, who was more conformist than me and was content to care for my father as he approached middle age, I remained open to the possibility of leaving Iraq. Things just weren't the same any longer, and I felt a pressing desire to move on. Moreover, relations with my old friends – the gang members – were becoming increasingly strained. As we grew older and more polarised in our developing characters – they, into young, and in one or two cases, handsome men; and I, becoming increasingly aware of issues with my gender – there was a pronounced loss of innocence, and I could not in all cases consider them solely as friends. On those occasions when we drank together, I instinctively began to flirt with them as a female. But it left me in a state of guilt and confusion.

20

The results of the Baccalaureate exams were out! Here was the announcement that determined one's life. Those who scored good marks could look forward to a future in architecture, medicine or engineering; those, conversely, whose performance had been little short of abysmal, would find themselves packed off to the Aski-Kalek Agricultural Institute, outside Nineveh, the city famously saved by Jonah. So desolate a location was this that the train that took the unfortunate student there didn't even stop at the station, but only slowed down, so the passenger, bags and all, would have to carefully jump from the locomotive. This, luckily, wasn't to be my destiny. Not that, being the son of a school teacher, I could glean some former knowledge of the questions that formed the subject of the final exams. Oh no!

My father who, as you know, was very fond of relating anecdotes, told us that one day he was invited by a rich feudal sheikh to attend a sumptuous luncheon along with some of his fellow teachers. Why he should be invited struck my father as somewhat perplexing. Nevertheless, he attended, and sat down along with his colleagues to dinner, from which no delicacy was absent. Soon, however, between courses, the sheikh quietly intimated to my father that he would be greatly obliged if he, my father, would provide his son with some hint as to the forthcoming exam questions. Immediately, father put his spoon down and stood up, as if to leave. His colleagues looked at him and followed his example. At that moment the sheikh drew a revolver from his drawer and directed it at his own head.

'Sir,' he threatened, 'if you leave this house I'll shoot myself!'

The teacher at once hesitated, thought the matter over and replied:

'On one condition only will I remain. That is, if you agree never to mention the matter to me again and, moreover, allow me to fail your son's paper this year.'

'But he'll have to repeat the final year again!' the distressed sheikh replied.

'That's correct.'

Ultimately, the sheikh relented, luncheon was resumed, and his lad had to remain an extra year at school before graduating.

I had achieved sufficiently good results to guarantee me a place at Baghdad University, where I would study architecture. Of course, my father was overjoyed at this outcome. To reward me for my effort, he kitted me out with architectural drawing instruments and books. When the end of the holiday finally came, he gave me a hearty pat on the back and sent me off to college with his blessing.

The University of Baghdad consists of many colleges arranged over a vast campus, each department having its own refectory and students. Every discipline hosted students unique to that discipline, such that you could identify their field of study by their external appearance. I had heard that the canteen located in the Department of Economics offered greater variety, apparently required by those who were destined to be the business people of the future. Taking my position in the refectory que with tray in hand, I surveyed inquiringly the dishes on offer. I felt a furtive tap on my shoulder. Somewhat absorbed with my choice of food, I initially ignored this intrusion into so important a decision. However, the tap was followed by another tap, this time more forceful than before. I turned around and (who would have believed it?), there, before my eyes, was Mohammed, the Mohammed of the peasants' village, the Mohammed of the watermill, the Mohammed who danced like an angel – in a word, the inimitable and lovable Mohammed. We embraced. It was like awakening from a heavy dream. My being was quickened, my body scintillated with life and fervour.

'Mohammed, I can't believe it. It's actually you. It's been so long!'

Previously I had believed that the feelings I had for Mohammed had been eradicated, that he had become a mere figment of the past – now I knew that those feelings had simply remained dormant within me, awaiting only the opportunity to emerge. All those childhood memories returned to me; they made me feel warm inside; but now a new feeling was attendant upon them, something I could not define. I picked up the nearest plate of food, and together we sat down, lost in recollections of the past and thoughts of the future. In such manner the entire afternoon was consumed.

After being withdrawn from the ballet school, it transpired that Mohammed had attended a regular state school in Al-Za'franiya, at which he unsurprisingly excelled. Now he was studying economics, with a view to modernising agricultural methods and creating some kind of farm or other. Clearly, he was one of those industrious students who give their entire being over to their studies, grateful that the opportunity to improve their minds had been given them. He was aware of the situation with my mother, and sincere in his condolences – she had been a second mother to him, he said. He placed his hands on my shoulders, looked into my eyes as if verifying that it was actually me before him, and again drew me to himself.

'You remember that day when we vowed never to lose one another? – we didn't make a good job of it, did we! Now, we'll began anew.'

'Yes, yes – forever, never shall we part again!'

'Come on, let's forget about this,' Mohammed urged, pointing to our paltry lunch. Accordingly, my intention to leave Iraq was put aside, at least for now.

21

As the months passed we became continually closer. Being students gave us the opportunity to meet each other frequently, almost every day in fact. It wasn't quite the same as before, but still we thoroughly enjoyed ourselves. We had much to talk about, but still there was that occasional lull in conversation that somehow demanded something more from our reunion than could be provided by words.

Some few weeks later we decided to skip college one afternoon. We sauntered into the city, pressing languidly against the searing afternoon heat. Mohammed was not familiar with the old quarter, and I wanted to show him my grandfather's shop in Al-Rasheed Street. We made good time, passing through the crush of pedestrians with great agility. My friend shot off in front.

'Come on,' he shouted, 'are you walking on eggs!'

'Slow down, you don't know where we're going!'

He laughed, as was his custom, his features those of a mischievous cat that submits to the attention of any stranger's hand.

'Here, over here! You've gone past the shop!'

Outside I saw Taqi, the old merchant. I hadn't seen him for a long while. He didn't recognise me at first, but I could not mistake his oversweet saccharine features and dominant paunch.

'Hadji, you remember me, Sami? This is my old friend, Mohammed.'

'Of course I remember! How could I forget a pretty face! I don't see you at your grandfather's shop anymore. He doesn't admit it, but he's lost without you.'

He looked me up and down; and, turning to Mohammed, added:

'Pleased to meet you, young man.'

Taqi held out his hirsute hand.

'I've just come to see your grandfather,' he began, 'but he's not in his shop. Fouad's on his own.'

'I haven't seen him for some time! I think I'd like to see him!'

'Well,' the other replied, 'he's just the same sombre soul as he's always been. He wouldn't laugh for the world!'

He looked at us both with importunity in his eyes as if waiting for one of us to reply. It was awkward.

'What are you lads doing nowadays?' he began.

'Oh,' I replied, 'we're both at college. He's studying economics,' I gestured toward Mohammed, 'and I'm studying architecture.'

'So, you're not going to follow your old grandfather in the merchant's trade?'

'No, I want to do something creative, in architecture.'

A young lad stopped beside us; he wore a dirty dishdasha that barely extended below his knees; his hair was knotted and tussled; the first sign of soft down upon his upper lip. The Ba'thist's new initiative to eradicate illiteracy didn't seem to have reached him! The lad held out his hand, a hand encrusted with dirt; his fingernails banked with ebony

107

grime. Taqi gave him a few fils, and shooed him away like a pestilential fly. Mohammed had wandered off across the street, where he was watching the brass workers hammering out a fat-bellied urn.

'OK, we'd better be off.'

I hastened to move away.

'Listen . . . you know where I live. You can always come and see me some time – and bring your friend along if you wish!'

'Thanks, Hadji. One day soon, God willing, we'll visit you.'

Mohammed and I slipped into Baghdad's famous cinema, The Rex, one of those old colonial piles, with plush, red velveteen seats and oak wainscoting, pitted and mottled where the varnish had flaked off. Only higher up did it show its pristine originality. No one was present at the screening, which played out to an empty house. It was usually the icy cold atmosphere that brought customers to the cinema, but at that time of day most people would be hiding from the sun in their homes.

Mohammed slouched onto one of the worn, threadbare seats, his limbs stretched out at full length over the seat in front. Head slumped over the backrest, he fixed his lustrous, guileless eyes, on the panoply of lights that encrusted the ceiling like so many stars in the firmament.

'I'm going to buy this place when I get rich,' he began, 'we can just sit here all day, watching the movies. And if anyone came in whom we didn't like, we'd just throw him out!'

I laughed, but Mohammed didn't follow my initiative. He paused, a mysterious, introspective tone informing his demeanour. It was that same otherworldliness that I had noticed as a child when we visited the watermill together to watch the sun setting over the Tigris.

He continued:

'Night would follow day and we wouldn't even know what time it was! Outside, everyone would be going about their work; children rushing off to school, their parents chiding them for their sluggishness; and the men would exhaust themselves earning a living. But all the time, we'll just sit here, as if we were on the moon!'

'Wouldn't we get bored?' I queried provocatively, sitting on one of the steps that ran between the seats.

'We could never get bored, Sami. When one movie ended, we'd just watch another. And when all the movies had ended, when the last reel had spun out its tale of weal and woe, we would have each other.'

'Didn't you say you wanted to get rich and modernise agriculture when you finish university, and start a family?'

Sitting upright in his seat, he looked at me with a sense of betrayal.

'Is that what you want Sami? Can we just forget the past, our friendship, go our separate ways now that we've found one another once again? Didn't we say we'd never leave one another . . . didn't we? Why can't we just carry on like this?'

'We can't. As far as people are concerned, we are two young men. It would seem odd.'

'But we're not like other people. We've got to do our own thing in life. Don't you feel the same?'

'Oh, Mohammed, what about our families? What about society? What about everything?' He rose from his seat.

'They can take care of themselves. Are we to sacrifice our life to everyone around us? Who are they to tell us what to do? What does anything matter, if only we're happy? Is it not good to be happy?'

What Mohammed said shocked me. Previously, he appeared so concerned with his studies. Now he seemed to want to throw it all away on some childish, absurd, dream. For all that, I appreciated the warmth he felt for me, and was, in some strange manner, touched by his seriousness. Maybe what he said was correct. If we all followed the same path as our parents, surely there'd be no progress, and stagnation would follow. After all, the West was undergoing so many changes, and the youth of Iraq were enthusiastically imbibing everything that came from that direction. People were having fun, expressing themselves, regardless of their peers' criticism.

I could hear footsteps approaching, muffled by the matted carpet. The rear door of the cinema slowly opened, revealing the stern face of a male usher. He shined a torch into our direction.

'You two, the film's finished. If you want to stay for the next show, you'll have to buy another ticket.'

I could see that Mohammed was going to ignore him, so I had to speak.

'We're going. We've already paid a hundred and twenty fils.'

He looked at me haughtily.

'It's not your father's cinema is it?'

The usher's interference was almost welcome. I cannot speak for Mohammed, but I felt that our innocent conversation might develop into something that would have been beyond our control. In the darkness of the cinema, like a young couple courting, our hands could have involuntarily touched, the touch giving way to a clasp pregnant with intimacy.

Outside, Mohammed resumed his usual balance, as if responding to the sun's cheerful face. But he was not the same as before. That weightlessness, that devil-may-care attitude was gone. I put my arm around him, and he smiled.

'Don't be sad Mohammed, you know I was only teasing! We'll always be together, and nobody can prevent that.'

He looked me straight in the eyes.

'Will we?'

His tone was one of scepticism.

'Why shouldn't we? Whatever we do, we'll always stick together – agreed?'

'Agreed.'

22

Iraqis are avid talkers, and Abbas was no exception. The garrulous old fellow could not survive without the willing ears of his friends to imbibe his effusion of words. When, each evening, they met in his yard, as the sun lay hard against the horizon, he spoke to his peasant friends with much deliberation, forcing his eyes into a penetrating squint whenever he deemed a point to be of especial profundity. Together they smoked, drank vast quantities of tea, and sent up their bland discourse deep into the night sky.

However, that was before Abbas become a member of the Ba'th Party. Now, his evenings were completely absorbed with what he referred to as 'political business.' As the local representative of the farmers' union, Abbas would retire around seven in the evening to the purpose-built concrete hall erected at the end of the dirt track, where it met the main road to Baghdad. Here he joined company with other trade representatives; each took turns in mounting the platform and discoursing on the revolution, the great strides made in industry, and the future of Iraq. The usual coterie of peasants, those whom previously sprawled out in Abbas's yard, attended these gatherings. Seeing their hero perched

111

on the stage, his mouth full of political slogans, their awe could not have been greater. The womenfolk did not attend these meetings, but remained at home with the young children.

After ten years of marriage, Abbas had grown disenchanted with his second wife, Zakiyah. Those days when the peasant was wont to anticipate her every wish, now lay irrevocably couched in the bosom of the past. She had become deeply jealous of Salha, who still possessed dominance over her husband's affections. Sometimes they battled like a pair of turkey cocks thrown hastily together in a small enclosure. The only element, in fact, they shared in common nowadays was the mutual distaste they felt at seeing one another. He said her cooking was fit only for donkeys; she, casting a malicious glance at Salha, that he didn't know what good food tasted like; he spoke of marrying once again; she rebuked him with ignoring her – and so on and so forth. In a word, she had grown shrewish and bitter, and at every opportunity wished to undermine Salha's position in the household.

Salha, conversely, was the model of magnanimity. She was never angry; she never cursed. No ripple of disquiet ever traversed her cheeks; and her eyes, in others the willing betrayer of the emotions, remained still and calm, like a bottomless lake, whose surface remains ever placid. Perhaps it was this absence of resentment that had undermined the years' insidious attempts to chisel away the grace and natural beauty of her features. Like a painting set amidst the living occupants of a household, Salha looked on, ageless, as those around her saw their appearance submitting to corruption.

It was thus a great relief for Mohammed when, as a child (for it was not long before Abbas became disabused of Zakiyah's false charms, and the problems began) we met and he found relief from this noxious atmosphere in the escapades the two of us enjoyed. But still, she watched the young lad like a hawk which, from its aerial heights, prepares her sharp talons to snatch up her prey as soon as occasion arises. He, Mohammed, was Salha's child, and the enmity she felt for Salha she transferred to him. Failing to find any genuine misdemeanour with which she could accuse the lad, she often fell to concocting stories about him. To see Abbas reprimanding the young man for something of which he was innocent gave her great relish. Naturally, her husband grew wise to the nature of her stories, but still he went along with Zakiyah, if for nothing else, but to keep the peace. Soon, however, he turned his back on the problem, and let things go on without his interference. It was only when Salha petitioned him – and that was seldom – that he intervened. He still respected her deeply and secretly regretted the day when he had linked his life with his second wife. But, with his head now buried in politics, he cared little for what went on at home, demanding only that he obtain relative peace and quiet among the warring factions.

But this was not always the case, and when he returned home, his head still enveloped in utopian dreams, and found Zakiyah sulking, the divergence between the ideal and the real would be just too much for him. Then, he would break into uncontrollable fits of shouting, bursting upon the household like a tornado raging through a densely populated city. Zakiyah would gather the squealing children around her, pressing them to her quivering breast, more to protect herself than for their safety. From there she remonstrated with Abbas, heedlessly casting accusations at Salha, who looked on silently, waiting for the storm either to burst or pass by. When, finally, it did burst – when the old fellow could no longer restrain his fury – then what was previously an ugly scene turned utterly repulsive. Taking up Zakiyah by the hair, he would throw her forcefully against the wall, which responded with a dull thud, indifferent to the damage he might inflict on her. The poor woman fell to the ground, and again he grabbed hold of her, repeating the same action over again. He struck her, beat her about the body, all the time shouting fearsome threats. When his anger was sated, she would then be thrust in with the animals, where she was commanded to remain. There she would sleep. If she wished to behave like an animal, so Abbas urged, she might as well live with them. All the while Salha and Mohammed remained motionless. Neither cared for Zakiyah, and the old fellow only glanced menacingly at them both, but never went any further. His conscience would not have allowed him.

On those occasions when these grisly scenes occurred, Zakiyah would remain deeply subdued for some time. Her spitefulness abated; her cavilling subsided; and, most importantly, her watchful eye over Mohammed and the other children turned inward upon itself, where it no doubt caressed its woes in balms of self-pity. These periods persisted for a number of days, sometimes extending to a week. Ultimately, however, Zakiyah would once again find her centre of gravity and the whole business would begin anew.

23

Following our visit to the cinema, Mohammed and I avoided being together on our own for some time. I was fearful that I might say or do something that would place an obstacle in the way of our friendship, and put me to shame. I do not know whether the interest I received from boys, stemmed from me being a woman, or from them being gay, or simply from their sexual frustration due to the separation of the sexes. In a society where there was more integration, perhaps no one would seek to indulge this 'unnatural practice.' For the most fearful punishment awaited anyone rumoured to have indulged in such practices, whether innocent or otherwise. Nothing, in fact, attracted greater ignominy. In some places it was even a capital offence; but it was the shame, the irreparable shame that would attend the subject of such an accusation that was the worst of it – a fate even worse than death to an Arabic man.

But with the progress of time, and the function of mind that suppresses what is not congruent with the will's intention, we became more complacent towards the urges that, I'm sure, we both felt. And while the relationship between Zakiyah and Abbas gave rise to much unhappiness, that between Mohammed and I burgeoned like a tall tree in springtime that first puts forth its delightful blossom, casting a healthy fragrance over everything within its compass, and then, all at once, bursts into sweet and wholesome fruit. But, all the time, as we enjoyed those light and ethereal delights our friendship yielded, deep below, like the hidden and ever-branching roots of that same tree, a more subterranean development was taking place, a frightening yet alluring intimacy that at first evaded our consciousness, but soon made its presence felt by its very strangeness. It was this intimacy that had sought to manifest itself that day at the Rex, when it was interrupted by the usher's timely appearance; and that would slowly, albeit with some interruption, gain increasing ascendency and acceptance. Each time we met, we allowed ourselves to go a little further without, however, acknowledging, be it verbally or otherwise, what we could both clearly see would be the object of these intimacies.

As we both attended the same university, Mohammed and I saw one another every day. After college we would head off to some ice cream parlour, bar or to find a shaded niche beneath the awning of one of Baghdad's many tea shops. No one would have believed we came from such diverse backgrounds. In humour, outlook and idealism we both shared common ground. We laughed at the same things, had similar interests in music, and found the same subjects entertaining. Yet, this did not stop Mohammed making jokes at the expense of my flared trousers and flyaway collar.

'You look like someone out of a western pop group – one of those hippies. . .' he would taunt, '. . . wait till you're a bit older. You'll laugh when you see a photograph of yourself.'

I was too considerate to remind him of the tattered outfit he was wearing; in terms of quality, there was little between

116

it and the shoddy clothes he wore that first day he attended school with me.

When a university trip was announced – an excursion to Iraq's southernmost city, Basra, the country's only port – we had no scruple about being the sole occupants of our own room. For there was little interaction between us and our classmates, and we frequently declined invitations to join them in their pastimes, remaining in one another's company perhaps too frequently than was prudent to avoid suspicion. At a time when the other boys talked of nothing but women, and carried heavily folded images of Western actresses in their pockets, our disinterest attracted comment. I'm sure they spoke of us behind our backs; it could all be seen in their glances if only one looked for it. But what Mohammed and I shared together was worth more than their approbation, so I didn't care much what they thought, and didn't alert my friend, who was often hopelessly oblivious to their innuendos, when I became aware of their scorn. After all, we had done nothing wrong.

It was during the college field trip that things took that final step from where there could be no turning back. That most tiresome day had been occupied with visiting a local container operation, taking meticulous detail of the destination and origin of the freight that went in and out of the port, the intricate working of the oil export business, how many barrels were dispatched per day. . . and so on and so forth. You can imagine how utterly tedious these details must have been to Mohammed and I. Indeed, we just could not understand how all this was taken so seriously by other students. How could anything be worthy of such gravity so far as the world was concerned?

'How tedious is the business of life!' Mohammed cried.

'They act as if there was nothing else but barrels and crates!' I added sardonically.

117

After all, wasn't all this bustle just a matter of putting food on the table and roofs over people's heads? Surely that could be achieved with a lot less effort!

How pleased we thus were when we escaped from this artificial world, which sought to overwhelm us in its cardboard embrace, and return to the pure air of our own company! We straight away made for the promenade that skirts the water's edge, and purchased a couple of bottles of beer from Basra Hotel.

Looking out at the deep murmuring sapphire waves, my friend commented:

'It's like a passage to another world!'

'From here. . .' I added, '. . . the water joins the Gulf, and, thousands of miles beyond, merges into the Arabian Sea.'

Like the sun as it hovers overhead, my friend looked on, as if absorbing the ocean's superfluity, which would then rain down upon his imagination when he returned home.

'Come on,' I interrupted, 'finish your drink. We'll take a walk along the front.'

Basra is a place of infinite beauty. Chiefly, it is known for its abundance of dates, which are shipped all over the world, but for us Iraqis, it is the Beirut of the Gulf. Not that one expects to see expensive yachts moored along the water's edge! But it has that inimitable holiday feeling; a lengthy and very beautiful promenade flanked with newly built hotels, lush date palms, and a population of extremely warm and generous citizens. We haltingly traversed the front, frequenting many of the open-air bars, and consumed a little too much beer. A delightful heaviness suffused my feet, which made my torso and upper limbs feel light and aerated. If these feelings could only be sustained indefinitely, I would have had no scruple about abjuring the serious business of life for the blissful feeling of unity thus engendered between myself and the world about me! How gregarious a person becomes; how joyful beneath a clear blue sky with a few bottles of beer flowing through their veins!

Making our way rather precariously along the promenade, Mohammed and I stumbled clumsily into one another, laughing at the phantoms of our imagination, and creating a most impolite hubbub that both amused and embarrassed those about us. Occasionally, when our feet refused to carry us further, we sat upon the concrete parapet that separates the water's edge from the promenade. Here we joyfully contemplated the Shat Al-Arab. Staring at that immense blue, I almost felt it to be a part of me, an extension of my body. Mohammed wanted to order more beer, but well I knew that a joy so elevated quickly reaches its maximum before it becomes immovable and begins to regress.

At its far end, we left the promenade and ambled across to the old town of Basra, from where we made our way back to our hostel room. Much of the mirth that characterised our behaviour only moments before remained outside with the shutting of the door. It was a serious moment in which we gazed into one another's eyes with an intensity unobstructed by inhibition. We were both virgins and far from adept in the dictates of love; but somehow we let our instinct overcome our ineptitude, and embraced one another. Our lips met in a passionate, raw kiss, offset by a delicate savour of tenderness. Then the damn that hitherto brooked our feelings all at once came crashing down, its waters throwing aside any further obstacles that stood in its way. Herein was an intensity I had never experienced before; a demanding, autocratic, and overwhelming surge of passion that refused to be any longer retarded. When our love-making finally ended, it was as if we had been possessed by a power beyond ourselves, a jin or spirit. For this glorious interlude would be construed thus by anyone who knew of our actions.

But it must forever remain an unfathomable enigma why our compatriots regarded these innocent pleasures with such opprobrium. Why the two of us shouldn't express our love for one another, just as a couple; that a little more love should be manifested in a world where suffering is so prevalent; how can this be wrong? It was not so in the old days, when the ancient poets expatiated on the delights of this love now prohibited. They referred to their male paramours as 'pretty boys,' a word no longer found in the Arabic language; and instead of 'homosexual,' that of 'deviant' is the most euphemistic term that can be applied to the act, its colloquial concomitants being a mixture of the grossest and most vulgar abuse. These expletives are so ugly as to defy expression.

24

As the final effects of the alcohol dissipated, I became increasingly aware of the enormity of what Mohammed and I had done. I was frightened, and didn't know what I could do to extricate myself from this shameful act. I felt like an outcast, somehow shut off from the moral approbation of society. No one would forgive this, and standing alone is a fearful thing. I panicked; I wanted to run away and never see my friend again. Then, I could just continue as if nothing had happened. It might even have been a good thing to start a fight with him, to prove to myself, at least, that this mess had been none of my doing. It was all his fault. Mohammed had led me astray. I hated him; I wasn't one of those deviants that everyone loathed! It was all his fault. Oh God! What would everyone think? I could imagine my father looking at me with his pleasant magnanimous features. He didn't deserve this!

Mohammed still lay asleep beside me. So sound was his repose that one would have believed him innocent of any sin. He even snored faintly, as if to irk me on purpose. I paced backwards and forwards, until at length my friend's apparent indifference made me angry. No, I'll not let him sleep!

'Wake up! Wake up!' I shouted, 'what are we going to do? What are we going to do?'

I threw back the shutters, suffusing the room with a penetrating light. My friend's eyes slowly opened as the brightness infiltrated his sleep. Shielding his face with his hand, a soft smile informed his lips.

'Well, what are we going to do Mohammed?'

'What's wrong?' he urged faintly, rubbing the sleep from his eyes, caressing his aching forehead. Sitting upright in bed he began:

'Has something happened?'

'What do you mean – has something happened? Don't you remember what we did last night?'

He pondered for a moment, while he recalled the previous day and how it had ended.

'Oh!' he began, 'it was quite a day, wasn't it! What with all that drinking!'

'You know what I'm referring to Mohammed – what we did last night.'

He looked a little hurt.

'You regret what we did?'

'Yes, no – I don't know!' I replied, continuing after a pause, 'Anyway, that's not the point. What are we going to do? I won't be able to look anyone in the face ever again! O God!'

I clasped my hands to my face in despair. Mohammed stepped from the bed and put his arms around me.

'Don't!' I cried, recoiling with disgust, 'This has got to stop! We can't see each other ever again!'

Mohammed took me by the arms, holding them tightly so that I could not break free.

'Listen to me,' he demanded, 'Listen to me. We have done nothing wrong – do you know that? We have done nothing wrong.'

He stared into my eyes, but I averted my gaze.

'Look at me . . . Susan. Look at me. What we did was not wrong – you understand that, don't you? Ever since we were children, I've looked at you, accepted you, as a girl.'

'But, Mohammed, I don't know if I even accept myself? Maybe I'm wrong?'

'You're not wrong! You know you're not wrong! You can feel it, deep inside!'

'Oh Mohammed, but everyone says it's wrong!'

'Have you harmed anyone? Have you caused anyone pain?' he continued, 'Well, have you?'

'No . . . but I don't know. I just can't make myself believe that what we did wasn't shameful!'

'I know it's hard, Susan – and don't you forget who you are; don't let anyone tell you who you are – but it won't always be so. You'll come to terms with it eventually.'

He let my arms go.

'You're right . . .' I quickly rejoined, '. . . it won't happen again. We must never give ourselves the opportunity.'

'No, Susan, there's no turning back now. You'll see that I'm right.'

'How can you be so calm? It's even worse for you. If your family found out what you'd done . . .'

'I know,' he replied, 'but they won't ever find out. No one will ever know – it's just between us.'

'But people will be able to see it in our eyes. They'll know we're guilty!'

'No they won't,' Mohammed reassured me, 'No one will see anything if we don't want them to see.'

After the events of that fateful night, things had become quite different between us. Our conversation was of the most superficial kind; we spoke of our college work, made uninteresting remarks about the scenery, and commented on the humidity that characterises the weather in Basra. We avoided returning to our hostel room until as late as possible, and then we would immediately get into our respective beds, say 'goodnight' to one another, and turn the light out. Yet, I slept very badly, and until the early hours of the morning stared blankly at the ceiling. I know that Mohammed was doing the same, as he always snored lightly when he slept, but now, but for the occasional sigh, he remained silent.

If previously we had appeared aloof, now our paranoid reticence, even frailty, made us stand out among our classmates. We quickly became the object of their open mockery and suspicion, which we both did our best to ignore. But this was no longer possible when one of their number, Hassan in fact, referred to Mohammed and I as 'poofs.'

'What did you say?' I demanded.

'Nothing, I didn't say anything,' Hassan timidly replied. No doubt he thought we were too unmanly to stand up for ourselves. But I wasn't having any more of it.

'What did you say?' I repeated.

'I called you "poofs" – so what you going to do about it, sissy girl! Don't think we don't know what you are; there's something wrong with you. You're a sissy!'

With that I fell upon him, releasing all those suppressed feelings that had been accumulating over the past few days. Another boy appeared and grappled with Hassan, as Mohammed grappled with me.

'He's gone crazy!' Hassan shouted, smoothing his ruffled hair down with his hand.

'The pair of you . . .' he continued, '. . . you're bloody nutters!'

I had lost control of myself, and now regretted my action. His assertion had cut me to the quick.

'They know – I told you they'd find out' I muttered to Mohammed.

At the close of the week, we boarded the train that took us back to Baghdad.

25

Mohammed was correct – there was no turning back. What my reasoning and prejudice could not construe otherwise than as reprehensible, my senses, or rather the feelings I had for Mohammed, propelled me in the opposite direction. However much I deplored and sought to dissociate myself from what had occurred, I could not find the will to oppose what one part of me felt to be innocent. The absolute secrecy demanded by our actions made us keenly aware of the necessity of finding a place to meet where there could be no chance of discovery. We ceased loitering around the city after college and instead went directly to our respective homes in Al-Za'franiya. No longer was it enough for us to sit around in bars or cafés or watch a film at the Rex. It all seemed so much wasted time. There was only a single place that would serve our purpose, a place we had frequented much in our childhood and, a few months earlier, visited as a matter of nostalgia. That place was the old watermill. At first, we met once, or at most twice, a week, fearing that these recurrent trips, if anyone should notice, would give rise to suspicion. After all, what could two people of our age be doing hanging around a dilapidated mill? For nothing remains hidden in

Al-Za'franiya. Wherever a person went, someone would always be aware. Gossip is as old as human communities, whether born of malice, boredom or just idle curiosity. So we watched our steps very closely; left our homes separately, and absented ourselves for a minimum of time.

Abbas, Mohammed's father, endeavoured to encourage his son to get involved in local politics. He wasn't a man to be easily contradicted, and notwithstanding my friend's petitions to the contrary, the old fellow expected to see him attending the concrete hall, where discussion took place, every evening. Yet it was not difficult for Mohammed to escape for the hour or two necessary for our assignations. The hall was very crowded, and the young man's absence would probably go unnoticed. Of course, I didn't have to endure such restrictions. Father was a man who understood the need for solitude, and when I explained to him that I found it greatly beneficial studying alongside the Tigris, he had no difficulty understanding me. When he saw me leaving the villa with a pile of books tucked snugly under my arm, he could not have been more satisfied. But like every object of human striving, the frequency of our meetings became woefully inadequate. What had begun as a twice-weekly affair ultimately became the occupation of anything up to five nights in every seven. Not that on each occasion we indulged in our love-making. Sometimes we would just talk about the future; how we'd emigrate to the West when our studies were completed; or we'd just watch the beautiful scenery.

At the time of our meetings – it was always sunset – when the orb of the sun slowly descended on her journey to the antipodes, and threw a ruddy, orange glow over the Tigris and the surrounding areas, the view was magnificent. Everything took on the hue of the sun's rays, absorbing, displaying, and reflecting them according to the quality of each element. The Tigris twinkled with the tremor of her opaque, incessantly gliding waters, adding a hint of deep brown to its splendour; the earth took on a uniform evanescence, speckled with knotty patches of dark brush; the mill, from its lofty position, threw off a burning orange that seared against the sheaths of shadow that lay about the old building.

Such was the scene before me as I secreted myself within the little niche within the mill's precincts that could be observed only from across the darkening waters. For I always arrived first – it was how we planned our meetings. During that time, I often pondered what I would say to Mohammed. I never arranged for things to develop in any particular way, and I'm sure my friend felt the same. It wasn't as if I thought 'today we'll make love.' Nothing of that sort ever crossed my mind. When love came, it was a purely spontaneous affair. I liked to tell myself that it had taken me off guard, that I could not be held responsible for whatever occurred. It helped to mitigate my continuous, albeit lessening, feelings of shame.

But soon I would become anxious, and repeatedly look at my watch. When time seemed to cease in its progress, and the minute hand remained stationary, I focused on the larger second hand. At least it was moving! Time brings everything, I mused, and so it too would bring Mohammed to me. When he was late, I was consumed with doubt, and wondered whether he had decided not to come. Heaving a sigh of despondency, I would fall back onto the steps on which I sat, their brittle resistance calling up images of mortality in my mind. These steps, which rose about six feet from the bank, were constructed of blocks fashioned at a time when ancient Babylon was still a power. Yet, here they lay, as if on their first day; here they would remain, long after I and Mohammed were gone, perhaps even after there were no humans to inhabit the earth. A busy swirl of delicate interstices marked their tawny surface. I traced out the figures with my fingers, striving to make sense of these rough hieroglyphs. Were these striations not akin to those that pass across man's forehead as he ages? Did these blocks not exhibit some semblance of sentience in their aged demeanour?

And then Mohammed would arrive, often out of breath. Straight away I would forget my concerns and, as if transported into another world, throw my arms about him and kiss his cheeks. He would utter his excuses; explain how he had escaped from his father's watchful eyes; and how he'd make sure he got away earlier on the morrow. But, of course, the same thing would happen the next day. Yet, all this prevarication and mystique served only to heighten the pleasure we shared in the brief time allowed us.

26

'Look. . .' Mohammed began, 'look what I've brought.'

It was just another of our meetings at the watermill. Suspended over my friend's right shoulder was a mono cassette-recorder, one of those top-loading, rectangular devices popular with teenagers at the time. He drew the machine around to the front of his body and pressed the play button. A thin, rather metallic sound issued from the machine. It was the music from Tchaikovsky's Swan Lake. I threw myself into his arms and we danced the black swan scene in pas de duex. Despite my initial elation, I was frightened that someone might see or hear us, however remote the setting. I'm sure Mohammed enjoyed seeing my face contorted into a worried grimace.

'Let's go inside, upstairs. No one will be able to see us there.'

We ascended the rickety ladder, carefully avoiding the missing runs.

'Nothing ever changes up here. It's as if time has no power over this place.'

Mohammed put his cassette-recorder down, the music still playing, and moved closer towards me. What followed was one of those passionate exchanges, too mundane now to be of extraordinary significance, yet too ineffable to be articulated in merely physical terms.

The shrill creaking of the old mill door closing on its hinges cut into our love-making. We lifted our heads, taut with anxiety.

'What was that?' I whispered.

'Oh, it's just the old door. It's got a life of its own. . . don't worry!'

I had grown accustomed to accepting his reassurances – perhaps it was a form of vicarious complacency – and didn't give the sound another thought. Unbeknown to us, at that moment, the figure of a woman in a black abiya, covering her from head to foot, hastily exited the mill door and scurried away rapidly alongside the wall. Her heart was pounding violently, her breath broken and intermittent. It was Zakiyah, that watchful, suspicious creature, who couldn't resist seeking out mischief. Creeping like a stealthy sneak-thief beneath the swaying ears of barley, hiding behind the date palms, she had been following Mohammed and I over the last several of his visits. Until that day she had not found the courage to enter the old mill, from the ground floor of which a clear view into the ceiling's aperture could be descried. But now she knew everything. Even if she could not have seen us, the sound we made was as unique as it was unmistakable.

Upon leaving the mill, Mohammed and I walked slowly back towards the suburb, reminiscing over what we considered 'the old days.' Sometimes we laughed; at other times a subtle melancholy infected our discourse. Everything gains a subtle, alluring mystique as it falls into the unrecoverable abyss of the past; even those unhappy, tearful moments when we thought life could never get worse appear detached from the suffering that actuated them. It is as if we looked on objectively, wondering how we could ever have been concerned, why we fought madly, like a man forcefully bound in a straight-jacked, against situations which, in themselves, were of little consequence. But then we remember that the past we look on is a past where we no longer are; that if repeated, we'd do exactly the same thing, and so fight against our chains once more.

Both of us, as we walked home, gazed at the ground. It was only a short distance before we would have to leave one another and travel our respective paths. Only the shrill cry of cicadas and the cooing of a few late pigeons, coupled with the subdued wash of the gentle waters lovingly lapping the banks, enriched the silence. It was now dark, and the vast awning of tiny stars reached across the convex heavens. I looked furtively at Mohammed's profile; he appeared an exemplary human being. Inhabiting that ephemeral period that separates youth from manhood, Mohammed's features hinted at a graceful, nascent beauty about to burst forth like a blown rose upon the cusp of life's springtide. His skin was pale, smooth and flexible, much unlike the tardy, charred features of his compeers. Sprinkled lovingly across satin cheeks, a fine lawn of golden down clung, intensifying into bristles around his strong saffron lips. His nose was of a medium width, gently narrowing in its ascent, where it met the curve of his ample brow, upon which soft, dark curls coiled like so many pythons lowering from a dense tree top.

We uttered our rather subdued goodbyes, and Mohammed set off slowly as if without a care in the world, before looking back briefly and disappearing into the darkness. I remained motionless, my body pulsating with adrenalin. By turns I felt deeply troubled, profoundly humiliated, and wonderfully elated. The sound of that creaking door kept repeating in my head. Could anyone have seen us? Surely out here, in the darkness, in an attic moreover, it couldn't be possible.

27

Upon reaching home I went straight up to my room and sat at my desk. I tried to concentrate on my college work, but it was of no use. I couldn't stop thinking about that creaking mill door. Its eerie sound kept repeating inside my head. I heard steps outside my room, and the door opened. It was Zaid.

'Can't you knock before you come in?'

'You're in real trouble, Sami. What have you been up to? Abbas is at the door waving a pistol in the air and demanding to see you!'

I flushed, as if a current of electricity passed through my body.

'I . . . don't know. I haven't done anything . . . What's he saying?'

Zaid led me onto the landing.

'Come and listen, but make sure they don't see you.'

I could make out some broken fragments of Abbas's raucous and angry voice. He was furious. What I heard was enough to convince me that he knew about Mohammed and I. Yet, it couldn't have been him who had seen us at the mill, because he would have gone for us straight away.

So, there was someone else involved, someone responsible for that creaking door.

Just as a cornered animal sometimes runs straight into the jaws of its predator to expedite a fearful necessity, so too I decided that I would rush downstairs and confront Abbas's accusations; better to get everything over with, I thought, whatever the consequences. But Zaid grabbed hold of my arm.

'What do you think you're doing? I don't know what you've done, but if you go down there now, you'll be in serious trouble.' He paused for a moment.

'I know . . .' he continued, '. . . Go upstairs onto the roof. Lock the door behind you.'

I could see the wisdom of his words, and sped up the stairs without further hesitation, locked the door behind, and ascended the narrow staircase that led to the roof.

'I'm done for,' I muttered to myself.

Zaid's pigeons warbled indifferently from their enclosure. In profound anxiety I paced backward and forwards, cursing the weakness that had made me submit to my inclinations. Occasionally, I glanced over the edge of the room to see if Abbas was still at the door.

Climbing over the low parapet that surrounded the roof, I grabbed hold of some overhanging branches of a eucalyptus tree, sprung onto the main trunk, and shimmied to the ground.

Out on the dirt track, my spirited, frantic running – it was my intention to get to Mohammed before he could return home – attracted the stray dogs that scavenged through the suburb. They barked hoarsely, vociferously, skidding on the dust as they set off on my heels. The heavy thud of my feet combined with the barking of the dogs caught the attention of Mohammed as he was just pacing nonchalantly towards the hut. He stopped, looked for where the sound was issuing, and straight away caught sight of me. Panting with exhaustion, I howled:

133

'We've been seen! We've been seen! Your father's at my house. They're going to kill us!'

'What?' he cried, 'We've . . .'

'Yes, we've been seen! That creaking door – I told you! We've got to go. Follow me!''Where?'

'Just follow, we're going to the city. There's a bus to Baghdad at eight. I've got some money. We're getting on it!'

Mohammed followed on my heels, all the time looking behind him. He didn't say anything. For the first time in his life, he seemed to be speechless with fear. As we left the suburb, we briefly paused for breath, and gazed backwards over our tracks. All that could be seen was a small row of lights coming from the teachers' villas. Perhaps at this moment Abbas's hut in the village was in an uproar, his family chasing around hysterically, looking for him. And my father . . . what would he be saying now? But out here, beyond the suburb, on the road to Baghdad, everything was silent. An old red single-decker bus pulled up, its breaks screeching. The door flung open. We jumped in. The driver looked on suspiciously while I fumbled with the small change in my pocket.

It was a that moment that, stepping from the darkness into the bright lights of the bus, that I felt the full extent of the void into which I had stepped. I wanted to curl up in my bed, awaken late in the morning, and find everything in its pristine, monotonous regularity. What this mad dash would ultimately achieve was merely a delay of the inevitable; we couldn't simply cut loose from our families, take up selling boiled chickpeas for a living, and sleep in a dirty corner somewhere. Eventually, we would have to return, and the whole business would be waiting for us, just as we left it.

Occasionally the bus stopped to pick up a passenger; at this time of evening there were not many people travelling from the suburbs towards the city. Most of the seats around us remained empty. Outside, a few cars passed in the opposite direction; beyond the road, a few scattered lights marking the existence of isolated dwellings. Mohammed had not said a word since we left Al-Za'franiya. He gazed lifelessly out of the window, his features motionless, his eyes, vacant. The expression on his lips was one of severity. I didn't know what to say to him, but I needed his comforting words now more than ever before.

Less than an hour later the bus terminated in the centre of Baghdad. Like the bus itself, the terminal was partially deserted. I couldn't help but think that we had done something utterly crazy.

'What are we going to do now?' Mohammed urged me.

'We'll go to Al-Rasheed Street . . .' I replied '. . . maybe we can find that fellow we met outside my grandfather's shop.'

'But what will we say to him at this time of night?'

'Let's not worry about that for now. Come on.'

Quickly traversing the slowly emptying thoroughfares, we reached Al-Rasheed Street. Even the ubiquitous chickpea sellers and vendors had departed for the day. The clanging of the brass market had fallen into silence. The clamorous bustle had concluded in stillness. All that could now be heard was the grating of iron shutters being pulled down over a few late-night shop fronts. Only the subdued light from a handful of restaurants and cafes cast a luminescence over the pavements. I thought again about the prudence of looking to the old merchant for a place to stay. He was too close to my grandfather, and I couldn't take the risk of our prospective host telling him of our predicament.

'We can't go to that fellow's house,' I announced to a disappointed Mohammed.

'Why not? Where are we going to go then?'

'I've got an idea – just follow me.'

28

Towards the end of Al-Rasheed Street, we entered a narrow alleyway, leading into a badly lit courtyard, littered with broken tea chests and heaps of rubbish.

'There it is!' I cried, pointing towards an open doorway, a sign above the threshold reading: '*Hadji Mahdi, Merchant of Fine Imported Fabrics.*'

The sign was partially lit at one end by a flickering bulb, illuminating the dilapidated condition of the lettering. From the expression on his face, Mohammed didn't appear to like the look of things, and hung back as I moved towards the doorway.

'What's wrong?' I asked.

'Are you sure you know what you're doing? I don't like the look of that place!'

'I know Hadji Mahdi. I met him when I worked with grandfather. He owns a little place out the back where he lets his customers from Basra stay. I'm sure he'll let us sleep there.'

Not completely satisfied, Mohammed nevertheless followed me in.

Within the shabby vestibule was a large oak desk, heaped almost to the ceiling with old ledgers; opposite, a huge

136

portmanteau blackened with age (also piled up with old paperwork), sprawled lazily against the wall, like an old resident of the place. The crumbling ceiling and yellowing walls did little to uplift our already low moods; and, if I had not known Hadji, I would not have chosen to enter the room to the left of the vestibule from where muttered conversation could be heard. I grasped the handle, held in place by a single screw, and pushed the door open. Beneath the dense atmosphere of smoke, lay a somewhat unsavoury-looking fellow, sprawled out on a matted rug before me. His hair was heavily pomaded and parted into a slick sheet across his balding head; he wore an unevenly trimmed moustache; and his neglected, greying stubble reached almost to his upper cheek bones. He drew deeply on a battered hurly-burly, releasing a gust of silver smoke up towards the ceiling. Three or four men leaning up against the wall about a foot away sipped at small glasses of arak, a strong Iraqi liqueur made from dates.

'Hello,' I muttered.

The fellow sprawled out on the floor drew himself up on his right elbow, peering intently across the smoky room.

'Good evening,' he replied.

'Is Hadji here?'

'No,' the slurred voice of one of the drunken men interjected, 'he doesn't come here often.'

'We're looking for somewhere to stay the night. We don't have much money, but I can pay you later.'

The features of our interlocutor remained emotionless. Again, I turned to the other man, who was taking a deep draw of a pipe.

'We don't have anywhere else to go. Otherwise, we'll have to sleep in the street.' Mohammed and I looked blankly at one another. Perhaps our anxiety was at that moment distinctly marked on our faces, but having finished propelling a cloud of smoke in the direction of the ceiling, the fellow explained:

'If you haven't anywhere to go, I've an old mattress upstairs. You can sleep on that tonight.'

'Thank you, sir, we'll pay you for it in the morning.'

'There's no need for that. It's on the first floor, right at the top of the stairs.'

'Thank you,' Mohammed added, as we both moved towards the exit.

'Have you eaten anything?'

'Thank you very much,' I replied on behalf of both of us, 'but we're not hungry.'

I found the room indicated. I couldn't push the door open very far, because the mattress the fellow had spoken of was wedged against its interior. When finally we managed to squeeze through the tiny gap, the light from the landing weakly illuminating its interior, we found the entire floor strewn with mattresses. Opposite the door I could make out an old washbasin; a single tap jutted from the wall above, the water dripping rhythmically every five or six seconds. There was nothing else in the room. I looked around to see if Mohammed was still there.

'Go in . . .' he urged, '. . . I'm right behind you.'

The floor creaked under our feet, as we stepped between the mattresses.

'Which one are we supposed to sleep on?'

'I don't like the look of any of them!'

I slept in my clothes that night. It gave me consolation to know that I was ready to go, should anything untoward happen, and, moreover, protected me from the filth-encrusted mattress. Mohammed too remained clothed. We uttered a few words to one another – mere trivialities considering the uncertainty we had disposed ourselves to – and I slowly fell into a half-conscious state between sleep and wakefulness, where awareness of the outside world persists, yet painted in surreal colours. Passing across this soporific stage, I was aware of the exterior lights being extinguished from the shop; heavy footsteps traversing the wooden staircase; and the door that opened onto the room being successively thrown open and shut as each occupant took up their place on a mattress. The tap continued dripping away, sometimes gathering its tiny droplets together into one large drop, that varied its accustomed rhythm. Soon the last remnant of consciousness was smothered, and I fell asleep.

29

Early the next morning at sunrise, I was awoken by the familiar sound of the muezzin, crying 'Allah Akbar,' the sonorous voice rang out from a loud speaker at the top of the minaret. It was a call for morning prayer, reminding the faithful that it is better to pray than to sleep. I looked around the room, now partially illuminated by the sun's first rays. The mattresses were already empty.

'Mohammed, are you awake?' I whispered.

'Yes,' he replied, 'I've been awake for the last hour. I just kept thinking about what we've done, running off like that. Do you think we did the right thing?'

'What else could we do?' I replied sententiously, gazing up at the smoke-stained ceiling, 'your father would have killed you!'

'But you didn't need to come with me – you would have been alright at home. Your father's not like mine.'

He glanced at me knowingly, seeking some words of reassurance.

'Do you think my life would be any better if I'd have stayed behind?' Mohammed smiled a strained smile, unable to disguise the frown which tipped the extremities of his lips.

I jumped onto my feet, throwing off these heavy thoughts.
'Come on. It's early and we've got plenty to do!'

I trudged across the mattresses and filled my hands with
cold water from the washbasin, splashing it onto my stiff
features. For a moment I felt invigorated.

'Let's go!' Mohammed was soon on his feet and, forcing
aside the heavy atmosphere that threatened to encompass us,
quickly seemed to fall victim to the ebullience I was feeling.
He stood before a small shard of broken glass that hung upon
the wall, vainly attempting to smooth down the hair around
the crown of his head, and then took a drink from the tap.

Almost on tiptoe, we quietly left the room and shut the
door slowly behind us. The fellows whom that previous
evening looked somewhat worse for ware, were now up and
about, as sprightly as spring lambs, hauling heavy loads
across the courtyard. I recognised the man who had been
smoking the pipe.

'Thank you, sir. The mattress was fine.'

'I didn't think we'd be seeing you this early!'

Mohammed and I thanked him for his hospitality, and
departed.

We entered the meandering lanes that compose the body
of the souk. Within the next hour, each side of the narrow
walkway would be decorated with a multitude of brightly
coloured goods. Even now the merchants and traders were
hard at work, some laying out multicoloured spices – deep
reds, mustard yellows and sage greens – in hollow basins,
emitting splendid odours of amber and saffron that swept
across souk; others wielded large wooden poles, upon which
they hooked up rugs, suspending them on hooks above and
around the entrance to their shops. A small film of steam
began to rise from the chi-chee's samovar.

I wanted to see if grandfather was in his shop before leaving
the souk. Surely, I thought, if he were still standing there,

speaking with his customers, things couldn't have been that bad. The sounds of the brass and silver smiths indicated that Mohammed and I had reached Al-Rasheed Street.

'What are we doing here? We've travelled more or less in a circle!'

'I know! I just wanted to see my grandfather before we go.'

'But I thought you didn't want your grandfather to see us?' Mohammed queried, visibly confused.

'I don't. That's why we need to keep out of sight.'

Seeing that hard-working man in his shop, everything running apparently as normal, gave me a sense that all was not as bad as it seemed. Fouad was there, rushing about as always – he had now gone completely grey, although he was only about twenty years my senior – the same faces appeared at grandfather's counter as when I was a child; the same cups of tea that had been consumed a thousand times were once again consumed. And, most importantly, I saw my grandfather's face occasionally light up with a smile, as one of his customers uttered some happy expression or anecdote. I felt the warmth emitted by that smile as if I stood there in his place.

Mohammed's attention was directed to the shop adjoining that of my father's – Fadil the barber. Beside a narrow red door, a dusty pane of glass partially concealed, partially revealed, the interior of this antiquated shop. Nothing had changed since it had first opened its doors, when my grandfather was himself a young man. Three or four timeworn prints decorated the walls – an actor from the 1950s; a scene from old Baghdad; Mecca during Haj. Small dark patches indicated where a number of similar images, now lost or broken, must have hung. At the far end of the room, beneath a coat hook from which hung half-a-dozen strops and a large pair of scissors, was a dish of syrup, dotted with flies. Suspended idly from the ceiling, a dark wooden fan with

142

gilded trim mocked the barber on summer days by refusing to work. Sometimes it sprung into activity; but most of the time it remained motionless, choosing only to work when it was good and ready. Occasionally, it would be galvanised into action by a solid swat with a broom handle.

Fadil had spent much of his life within the shop. No one could actually remember the time when the barber's shop had not been there. In my grandfather's day, Baghdad barbers were much respected. Not only did they shave their customers, but they could also pull out an aching molar or conduct minor surgery. He was a squat, spare man, the ample girth of his belly making up for his diminutive height. Around his paunch was fastened a blue cotton apron over the top of a red chequered shirt. He had a 'horse shoe' of greying hair that covered an otherwise smooth head. A serious man, he only became alive when debating politics with his customers. Then they would be aflame with ardour, ready to take on the presidency of Iraq. And his customers were loath to contradict a man who, apart from being a keen frequenter of the opium pipe, waved a razor-sharp blade above their heads to emphasise any point of discussion. Nevertheless, all his customers were profoundly devoted to him, and would have rather predeceased Fadil than have to find another barber they were comfortable with.

'Aren't you hungry?' I asked Mohammed.

'I'm starving!' he replied, smiling.

I pointed to a bubbling cauldron of boiled chickpeas, tended lovingly by a young lad, barely tall enough to see over the front of the mobile stall.

'Those chick peas smell good!' I cried, 'let's get some.'

'Don't be frightened to add more!' I urged the young fellow laughingly, as he tentatively filled our bowls.

Mohammed also laughed, and we fell upon this meagre fare as if it were a rich banquet. A wise man once said that we should always sleep as if upon a bed of feathers; always drink as if quaffing divine nectar; always eat as if at the table of a king. I was beginning to understand what he meant by this. Calling over a passing chi-chee, I asked for two strong, sweet cups of tea. Despite its being hot, I swigged it down, savouring the sugary aftertaste.

'Another one!' I cried, 'More, Mohammed?'

He was too busy catching up the last few chick-peas out of his bowl, which he held close to his face, to notice what I was saying. The morning chill was giving way to the thirsty sunlight when we entered the main square of Medan. I had plans for that day. I wanted to show Mohammed a part of Baghdad he'd never seen before. We took the bus to Zohra Park.

'You said you've been to this club before?'

'Oh, we used to come here most weekends. My father has been a member since it opened.'

'But what's it like?'

'You'll soon find out. We're nearly there . . .'

30

A neat outline of palm trees delineated the perimeter of the country club. Mantling the lower portion of the foliage, a thick growth of eucalyptus trees concealed a wire mesh fence that prevented non-members entering the grounds.

'There it is!' I shouted excitedly.

'Wow! It's magnificent!' Mohammed responded.

'You wait till we get inside . . .' I cried, '. . . this is nothing. They've got swimming pools, sun loungers, a bar by the pool – everything you can imagine.'

The bus had dropped us off a hundred yards or so from the club. We sprang along nimbly on our heels, as if without a care. But having spent the night fully clothed on that dodgy mattress, I did feel a little embarrassed to enter the club. All those who visited the club – ex-patriots, my father's middle-class friends – always dressed immaculately. It was the club rules. Whether they'd let us or not hadn't crossed my mind. I might pass muster, but Mohammed was a little threadbare at the best of times. I'd just have to be stubborn, and use my right as a member to invite a guest. So, I pulled my trousers up, tucked in my shirt, and brushed myself down.

'Just leave the talking to me.'

The grounds were fronted by a majestic iron gate that opened automatically to let cars in and out, beside which, a smaller gate, flanked by a porter's lodge, gave entrance to foot visitors (which, admittedly, were very few). The porter, who guarded the gates as if it was a military checkpoint, was an officious, yet polite man, and I knew he'd be out like a shot as soon as Mohammed and I entered the gate. And, true to form, he popped out like a jack-in-the-box before we had closed the gate quietly behind us.

'Good morning!' I uttered confidently.

'Good morning to you, sir. . .' he replied, '. . . what can I do for you, young man?'

He looked me up and down, disdaining even to acknowledge Mohammed. I smiled with affected aplomb.

'We want to come in, sir. Just to have a look around, a glass of beer.'

My request didn't seem to have registered with him, so I paused, and began again.

'You know me sir – my father's always been a member here.'

He rolled himself onto the heels of his flawlessly polished shoes, so as to appear taller and more important than he was.

'Of course, I know your father, a fine man. You're Sami, aren't you?'

'Yes sir . . .' I replied, '. . . and this is my guest,' I added, gesturing to Mohammed.

The porter attempted to smile courteously, and finally uttered:

'Welcome to the club!'

Passing the lodge, Mohammed caught up beside me.

'What an odd fellow!' he snickered, 'is he always like that?'

'Always! Don't look back – he'll be watching us!'

To left and right, deep green lawns, strewn with scores of ever-active sprinklers, were laid out in the Western fashion, giving a crisp, moist feel to the atmosphere. Edged with neatly trimmed box and yellow wild roses, the lawns terminated, some hundred metres or so from the porter's lodge, on both sides of the road that divided them, into sweeping semi-circles, filled with small stones, and elongated into an oval, giving vehicles space to manoeuvre. Beyond, the colonial pastel-orange façade of the splendid clubhouse, watched over by magnificent date palms at either side of the entrance that shot high up into the faultless sky, awed the visitor into submission. Mohammed was clearly intimidated.

'I can't go in there!'

'Just follow me.'

Two doorman, smartly dressed, blithely swung the large polished glass doors open.

'Good morning young sirs.'

Mohammed beamed at them, all the time smiling and nodding maniacally, nearly tripping on my heels as he did so. We strode nimbly and without pause through the air-conditioned foyer; and then through a large dimly-lit lounge where several members were quietly importuned by a throng of staff who milled about, and out the rear door. Here the vista opened onto a huge patio with a swimming pool sunk in the middle. Bathers lay relaxing on sun loungers under white parasols; some read newspapers or sipped drinks, served by a dapper fellow wearing a bright red bow-tie who issued periodically from a bar topped with palm fronds; others sat at the edge of the pool, dangling their feet in its warm water. A subtle medley of Western music quietly played in the background.

'It looks great!' gasped Mohammed. 'I didn't think we had anything like this in Baghdad!'

'Let's sit down over there, otherwise we'll draw attention to ourselves.'

The barman came over to us.

'What would you like sir?'

'Do we have enough money?' whispered Mohammed.

'Have whatever you like – it all goes on a tab here – we don't have to pay anything.'

Mohammed perused the leather-backed drinks menu.

'I never knew there were so many different drinks! What're these?'

He underscored the heading of a list of liqueurs with the tip of his index finger.

'May I take your order sirs?' the waiter repeated impatiently.

'Let's just have a beer. . .' I suggested, '. . . two Farida's please waiter.'

The waiter briskly returned, and removed the caps nimbly and artfully from the bottles, a creamy foam escaping down their chilled sides. The odour was delicious. Mohammed took up a bottle, and drew off a huge gulp.

'That's good!' he announced, leaning back heavily into his chair.

'Slow down,' I warned, 'you'll get drunk!'

'I could drink this stuff like water and it'd never make me drunk!' he urged, taking another deep swig and drawing a small platter of nuts and crisps towards him.

'We'll see,' I retorted knowingly.

I too took a large swig from my bottle, perhaps subconsciously not wanting to be outdone by this young tyro, and sank back into my recliner with a self-satisfied air. Soon I fell into a vacant reverie, and watched the delicate breeze tickle the fringe of the parasol.

Very quickly the beer made its mark on Mohammed's features. His eyes began to glaze over, their stillness exhibiting the appearance of the artificial eyes of a waxwork; his features quiescent, glowing with that summer calmness that

148

precedes the raucous volubility of the inebriate. It was not long before I felt my legs becoming heavy and torpid, as the alcohol traced a limbering path through my body. I called the waiter over and confidently asked for two more beers.

'Paradise must be something like this,' murmured my companion.

'Do they have beer in heaven?' I laughed.

'Perhaps then. . .' he continued, his words unencumbered, yet halting, '. . . perhaps heaven's a feeling rather than a place. Perhaps I can simply close my eyes, and there I'll be – in paradise!'

'You're crazy Mohammed!' I cried, raising my bottle.

'To the drunken philosopher!' I toasted.

'I'm not drunk!' Mohammed replied with a slight slur.

He made to rise from his seat, but leaned so heavily on the edge of the table that it was almost overturned. His legs gave way beneath him and he fell backward, chuckling.

'More beer! More beer!'

'Behave yourself! You'll have us thrown out!'

31

Two men seated at the bar rose from their seats and walked over to us.

'Now you've done it! We might as well just get up and leave.'

They were immaculately dressed and puffed away contentedly on thick cigars. Perhaps in their early forties, both were of medium build, one a little taller than other. I could tell they were important customers. They were clean shaven, somewhat handsome in their flawless fine suits that gave them an appearance of great importance. It had not escaped my attention that these same gentleman had, for at least the past hour, been casting furtive glances in our direction. The shorter man took the lead. As he drew nearer, I discerned a somewhat mischievous look in his eyes, that made me feel a little uncomfortable, whilst alleviating the fear that their approach caused. Mohammed chuckled inanely, notwithstanding my attempts to restrain him.

'May we take a seat?' the shorter fellow asked.

'Of course, of course!' Mohammed blurted out, 'Let's have some more beer!'

The two gentlemen sat down, one on either side of the table. The larger one clicked his finger condescendingly in the air 'waiter, four beers.'

Mohammed had clearly had enough by now. I feared for the worse and didn't appreciate this fellow more or less drowning the young man. For all that, it wouldn't do us any harm to forget our troubles for a while.

'To your health!' the mischievous fellow announced.

'To your health!' we all repeated in unison.

'What are you fellows doing here? I don't recall having seen you before!'

'I know this young fellow, Khalil . . .' said the taller of the pair, gesturing towards me, '. . . I have seen you come in here with your parents.'

'That's right, my name's Sami.'

'Yes of course, of course. I'm Aziz, and this is Khalil.'

'And your friend?'

'Mohammed; his name's Mohammed. He's not been here before.'

'Well. . .' urged Aziz, '. . . he certainly looks like he's enjoying himself. Young people should enjoy themselves. When you get older, you have to work, look after your children – then there's nothing but responsibility – never any time for enjoying yourself.'

He smiled and relit his cigar, which had smouldered away idly until half its length had been consumed.

'Ever smoked a real Cuban cigar?'

Aziz offered me the cigar. I politely took a puff, and grimaced at its infernal taste.

'What about you, Mohammed? You look like a man of the world.'

'He doesn't smoke,' I objected.

'Of course I smoke – give it here.'

Mohammed grabbed the cigar and masterfully drew in its rich fragrance. For once his show of bravado surprised me. I couldn't recall him ever having smoked before. But soon, with a splutter and a cough, he brought up a handful of undigested nuts, and the cigar fell to the ground. Khalil and Aziz doubled up with laughter.

'You're hilarious, Mohammed.'

My friend wiped his mouth with the sleeve of his jacket, and fell into violent maniacal convulsions.

'You like western music – the Beatles?' Khalil asked, 'just hold on a minute.'

Again, he gestured in his condescending manner to the waiter and whispered something in his ear. Immediately, the sound of the Beatles' 'Lovely Rita,' replaced the gentle afternoon somnolence.

'Louder waiter, louder!' Aziz shouted. 'We can't hear over here!'

The waiter looked disturbed, and in a mousy whisper added 'Sir, you'll upset the other members.'

But any scruples the poor man had were promptly silenced by our host's steely expression.

I cannot remember how many beers we consumed that afternoon. Things became progressively hazier, insular; I think that all four of us must have been pretty much soaked when we finally left the club. Amidst this raillery, I recall seeing Louise, who had returned to Iraq from England. She came over to our table, asked to speak with me privately, only to be met by looks of incomprehension and rude laughter from my companions. I really did want to speak with her. She knew my father, and might relate our whereabouts to him. But it was as if I was dreaming, where the most mundane operation becomes monumentally difficult; and though I took immense pains to draw my faculties together so that I could speak something coherent to her, everything just came apart every time I tried. Understandably, she did seem a little upset.

Beyond all this, I wondered why we hadn't been ejected from the club; all the other members had slipped away, probably disgusted at our behaviour. The only way I could explain this was by assuming that our hosts were important persons and their patronage carried weight. Mohammed was completely wasted. Before his lights were finally extinguished, he made a great commotion about wanting to swim; but for Kahlil's quick responses, he would have dived headlong into the pool fully clothed. God only knows how we'd have fished him out! It was this episode, that gave rise to Aziz's or Kahlil's suggestion – I can't remember whom it was now – that we go to his place, where, so he said, he had a magnificent swimming pool that made the club's look like a mere paddling pool. He owned a large villa in Monsoor, a beautiful palatial building. There we would find everything to be found at the club – sun loungers, a fine stereo, a bar. So, we accepted his invitation – after all, we had nowhere else to go – and left the club.

32

The uproar Mohammed and I left behind in Al-Za'franiya continued late into the night. It was similar to when someone accidently steps onto an ants' nest, and all its tiny inhabitants come scurrying out to register the disorder. The question on everyone's lips was why these two young men had taken to their heels so unexpectedly. For the real accusation remained without a voice. For all his bluster, Abbas was yet unconvinced by Zakiyah's story. Even our departure failed to persuade him of the truth. A matter of such moment, with such profound implications, had to be looked into.

When Zakiyah arrived home after leaving the watermill, she found the house empty. Abbas, as usual, was ensconced at the newly-erected concrete structure where he and the other peasants acted out the part of politicians for two or three hours every evening. Seeing the hall's flimsy wooden double-doors open, and his wife standing distraught on the threshold, Abbas's first instinct had been to immediately send her home with a few sharp words. This instinct had promptly been transformed into action. He stomped impetuously across the tiled floor and gestured the wily creature

outside. When she remained impervious to his vitupera-
tions, he cast a stealthy glance around to make sure no one
was looking and escorted her outside. Taking Zakiyah by
the shoulders, he shook her like a rag doll.

'What are you doing here? What's happened, coming
here showing yourself to men?'

But still she remained silent, a steely inflexibility in her
eyes. There was a venomous contentment in that glance that
gave her the ability to resist whatever this man threw at her.

'It's your son, Mohammed, you should be shouting at. . .'
she began, '. . . if you were ever at home, this could have
been avoided.'

Abbas was beginning to lose his temper.

'What are you talking about, woman? I haven't got time to
be listening to you. Can't you give it a rest for the night?
Mohammed's been doing this; Mohammed's being doing that!
Always the same. Don't you understand – I've had enough!'

She gloated, and savoured the anticipation that heralded
her revelation.

'At first I ignored it. But then he started disappearing
more frequently; in fact, every night, shortly after you left
with him, I saw Mohammed walking past and again, a
couple of hours later, he'd go back in the opposite direction,
towards the hall. So, I thought to myself: why don't I follow
him; see what he's up to.'

'Get to the point. No need for this introduction.'

'Well. . .' Zakiyah continued, '. . . careful not to be seen,
I followed him. And it was always the same place he went
to – the old watermill. I thought to myself, "what's he doing
in there – all on his own?" But that was it – he wasn't on
his own.'

She paused, and waited for Abbas to prompt her.
'Well?'
'Well, he was with that boy, Sami.'

155

'Is that it, woman? You've brought me out here to tell me that?'

She didn't want to let everything out at once.

'Wait, Abbas, wait. There's something else you'd better know about.'

'Later, later.'

'No, now!'

He began to move away, but she ran after him and clung to his arm.

'Don't you want to know what they were doing at the mill, up there – all alone – what they were doing time and time again?'

The poor man was confused. If he had been anyone else, one might have felt sorry for him.

'What were they doing? What could they have been doing?'

For once Zakiyah appeared bashful, hesitant.

'They were. . .'

'They were what?'

Having reached the point she had so looked forward to conveying, she found herself lost for words.

'They were what?' Abbas repeated.

'They were. . . doing unnatural, shameful things!'

'What are you talking about – shameful things! God help me if I don't let you feel the back of my hand! Come out with it woman!'

He lifted his arm, ready to knock Zakiyah to the ground, should she continue to prevaricate. She knew it was now or never.

'They were. . . having sex. Yes, Mohammed and Sami were having sex! Diabolical, God-forsaken, devilish sex.'

It was too late. Abbas's arm came down on the poor woman's face with a penetrating thud, sending her crashing to the ground.

156

'You wash your mouth out, you filthy liar. Shame on you! Just you wash your mouth out, you dog.'

Despite wishing not to believe her, his first thought was to look inside the building. He had taken the lad with him that night, as he did every night, and couldn't recall seeing him leave. Surely, he would be aware if Mohammed had gone absent every night! He wasn't a complete fool! Thus, he hastily peered through the doorway, looking right to left and, as Zakiyah had affirmed, the young man was not there.

He then stormed off in the direction of the mud huts, intent on settling the matter directly with Mohammed. If he was coming that way, surely he couldn't miss him. But when he found no sight of Mohammed, he began to waiver, albeit with much resistance, of his son's innocence. Still, he couldn't just sit about waiting. And rather than rushing to the watermill, which would seem the obvious place to start, he picked up his old service revolver, gripped it firmly in his right hand, and made to leave in the direction of our villa. Here was something material that he could throw at my father; for he couldn't forgive the other's glib and self-assured features when he had thought to charge him with communist sympathies.

The commotion outside the political association had attracted the attention of its inmates. Most of them thought that Abbas and Zakiyah were having one of their usual squabbles, laughed the matter off, and continued with their business. However, two or three of his closer companions watched the altercation develop from between the apertures in the closed shutter. When Abbas left his wife laying on the ground, they rushed out, lifted her up, and tried to pacify her. For by now she was in a fearfully distraught state, almost regretting her disclosure. Such, in fact, was her condition that they decided it would make sense to escort her home.

It was at this point that Zaid burst into my room and informed me of the situation. Luckily, my departure went unnoticed. Abbas was soon persuaded to depart. The peasants that had assembled outside in response to the fracas thought that the old fellow had finally cracked. With great difficulty father convinced Abbas to lay aside his revolver and wait to see what transpired. He chided Abbas, urging him to refrain from such assertions.

'That kind of slander can cause serious damage,' he urged.

For a moment the poor old fellow thought that Zakiyah had misled him. Certainly, it was not beyond her to fabricate stories when it suited her. But the next moment, he remembered that Mohammed had mysteriously disappeared, albeit the fact that the young man was not at the club or at home did not warrant drawing the conclusion that Zakiyah was telling the truth. In fact, Abbas was in a complete muddle. Eventually, tentatively apologising to my father for the interruption, he headed off back home, passing by the club on his way. Perhaps Mohammed may have even returned.

33

When the door was closed behind Abbas, father patiently composed himself before the mirror, so as to give himself time to reflect, to consider what he would say to me, and began the ascent up to my room. Zaid, who had been watching the affair from the top of the stairs, could see the disaster approaching and slinked off into his room. Father knocked gently on my door.

'Sami, are you in there?'

There was no response. Again, he repeated my name and, receiving no response, turned the handle and entered. The empty room, the open window, and the upturned savings-box immediately convinced him that there might be something in what Abbas had said. Though he felt angry, he also felt gravely humiliated. If it was true that a son of his had done what the old peasant had alleged, the shame that would be thrown on the family would forever remain indelible. Probably, he would have to move somewhere else in Baghdad, and even then his own conscience would condemn him, and he'd have to live with the shame forever. He sat down at the foot of the bed, and gazed sadly around, pondering where he went wrong. Was this the recompense for years of nurture? To have everything thrown back in one's face, as if it all meant nothing? Who was to blame? Could something have been done to avoid it? But, then, Zaid was normal, wasn't he? He arose, absentmindedly replaced several dinar into my savings box that had fallen aside in my rush to leave, closed the lid, and left.

That night must have been one of the most unpleasant in my father's life. He, as always, remained, at least externally, calm. He had a way of suppressing his feelings so they would not get the better of him. He thought of calling the police. But what could he say? That the son of Iraq's most prominent teacher and educationalist was gay? That he'd absconded with another boy? Perhaps he could contrive some excuse, and no one would be the wiser? Yet, wasn't his son's safety more important than anything? He must find out where his son had gone; where he was sleeping. He knew that I had very little money, and would soon be without any means.

'Let's wait. . .' father again reassured himself, '. . .he won't have gone far.'

Zaid, who did not disclose his suspicions, concurred:

'He's an adult now and knows how to look after himself. Let's just wait until tomorrow.'

'Yes, you're right,' he resignedly concluded, 'They're probably just messing about somewhere, and have forgotten the time!'

'They'll be back soon – you just wait and see.'

Father was deeply troubled, and couldn't refrain from shedding a tear when he retired to his study that evening.

If I had had the foresight to see the outcome of what I'd done, would I have considered running away? It is easy to be merciful in retrospect, but the sense of self-preservation – like that to propagate – is so fundamental an urge that to override it is almost impossible. Yet it was only a matter of time. The little respite I had gained was being dearly paid for in heartbreak and tears. How egoistic human beings are, when for so little, they see nothing objectionable in destroying someone's life!

34

Abbas, as we have seen, couldn't accept the matter so sedately. The energy that coursed through his wiry sinews wouldn't let him rest for a moment. As his credence increased, so too did his ire. Falling into a violent passion, he rehearsed all his former grievances against Mohammed and became fixed on retribution. He should have known that the lad would only be trouble. Right from the start he refused to get on with his siblings. He cursed as he had never cursed before, invoking the name of Allah and his Prophet as witness to the uprightness of his life. What had he done to deserve this? Now his honour would be blighted forever. It would have been better if the boy had never been born. Oh! What is the life of man but constant tribulation! But for all his anger, Abbas knew that no one could be allowed to suspect what had taken place. He could barely allow himself to suspect so heinous a crime. If word got out, the matter would be out of his hands; he would be expected to sacrifice his son, and didn't know if he was ready for that.

Gathering a few confused peasants together to look for Mohammed – who, but for their fear of Abbas, would have gladly gone home to their beds – the old fellow strode off into the night. They carried paraffin lamps to light their way. The four dots of light drifted slowly into the night like fireflies; from a distance, they hardly appeared to move at all. Abbas made straight for the watermill. He crossed the rugged soil, kicking up fragments of dirt as he and his companions marched along in their sandaled feet. No one spoke a word. Beside them, the Tigris coursed busily, whispering its melancholy dirge. The four lights halted. Before them, the gloomy silhouette of the mill rose up like a monument of ignominy that would remind the world of the shame perpetrated there until the end of time.

Abbas had to steel himself before continuing – he felt the gall rise in his throat. And the closer he came to the mill, the more nauseated he felt. Every gap in the mill's exterior, every aperture seemed to him to glow with white heat, as if Satan had taken up residence within.

'Look inside,' his voice echoed, cold, perfunctory, lifeless.

The peasants obeyed without hesitation.

'Upstairs and down. Look everywhere.'

Moments later they emerged, empty-handed, and found Abbas standing in front of the entrance, the flickering of the paraffin lamp casting a sinister, wavering shadow across his face.

'Nothing in there. Where now?'

'Go ahead. . .' he replied, '. . . I'll catch you up.'

They scuttled away as fast as their feet would carry them, leaving Abbas alone. Boiling with a rage he could hardly contain, he pitched his lamp into the opening of the mill. Whoosh! The slender yellow-blue flame shot up through the opening in the ceiling leading to the floor above, catching the brittle, dry date fronds. Beneath the crackling, snapping sound, Abbas smiled sardonically, uttering the words of the Qur'an:

'As for those who are wretched, they will be in the Fire, sighing in a high and low tone.'

The flames quickly spread, igniting the sky, catching up the peasants who scuttled away, in a ruddy glow.

'What on earth's going on!'

They quickly returned, fearing for Abbas's safety. But he had already departed.

This was a weight he couldn't carry. Someone had to be responsible for his son's undoing. It couldn't be otherwise. Mohammed had received a good and wholesome upbringing, always surrounded by the right kind of examples. Surely he could not have been ignorant of the utterly heinous nature of what he was doing? That his son should turn out a . . . The thing was so vile that it defied expression. It caught in his throat. If the young man had murdered someone, it would have been easier to bear. The whole ignominious affair must simply have originated elsewhere. Someone had put the idea into his mind. But, even if he could shift the blame, the shame would be absolutely unassailable. It was a stain that would resist any solvent. Here was an asymptote that could never be crossed. Either way he was condemned. And if the matter should reach the light of day, steps would have to be taken to show his unconditional repudiation of the act. For this was a matter of honour, and he would not shrink from doing whatever necessary to maintain it unblemished. If blood was demanded, then so be it. No one would blame him for it. This had cut Mohammed off from the mercy of both God and man.

35

The following morning two individuals, one from each community, departed from Al-Za'franiya – one on a donkey, the other in a car. The ten years that had passed since the marriage of Abbas and Zakiyah had not been happy ones. She was a young girl then, a perfectly ingenuous creature whose pretty, albeit rustic features, convinced her that she would find the first place in any man's heart, even if she had to share the same tandoor with another woman. But marriage seemed to have brought out the worse in her, and had caused those selfish proclivities, that reside within all of us, to manifest themselves.

She was an only daughter, and her two brothers exerted themselves to ensure that she would not jeopardise the family's honour. When the time came for her to marry, they were adamant that it would not be to someone from a different tribe. Didn't they have plenty of fine, strapping fellows who would keep her on the right path? Ones they could keep a close watch on? Wasn't Ali bin Salman such a man. He owned one of the largest plots of land in the tribe. Not forgetting young Munther! Now there was an honest, hard-working man if ever there was one! And there were plenty of others. Not that any of these fellows was brave enough to so much as glance at Zakiyah! The brothers placed impossible demands on their affections. But marrying outside one's tribe – that seldom worked out. Especially with a tribe such as the Sraji – they were not an honourable people. For years beyond number they had feuded with the Sraji. No one knew what the cause of this mutual animosity was, but nevertheless it made itself known by its effects on the tribes' relations with one another. Hence, when their sister's marriage to Abbas was finally announced, it came as a nasty surprise to the brothers, and they fought the union unremittingly right up until the time of the marriage, but all to no avail. It had all been finalised by then, and there was nothing they could do. Abbas had offered two fine oxen, complete with trappings, in exchange for the bride, and the father handed her over with his blessing. When the brothers begrudgingly attended the celebration, their funereal demeanours would have been more in place at a wake.

The first time Zakiyah returned to her own village seeking consolation for Abbas's treatment of her, complaining that she played second-fiddle to a woman twice her age, the brothers were profoundly satisfied. Not that there was anything out of the ordinary in the way Abbas handled his wife. It was, after all, a man's place to run a household as he deemed fit, and if the odd whack was necessary, then that was perfectly acceptable. But Salman, the elder of the brothers and a widower, sought to make something out of nothing, and tried to provoke their father into admitting that he had been right about the Sraji. But the old man was having none of it; he knew his son's complaints were nothing but ill will. Soon even Zakiyah herself grew tired of their using her to get at one another, and returned to her husband, more wearied by their overweening protection of her than the prospect of Abbas's temper. Thus began a cycle of perambulations between the two villages. Always the little grey-brown donkey would appear, tiredly rounding the undulations of the river that enveloped the village, Zakiyah jolting back and forward as regular as a time-piece on its back, her forlorn expression betokening the usual complaints.

When it was time for my father to leave Al-Za'franiya, he found Salem Tahir and Abu Hilal having a heated discussion at the end of the driveway. The subject of their discourse centred on ascertaining the grounds on which Mahmoud Al-Shaklee sold vegetables above the government's set tariff.

'We're just going around in circles!' gasped the mayor, throwing out his arms and revealing the palms of his hands, as if to say: 'it's nothing to do with me.'

'I tell you, he's going to get himself in trouble with the authorities if he carries on.'

Abu Hilal assumed a military expression that would brook no opposition. The two men looked at my father, as he opened the door of his car. The mayor chipped in:

'Abu Sami, you're looking a little sad today. I'm sure the lad's just playing around. Young men are like that – get silly ideas in their heads!'

Father smiled vapidly at them. He returned their greeting absentmindedly. It had been a wakeful night, and now my father was thoroughly exhausted. Still, he felt he had to do something, and decided to pay my grandfather a visit, and find out if he'd seen anything of us. It was a good place to start. His equanimity was by now starting to give way to anxiety, but still he was chary to involve the authorities in the search, for he could not jeopardise the matter getting out. Like every Arab, my father was a proud man, and a good name preceded a person in all their interactions with others. Everything, whether true or not, had to remain a secret. So, with the mayor and Abu Hilal still gaping, father headed off along the dirt track, and took the road to Baghdad.

167

36

I can remember very little of the journey from the club to our hosts' villa, and I'm sure Mohammed remembered even less. Only images of a shiny black car with leather upholstered seats; Mohammed and I being thrown from side-to-side as the car swerved along the highway; and Kahlil's expression as he glanced intermittently at us from the passenger seat. I was feeling sick from the drink, and thought the journey would never end. How Mohammed was holding himself together I don't know.

We passed through well-maintained streets, ornamented with symmetrically planted date palms. The villas were tall, majestic, and fronted with automatic gates. A sentinel, sometimes armed, stood attentively on the spot, displaying that well-disciplined demeanour only seen in trained military men. And then the car halted before an enormous mansion, buried in lush vegetation that permitted only a furtive peep at what lay beyond. The gates had opened before we arrived. They must have known we were coming. Two unmistakably state security men carrying machine guns immediately approached the car and opened the doors. They seemed to be adept at their job. But our hosts hastily withdrew without saying a word, leaving us in the hands of these intimidating men. I was a little uncertain on my feet, but eventually managed to stand unaided. Mohammed, however, had to be carried to the room allotted us at the top of a flight of stairs. There we were left. I laid down beside Mohammed, feeling more secure, and shortly fell asleep.

It was dark when I awoke, sometime in the depths of the night. Mohammed was still asleep. I switched on a lamp with a heavy shade that absorbed much of its light. The door opened. It was Aziz:

'Good evening young men – you've slept deeply! Is your friend's still asleep?'

I looked at Mohammed. One after the other, his eyes slowly opened. Confused by the strange environment, he sat upright, involuntarily raising a hand to his head as the pain shot into his eyes and forehead.

'Slowly does it young fellow!' added Aziz, 'perhaps you had a little too much to drink!'

Mohammed squinted, and smiled vapidly.

'Why don't you two get washed up and come downstairs. A little food will cheer you up. In the morning, when you're feeling better, I might be able to show you around the place.'

'Thank you,' I muttered.

Our host smiled politely and gently closed the door behind him.

As nimbly as his heavy legs would carry him, Mohammed crept over to the balcony and drew back the curtains.

'Where are we?' he asked, his eyes remaining fixed before him.

'Look, there's someone lurking about with a gun out there.'

'You can't remember what happened?'

'I can only remember being at the club, drinking. . . are we still at the club?'

169

Mohammed turned to me, letting the folds of the curtains fall back gently into place.

What a poor, bemused fellow he looked!

'And my head's killing me.'

He pressed the palm of his hand against his forehead and eyes.

'Look, sit down for a while longer.'

I put my arm around his shoulder and led him back to bed.

'The men we met at the club – you remember? – this is their house.'

I didn't tell Mohammed what I had learned from the exchange between myself and our hosts, namely, that they were high-ranking government officials, probably Saddam's cronies with a sexual appetite for teenage boys and girls. Such things were not unknown to those familiar with the regime. I wanted to leave at once, but I could not persuade Mohammed to depart, he was feeling so fragile and hungover. Moreover, it was too late, anyway, to get up and go immediately, trudging off into the abysmal night. Nevertheless, he was clearly disquieted by my obvious apprehension. While he looked at me for reassurance, within himself Mohammed was torpidly examining his recollections for the thread that would lead him up to the present. We agreed that we would leave first thing in the morning.

From downstairs the sound of music and the clapping of hands could be heard.

'Haven't they had enough!' muttered Mohammed.

I was inclined to make the best of a bad situation.

'Maybe it's not as bad as we think. . .,' I interjected, '. . . let's go downstairs and see what's going on.'

Mohammed, however, wanted to nurse his aching head, and go back to sleep.

'You'll have to go on your own. I need to rest some more.'

I arose and pushed the door wide open.

'Just listen to that – doesn't it make you want to dance?'

I clapped my hands in time with the beating of the tabla.

'Come on! They'll be wondering where we are by now. We certainly can't afford to upset them.'

Mohammed rolled onto his side and gathered himself up into a ball. He groaned. I closed the door once again, and sat on the bed.

'Are you upset?'

'Just go downstairs. Leave me alone for now, Sami. My head's killing me. Go on. Maybe they just like a good party. Go!'

I slipped from the room and followed the beat of the tabla, which led me downstairs. There, an ample vermillion curtain was drawn aside by a short servant, at once revealing a scene from the 'Thousand and One Nights.' The commodious low-ceilinged room opened at one end onto a large veranda, separated from the interior by a light drape that caught up the breeze from the ceiling fans and undulated erotically. Deep musk incense commanded the attention of the nose as did the bacchanalian music that of the ear. The musicians – two percussionists and one oudist who also sang – sat, cross-legged, upon a richly ornate rug, their gold-embroidered waistcoats catching up the dimmed light that cast a surreal glow over the whole. Heaps of velvet cushions decorated with braided tassels were cast carelessly upon a low divan that circumvented the room. In the centre, a myriad of silver plates, platters, bowls and goblets disgorged a heady mixture of sweet fragrances and rich meaty aromas. But no one was eating.

Two belly dancers – matchless female beauty, that robust Arabic beauty, full-bodied and unlike our svelte western beauties – swept across the floor, visually representing the music, their movements fluid, seamless. Every part of their bodies responded, with fitting appropriateness, to the rhythm. They flung their arms out, shook their hips and breasts, gyrated their heads, creating a dark, alluring whirl-pool of sable locks. On the low divan, several men, whom I had never seen before, clapped their hands and clicked their fingers in time. They didn't pay much attention to me. On the opposite side sat Khalil. He jumped to his feet when I entered, welcoming me in the hearty Arabic style, throwing out his arms, and kissing me on either cheek. The heavy atmosphere I left behind with Mohammed lifted at his jaded, yet joyful, appearance. It was another taste of that cynical disjunction in time between the now and the morrow, when a person can dance merrily in face of an unknown future.

'Get the young man a drink!' he commanded the small fellow who drew the curtain back.

'Come, sit next to me. What do you think? Good?'

I sunk into the cushions beside Khalil, who gestured to the musicians and dancing girls to cease. He clicked his fingers at the girls:

'Over here!'

They giggled inanely and sat beside me, a heavy odour of perfume and sweat emanating from their heated bodies as they slumped heavily onto the divan. Meanwhile Aziz had taken up the oud, causing the group opposite to emit a flurry of cheers. This was obviously Aziz's showpiece, something he had done many times before.

'I'm going to play you a dirge. . .,' he announced, '. . . as a young man, my father – God bless his soul – always used to sing this when he entertained guests. So I too shall play it to my guests, while the flower of youth still blossoms; while love still illumines our souls; while we can hope for a better tomorrow.'

Silence followed. Plucking away lightly on the taut strings, he sang Umm Kulthum's Othkorene, a song famous in the

1940s. Everyone knew that song, and everyone, including me and the belly dancers beside me, joined in. When he finished, he handed the oud back to its owner, clearly moved by memories of the past.

'Let's have something a bit livelier!'

And gesturing to the dancing girls, he enjoined them:

'Up, up. Dance girls, dance.'

As if we were puppets manipulated by the melody, all of us overcame our passing sombreness and warmed to the wistful and bright tones.

Khalil then introduced me to his friends.

'This is Sami. I met him at the club today with a friend – a little worse for wear, I believe – and they decided to join us here for a while, to liven things up a bit.'

'Splendid!' interjected one of the fellows, clearly saying what his friend wanted to hear.

'You see. . .,' Khalil continued, '. . . Sami's a young man now. To him, no doubt, life is full of fun and enjoyment – a playground. I was the same at his age. Everything's so simple when you're young; the book of life appears a blank page on which one can write whatever one wants. If only! But our lives are not our own, gentleman, our lives are not our own! We live as we must, and do as we can. So, while we can, we must enjoy ourselves. When you get older, you'll look on these tender bygone days as a lost paradise.'

He clapped his hands:

'Come gentlemen, enjoy! Enjoy life while you can!'

37

I sat with our hosts deep into the night. Of their identity, I was unable to glean much. All I could discover was that they were high-ranking diplomats and cronies of 'Mr Deputy,' as they referred to Saddam Hussain. Their type flourished under his regime. He was happy to let them believe they were big men, able to do anything pursuant of their pleasure, providing this did not detrimentally disturb the regime.

Thus, the company continued to indulge in revelry, with apparently unflagging spirits. Aziz kept coming and going. No sooner did he return than he was called away again. Khalil, however, remained close at my side; he seemed to take more pleasure in my unassuming presence than all of the other paraphernalia that held the party uninterestedly captive. It was not long before I came to the conviction – a conviction that would soon be confirmed – that it was for Kahlil's benefit that I was there. Mohammed, so it transpired, was a mere appendage; he was 'a little too rough around the edges,' as they euphemistically put it. I should have been offended at their estimation of my friend, but instead vanity rose up within me; I felt deeply flattered that a man of Kahlil's calibre should choose my company above that of others. How venial is the human soul! Despite myself, I did nothing to stand up for my friend, and even endorsed some of my host's unfavourable remarks. I could not see, or chose not to see, that here was a man who would concoct any ludicrous tale, split apart friends of a lifetime, for a mere moment's pleasure.

It was not long before he started taking liberties with me. He placed his arm around me, caressed my hair, tickled the nape of my neck, and finally placed his hand on my thigh.

'You don't mind me touching you?' he asked, confident of a favourable response.

'Look Khalil,' I responded with some firmness, 'I'm not like that. I'm not what you think.'

'And what do I think you are?' he queried in his debonair way, assuming a saccharine smile by way of endorsing my response.

'I'll tell you the truth, Sami: you're the boys who ran away – you and Mohammed, aren't you?'

I remained silent, but felt that dreadful feeling, somewhat akin to nausea, one experiences when caught doing something one should not be doing.

'Word gets around, you know. . . Not that it bothers me!'

He smiled, his expression failing to conceal the advantage he hoped to obtain from this knowledge.

'It's all right with me. . .' he again repeated, qualifying his comment with, '. . . but, of course, I don't know about your friend. They'll catch up with you eventually – it's inevitable – but. . . you know . . . Mohammed will feel the sharp end of this more than you will. He belongs to a people that like to do things in the old-fashioned way. They like to sort things out themselves.'

'OK, that's enough,' I interrupted him, holding my hands up, as if trying to deflect his words.

'We only invite people to our house when we know who they are. I made enquiries at the club when I first saw you and felt I really liked you. The club enquired with the Al-Za'franiya branch of the Ba'ath party, which is run by Mohammed's father. When I learned the whole story, I was quite shocked.'

'You didn't tell them where we are?'

'Of course not! Don't worry, Sami. For Mohammed's family, this could only terminate in an honour killing. They'll certainly kill him. You can stay here for the time being; no one can touch you if you're with me.'

He moved closer. I could see he was sexually aroused.

'Sami, I really like you. Right now, I can hardly control the urges I feel for you. I want to make love to you.'

What I had previously taken for innocent sentiments were now thoroughly defiled by his profession. I was almost lost for words.

'But Khalil,' I cried, 'I'm not gay.'

He laughed at my naïve outburst.

'Then what kind of relationship are you having with Mohammed? You don't have to be too intelligent to notice these things!' he taunted.

I tried to explain that it wasn't like that; that within I was a woman, no different from any other woman; that I was in the wrong body.

Khalil, of course, was having none of this, and assumed that I was just in denial about the true state of affairs, namely, that I was gay.

My relationship with Mohammed, I tried to explain, was one of love; the physical union we enjoyed within this love was something tributary to its existence. For a moment, I felt that I had stirred some vestige of empathy, even of understanding, in Khalil. Certainly, he was fascinated by the expression of my deep-routed dysmorphia, the horror even, with which I considered my own naked body.

'I spent some time in Europe, Sami, and I heard about people like you who believe they're in the wrong body. You can have an operation for that.'

'Are you sure? Is that possible? How?'

'I don't know any more than I've told you. It's just something I heard.'

Now I was agog, hanging on his every word. If this were true, my interview with Khalil was truly providential. I felt such gratitude for what he conveyed that I almost forgave him his sexual overtures. The urgency with which I had sought to leave now abated. This man – this lecherous, pleasure-seeking sycophant of Saddam – had illuminated what for me was the darkest side of my life. I had hope.

'How would you like to come out for a drive with me tomorrow, just the two of us?'

No doubt realising that I had become more pliable since his last admission, he now sought to gain further ground by presenting me with the prospect of further information.

'And I'll tell you all about how you can get help with your predicament?'

I was only too glad to acquiesce.

'I'd love that!' I broke in without hesitation.

'Excellent!'

Ultimately, I managed to slip away without making too many promises. But those I did make weighed heavily on me when I returned to Mohammed. It even crossed my mind that my friend knew that I had somehow betrayed him. Did he, perhaps, have some inkling of things to come? Could he, with his rustic simplicity, penetrate the reason for our presence better than I, who considered myself, albeit young, worldly-wise? But finding Mohammed awake upon my return, now captive to a lighter mood than that of earlier, I dismissed these thoughts as unduly paranoid.

He threw his arms around me, and asked me to forgive his earlier moodiness.

'I just felt a bit down – that's all! You didn't take offence, did you?'

These words cut me to the quick, and I confessed in my heart never to betray Mohammed, in howsoever small a manner again.

'Of course I forgive you – to tell you the truth, I was feeling a little bit down myself.'

He recalled our decision to leave in the morning.

'Leave,' I urged, 'where would we go? No. Let's make the most of our luck; try to enjoy ourselves.'

I didn't tell Mohammed that our hosts knew who we were. He questioned me about what I had been doing, seemingly unsatisfied until I had related every detail (with certain omissions) of that night's entertainment.

'They are not as bad as we thought,' I reassured Mohammed, 'I think we'll be safe here.'

With my disclosures complete, I locked the door and took Mohammed eagerly in my arms.

38

We slept late the following morning. Contrary to my expectations, no one woke us, and we were left to find our own way about. At such times, one feels keenly the absence of the common routine that shapes our lives; yet this comes not without a frisson of native excitement, the feeling of being master of one's actions. Anyway, we couldn't just sit there all day, hoping that someone would come and fetch us, despite the presumption involved in wandering off alone. So, wander we did. At the far end of the landing, the sun blasted through an open shutter. It was a beautiful morning air – such as one inhales in the West after a light summer-rain has freshened the parched grass. Here the source of the freshness was a rotating sprinkler. Outside, two domestic staff were scouring the base of an empty swimming pool.

Mohammed and I followed the landing until we came to the staircase I descended the previous night. A clattering of crockery led us to the kitchen, where we were informed that our hosts had been called away and would not return until later. They offered us some breakfast, which we consumed on a pretty veranda, where slatted wooden seats were arranged beneath a natural arbour formed of orange and lime trees. The perfume from the orange blossom was dense and piquant.

While we ate, Mohammed and I spoke briefly of our plans; how, notwithstanding what appeared to be the bleakest of prospects, we would somehow scrape together a meagre existence. We even spoke of going to live in England.

'Look Mohammed,' I concluded, 'I think Khalil will help us. That's the only way out.' Mohammed looked serious and unsure.

The breakfast was enormous, and we ate enough to satisfy us for the entire day. I broke off small pieces of khubz and threw them into a clearing, where some tiny birds picked them up and swept away enchantingly into the sky. When we could eat no more, and our excited musings had run to a mere trickle, one of the servants – a genial old fellow, conspicuous for his unaffected and genuine solicitude – suggested that we might like to explore the grounds. There were lots of unusual flora, he explained, that had been transported from all over the world. By the time we had finished, he added, the swimming pool would have been refilled and we could go for a swim.

With much effort Mohammed rose from his seat, accepting the old fellow's recommendations, and the two of us strode off along a narrow path covered in stone chippings. It was like one of those exotic, tropical collections one visits, perhaps while on holiday, where plants from across the world, usually so unsociable towards one another, recline cheek-by-jowl, lovingly and arduously kept in existence by their carer's untiring efforts. Small benches interspersed the lavish growth, quaint nooks encased by the humid air trapped beneath the overhanging foliage. A narrow waterway trickled furtively along, utility and beauty combining in a carefully concealed system of irrigation, before opening into a big pond where large fish swam unconcernedly between rocky outcrops. Mohammed and I stood upon a wooden bridge that spanned the pool and watched the fish flitting beneath our feet. Our reflections danced gently upon the delicate ripples.

For some time we remained silent, absorbed by the contrived beauty of our surroundings. Moving leisurely along the narrow pathway, our attention was taken up by a display of cacti: fat ones shaped like pumpkins; some tall and slender, bristling with spiky defences; others, almost fluffy in appearance, their spines deceptively concealed beneath a filigree membrane. Sometimes we walked behind one another; at other times, we squeezed side-by-side upon the slender trail. And when we did our hands would touch, involuntarily catching up one another in a tight and tender grip. It gave me a strange feeling at first, but it felt right, and with repetition this tender squeezing of hands soon became so natural as to put to shame the loveless world. Yet, neither of us acknowledged this furtive caress, and soon, upon the approach of a tapering curve in the pathway, our hands would once again fall apart.

As our guide had intimated, the garden was, indeed, vast, and soon we wearied of reading the tiny wooden legends giving the name and origin of each plant. Viewed in abundance, even beauty begins to cloy the mind, making it increasingly unreceptive to nature's exquisite creation. Touched by this sense of languor, and the imperceptible progress of the sun, we rallied with greater expedition along the pathway. Not without a certain poignancy, we stretched out upon one of the many benches strewed along the way, lovingly embraced by foliage. When we spoke, it seemed that we had been thinking of the same matter: everything was all very beautiful. But this exquisite morning, the hearty breakfast, those enchanting gardens did make us suspect

181

what might underlie our hosts' invitation. Of course, from my experiences the previous night, I had a pretty good idea as to where things were tending. Soon Khalil would return and expect me to accompany him on a drive to god knows where; and Mohammed would look on incredulous, wondering how I could be so duplicitous.

39

Stepping towards Khalil, who had just arrived, I furtively glanced to the right, to see if Mohammed was watching me. There he stood motionless, like a stock thrust immovably into the stubborn earth. Alone revealing signs of vigour, his ardent, indignant eyes pierced me to the quick. Hastily, I looked in the opposite direction, and smiled diffidently at Khalil. He looked at me quizzically, and turned about. Mohammed was gone.

'He'll be alright,' Khalil uttered reassuringly, smiling an avuncular, consolatory smile.

I responded with a weak smile, my features straining to visibly accept his reassurance.

'Oh, I'm not worried. Maybe he'll just be at a loose end without me, that's all.'

We stopped beside Khalil's large, immaculate car. It was one of those huge American cars, with the roof slung back, revealing maroon leather upholstery. I stepped in awe around to the passenger seat.

'No, the other side,' he urged.

'But, I can't!'

I was about to explain that I couldn't drive; that, as far as driving was concerned, my knowledge went no further than watching my father's hands and feet operate clutch and gear in unison. But what had Khalil to do with these formalities? He seemed to dispose of things as it suited him.

'Get in. Go on, don't be afraid. I'll show you what to do.'

The seat was hot and stuck to my legs uncomfortably. The car was huge and I could barely see the far end of the bonnet, its mirror-like chrome emblem refracting the cutting rays of the noonday sun, dazzling my eyes and making me squint. Khalil sat beside me, easing himself with great facility onto the edge of the passenger seat, from where he could control the car should I need help. His thigh pressed tightly against my own, and he gently rested his hand on mine, as I ineptly grasped the gear stick, pressing my hand firmly against its smooth leather contours.

'OK. Turn the key.'

I looked at Khalil knowingly, an ironic expression passing across my features.

'Sorry . . . but we must begin somewhere. . . you did say you hadn't driven before? OK, then, press down the clutch . . . move the gear stick into first.'

I could sense he was looking at me rather than paying attention to his directions.

'Right. Slowly lift your foot from the clutch and press down on the accelerator.'

The car spurted violently into action, and let out an offended screech. Khalil looked a little irritated.

'Don't worry,' he urged, 'we'll be fine in a moment.'

With Khalil to guide me, we gradually picked up a steady pace, until the car forged a somewhat abrupt path onto the highway. I giggled a little foolishly, my thoughts wholly consumed by the progress of the car and what Khalil would be thinking. The vehicle was so large I feared that I'd hit some obstacle at any moment. It seemed like driving a tank.

184

'You're doing fine . . . you're a natural,' uttered Khalil, smoothly, calmly, with a sugary beam that revealed his perfectly etched teeth.

I felt all the more comforted when he finally fell back into the deep hollow of his seat, taking a cigar from his breast pocket and adeptly tossing it into his mouth.

'See, you can drive!!!'

I laughed, this time with more aplomb, glancing around with self-satisfaction as other cars shot past us at what appeared lightning speed.

'Relax . . . relax Sami . . . Now move over to the other lane.'

He gestured towards the fast lane.

'They're driving so fast . . .' I retorted, '. . . I'll never get in!'

He gripped the cigar firmly between his lips, and muttered:

'You push the accelerator and I'll do the steering!'

This time Khalil leaned heavily on my thigh. He took the wheel forcefully, while I pushed the accelerator down until it hit the ground.

'Whoosh . . .' he cried, '. . . look, we're going nearly sixty miles an hour.'

I had never been driven so fast in my life, and let out a loud scream of exhilaration. Jolting the steering wheel harshly in clockwise direction, the great metal bulk flew into the fast lane, its tyres screeching as their resistant rubber scoured the smouldering asphalt.

'You'll kill us!' I cried, at the same time laughing uncontrollably.

'Enjoy, enjoy, Sami. There's nothing else but enjoyment!'

Behind us, two ebony tracks remained imprinted on the road.

We cruised along for perhaps ten or fifteen minutes. Khalil once again fell back languidly into his seat. The angular blue road signs swept past. Ahead and to the left, four tall, monolithic, structures, visibly corroded, with clusters of lamps attached to the top of each, indicated an old disused football ground.

'There's an entrance about fifty metres ahead to the left – take it!'

Khalil accompanied his command with a gesture of his arm. Inexperienced as I was, I lifted my foot sharply from the accelerator, the car slowing down rapidly, the vehicle behind swerving aside with a loud blast of its horn. Khalil raised his hand to the dashboard, opposing the force that thrust him forth. I could see he was piqued.

The exit road was overgrown with tufts of tawny foliage that broke forth indomitably through the disintegrating asphalt. From the overhanging palms, dates lay scattered on the road where they would decay unenjoyed; and desiccated fronds lay strewn along the wayside, blown into the shallow concavity at the edge of the road that was filled with all manner of debris. Soon the lane opened up, revealing two large rickety gates, flung wide apart, a rusty chain and padlock hanging uselessly, almost apologetically, from the meshed iron of one. Flanking each side of the opening, a disused ticket box stood sentinel, waiting interminably for that time when it would be relieved from duty.

'Now, be careful here . . .' Khalil urged, '. . . we'll be driving through a very narrow opening.'

We eased slowly through the passage formally trod by the football teams entering the field, the vehicle almost touching the extremities of the dusty brickwork wall.

'Right, stop there.'

Before us lay the huge pitch, only one or two tiny sods of parched grass remaining; for the most, it was a dust bath.

'Let's swap over.'

Khalil and I changed places. As soon as he was seated, he pushed his foot to the floor, throwing a fierce miasma of dust into the atmosphere. We skidded off, almost pitching into a spin. In such manner we indulged our juvenile predilections, each of us taking turns to create vast foggy clouds of dust that momentarily eclipsed the sunlight.

40

From the football ground it was only a short distance before we reached Khalil's farmhouse, or rather his luxurious country retreat decked out with rustic charm that only took the form of its previous role of a working farm without the utility thereof. For this, so I learnt, was just one of Khalil's many well-appointed adjuncts to his property in Al-Mansoor. The doors and shutters had already been opened to air the place, indicating that our visit was anticipated. I did feel somewhat nervous, and asked Khalil where we were.

Before leaving the car, Khalil bent over towards me. He seemed serious for a moment, as if he had something important to utter. Without preamble, he began, in hushed tones, presumably so to highlight the sensitive nature of what he was to say:

'Sami, I've brought you here so we can be alone. I'm not going to force you to do anything you don't want to do. You know how much I like you. In fact, I'm going to do all I can to help you go to the West - with Mohammed if you wish. You'll be able to pursue the path you are set upon. But in return I don't want you to disappoint me.'

There was something threatening in his voice. He continued:

'If I'm disappointed, then Mohammed can just as easily be bundled up in a car this afternoon and taken back to his parents, where he'll be slaughtered like a lamb.'

He paused for a moment:

'So, what do you say?'

It seemed as if I didn't have any choice. How could I live with myself if my refusal to please Khalil resulted in Mohammed's death? He had found my weak spot. Nothing comes without a price.

'OK,' I spluttered, 'whatever you want.'

Once inside the house, Khalil went into an adjoining room, leaving me inside the threshold. He quickly returned with two crystal tumblers and a large bottle of whisky, presented on a decorative silver tray. One of the glasses, which he left on the tray for me, was considerably fuller than the other.

'Someone's got to drive us back!' he retorted with stiff mirth, in response to my inquiring glance.

The light from the open shutter quickened its malty, transparent hue. Then, looking at Khalil, I queried:

'Isn't it a bit early?'

'Never too early, young man. As I keep telling you, you must lighten up a bit!'

It wasn't difficult for me to oblige. The whisky would numb my senses, and interpose a filter between myself and what was happening. It wasn't that I was averse to sleeping with this man, for I had made love to Mohammed many times; I just didn't feel able to generalise my feelings beyond Mohammed. I felt uneasy and intimidated by Khalil. Yes, he was an attractive and successful man, and could help Mohammed and I, but it was the circumstances, the contrived circumstances, that made his advances unsettling.

I swigged back the whisky, feeling it would both appease my host and commit some of my anxieties to quietude. It was acrid. The alcohol's ferocious onslaught burned my palette and throat, its consoling warmth caressing me inside.

'That's more like it!'

Before I could return my tumbler to the tray, Khalil had already grasped the bottle and suspended it over my glass, once again refilling it. He hadn't touched his own.

I had stepped unwittingly into a world in which I had no control. Strange, ironic even, that the liberty I expected to obtain by running away from my parents should lead, not to freedom, but to my becoming enmeshed in a web of constraints in which my very existence had to be purchased. What would Mohammed have done in my situation? Would he make the same sacrifice for me? I recalled his face as I departed in Khalil's car, overcome with indignation. Yet he had been so happy earlier that morning in the garden! Momentarily, I resolved that I would have nothing to do with Khalil. Let him do what he would, I mused, he won't force me to do what I didn't want to do. But then, I considered that the whole thing would be over quickly. It was a terrible muddle.

Not that I had long to ponder these questions. Khalil's time was limited (thankfully), and he couldn't allow his appetites to be stayed by my hesitation. Closing his arms forcefully around my waist, he lifted me from where I was seated. Only then, when I almost toppled over, did I realise how light my head had become.

'Hey there, I've got you. You won't fall!'

I felt weak and even submissive. When he walked me over towards the bedroom, my energy was directed more to standing upright on my feet, than to resisting his assault. In this condition of intoxicated ambivalence, he sat me down beside him on the bed, closely easing his body against my own. The unruly bulge in his trousers indicated that here I no longer was dealing with Khalil the charming socialite, but with the raw power of nature asserting its hegemony over human conventions. Clasping me close to his chest, his face only a few centimetres from my own, he spoke, his narrow eyes like those of a serpent. I could smell a nasty blend of cigars and whisky on his breath that had the odour of adulthood about it, which made me feel particularly uncomfortable.

'Come on, you'll enjoy it, I'm a much better lover than Mohammed.'

'No,' I yelled, 'you've got it all wrong. It's not like that!'

He held me tighter, forcing his lips against my own. Confused again, I pulled away, my waning strength melting before his overbearing onslaught.

'There's no where you can go. Complain if you want. Complain as loud as you like! No one's going to hear you.'

These words brought my responsibility to an end. Of this I was glad. I threw myself down onto the edge of the bed. Strangely, the thought of my father and the pain I had caused him came before my mind. I felt so alone, wishing I had never left home. I needed people to accept me; to be part of something; to be a normal person. How I craved normality!

Khalil paced slowly towards me, a disarming tone now in his voice:

'Oh, Sami, I didn't mean for things to happen like this. I only wanted . . . you know, I like you, Sami, I'd never do anything you didn't want.'

I was no longer master of my emotions and, against all reason to the contrary, I even felt pity for this man. Yet, I knew his wiles; I knew that men like him can manipulate their emotions at will, turning them on and off with the same dexterity with which women are said to be able to produce tears. Foolishly, I looked into his face, and I was overcome.

191

'Take off your clothes.'

Without attending to what I was doing, I slowly disrobed, my eyes turning on Khalil as he removed his shirt and trousers. His body was covered with dense, coarse grey-black hair, scarcely revealing the sluggish olive skin that lay beneath. It was not like Mohammed's body, smooth and firm, with only a few soft nubile hairs cropping forth intermittently atop his soft downy skin. It frightened me; this was a real man, and I didn't know what I would feel like in his embrace.

Khalil sat on the bed beside me. I felt unusually self-conscious completely naked before this stranger. My own body disturbed me; that part of me which should not have been. I hurriedly covered myself with a sheet. Thereon I complied with Khalil's wishes, albeit the experience was particularly unpleasant, my only relief being the rapidity with which it was terminated.

The return journey to Al-Mansoor was punctuated by extended periods of silence, giving way only to lame platitudes. There was now a change in Khalil, a slackening off of interest, or rather amiability, towards me. He was abrupt, discourteous, and visibly relieved, as indeed I was, when the car finally pulled up outside the villa. My first wish was to seek out Mohammed, repair our fractured relationship, and construct some plan for the immediate future.

41

While I felt my free will had greatly been reduced, I deeply regretted submitting to Khalil. The actions of that day created a barrier between Mohammed and I that somehow transformed all I said and did into duplicity. But Mohammed, being of a naturally generous nature, his anger and suspicion soon subsided – or, at least, I thought it had. Yet the guilt I felt at betraying him would not leave my thoughts for a moment, and merely intensified when I was in his presence.

I coaxed some money from Khalil and suggested to Mohammed that we take a walk to the town of Al-Mansoor. Just a short stroll through this opulent outlying district would take us into the heart of its expensive boutiques and restaurants. Though I had heard much talk of this illustrious area, I had never previously visited Al-Mansoor. It did not take me long to understand why this was so. Apart from a small souk tucked neatly away beyond the main thoroughfare, where cooks purchased groceries for their employers, the street was lined with very costly specialist shops. Some sold designer clothing; others, imported shoes for women. Perusing the handsome menus outside the restaurants, I had to look twice before convincing myself that I had not misread the prices! I thought that Khalil had been generous in his handout, but now I realised that, if Mohammed and I were to have anything to eat or drink, we'd have to find some more moderately priced establishment, which would not be easy.

But all the time Mohammed appeared quite bored. Unimpressed by all this affectation, he revealed himself as a true son of the soil. Conversely, I was inspired by what I saw, and determined that it would one day be my destiny to live the life of the inhabitants of Al-Mansoor. When I related this to Mohammed, he looked askance at me, as if surprised at discovering this superficial side to my nature. I assured him that I was not in earnest, but clearly he believed otherwise. It was as if he was beginning to have reservations about the future. That simple, uncomplicated nature of our interactions, those days at the watermill had, he thought, been compromised by our meeting with those two strangers at the country club. It had been a most inauspicious day!

Soon our wanderings were cut short by the sight of a group of workmen sitting on upturned buckets outside what we hoped would be a cheap cafe. For where there are riches, there is sure to be those poor workers who slave away embellishing their employer's residence for a meagre day's wage! Who would have thought that in Al-Mansoor one could buy a hearty plate of pacha? Yet such was the case! For the time being we became ourselves again, spoke with some of the workman, and almost forgot that at the termination of the day we'd once again return to the villa. Why didn't we just get up and go somewhere else? Many reasons militated against such a decision, the most pressing of which was the fact that we had nowhere else to go. Now Khalil had taken advantage of our impoverishment, it would only be a matter of time before he'd ask us to leave anyway, and I was hoping that he might give us some money, if for nothing else, then to alleviate the feelings of guilt that I mistakenly applied to him.

42

My father, and Abbas, Mohammed's father, both sought different means of dealing with the situation. Whereas my father was primarily concerned with my wellbeing, and clung to the hope that I had not met with some misadventure, Abbas viewed the incident from the perspective of honour and considered what he would do to maintain the respect of his tribe. If the matter came to light, Mohammed's actions would bring disgrace to his family's tribe, which would become the subject of perpetual ignominy.

Nor had Ahmed, Zakiyah's son, remained idle during the past few days. He conveyed the news of disgrace and dishonour to Zakiyah's tribe and his maternal uncles and grandparents. They sought assiduously to compel their daughter to reveal the secret she held about her stepson. Usually, she enjoyed the attention, and had always sought to profit from her complaints; whether authentic or fantastical, it mattered not to her. As a child, a scrape, a scratch, a harsh word was sufficient to bring on a flood of tears, upon sight of which her mother, a soft and docile woman who doted on her, quickly came to her rescue. With both the death of her mother and her removal into the household of Abbas, the results of Zakiyah's self-pity became greatly attenuated. No one cared to listen to her anymore.

But, in response to her brothers' insistence and, in particular, to Salman's, importunities, she suffered a long time in concealing the truth; for she knew that, once known, the grave question of honour would necessarily arise, together with the ugly consequences that surround its vindication. For honour, if vitiated, had to be cleansed or washed away; and the only emolument that had the properties to wash away a putative sin was blood. Cases of this remedial blood-letting punctuate the history of many Middle Eastern tribes, and the law is chary to get involved in these sanguinary events. The tradition runs too deep to be set aside by legislation, and seldom are stiff sentences incurred by the perpetrator if he is caught.

Zakiyah's elder son, Ahmed, who had been raised by his uncles, was becoming a muscular young man, and delighted in any opportunity to exhibit his strength. What a person will ultimately turn out to be can be gleaned from the child. In this respect childhood had not belied his proclivities. Even as a child, he would psychopathically entrap his friends into making assertions that could be construed as insulting his family's honour. This gave him an excuse to get rough with them. So, when he scented matters of greater import concealed beneath Zakiyah's reticence, he would not allow himself to be shaken off. Yet she continually skirted the subject, sent him up blind alleys, and led him almost to pull out his hair with her interminable prevarications and tale-telling.

In such manner she resisted her family's interrogations for two days; on the third day, however, she sat at breakfast with a different attitude. It seemed that during the night she had experienced some kind of devilish epiphany that commanded her to reveal the whole matter to Salman, come what may. When her brother asked her once again to reveal the truth about Mohammed, she offered up the entire story, even adding details that would enflame the good man further. At once his anger boiled over, and he scolded Zakiyah for letting him live in ignorance of his dishonour for so long; then he threw his arms above his head, paced violently around the room, even scaring his father and brother, who tried to calm him down.

When, finally, Salman grabbed his rifle from where it lay against the wall, even Zakiyah started to feel remorse about her disclosure. Salman, his other brother, and Ahmed pounced upon him, grappling violently to snatch the weapon away. The breakfast was scattered about the floor and trodden underfoot violently. It was an awful, frightening sight, seeing this otherwise peaceful household scrapping like wild animals, with Zakiyah looking on ineptly. Eventually, they managed to relieve Salman of his gun, and sat him down. But still he fought, at first physically, and then verbally, against their desire to pacify him. He upbraided Ahmed:

'You know what any tribesman would do in my position. It's clear that our honour has been tarnished. No one will say it hasn't. And if I don't straighten it, we'll be outcasts. Do you want that to happen? How then are we to hold our heads high in the community?'

Contrary to their desire, neither mother nor uncle could gainsay the truth of what Salman uttered. He handed his gun to Ahmed. All three looked at one another blankly, the older man slowly running the palm of his hand around his bristly chin.

'You go son. Go and do what needs to be done.'

Ahmed glanced at Zakiyah, almost wishing that she had remained silent. Finally, Ahmed rose from his seat, held the gun and tilted his egal to one side. He looked first at his uncle, then at Salman, the family elder, who, almost imperceptibly, nodded his head, as if ratifying the sentence. There was no going back now.

43

Father was a very resourceful man, a characteristic I would one day inherit from him. It was on Monday when Mohammed and I absconded; on Tuesday we visited the club; on Wednesday, shortly before noon, he could be seen stepping out of his car before the club, gently rebutting the valet's attempt to park his vehicle.

'I'm only going in for a minute, my friend. If I could just leave it here, it would be much appreciated.'

The small dark fellow, wearing a yellow waistcoat that was too small and a cream jacket that was too large, smiled with gracious alacrity and tapped lightly on the roof of my father's car.

'The car will be alright with me, sir. Take as long as you want.'

Father presented the fellow with a hundred fils coin and strode resolutely towards the club foyer. This was just one of many places he had searched after visiting my grandfather, calling at all the places Mohammed and I frequented, the cafes, bars, the ice-cream parlour, The Rex . . . Despite his lack of success, he remained adamant that he'd catch up with us eventually.

Within the foyer, my father was greeted by several members of the club's staff, a repetitive formality he found particularly trying at the best of times. Severally they addressed him with the same words they always did, gathering their gestures up into the same expressions, asking, as always, whether he'd like anything from the bar. He smiled, thanked them for their attention, and only with much effort broke free from their importunities. My father then perused the partially empty club, strolling with strained insouciance out to the tiled poolside, where most of the seats were uninhabited. The air had a faint odour of chlorine about it. This was a singular procedure, but the good man believed that if I or Mohammed had visited the club within the past few days, he would in some curious, yet inexplicable, manner be able to sense it. It was a faculty that had not hitherto let him down. When, for example, he returned home from teaching one of his classes, my father could say with absolute certainty whom had called at the house in his absence. Mother always said that his knowledge was based on some barely perceptible odour that the visitor in question had left behind, thereby demoting his intuition to a finely nuanced olfactory sense. Be that as it may, my father's sense did not fail him this time, and it would have been impossible to convince him that I had not been at the club the previous day. Not that anyone unequivocally contradicted his queries, but no one seemed particularly interested in facilitating them.

Only Louise, who emerged from one of the private rooms, quietly informed him, after much pressing, that Mohammed and I had indeed visited the club. However, she was very reluctant to disclose precisely with whom we had departed, but eventually revealed that we had left the club with two gentlemen, probably high-ranking government officials, whose identity she didn't know. All she knew was that they frequented the club often and lived in Al-Mansoor.

Father returned to his car. He wanted to think, to figure things out. After driving about a hundred metres or so along the highway, he checked his rear-view mirror to make sure the porter wasn't watching him, and pulled onto the tufted grass bank. Turning the key in the ignition, the engine came to a halt. The silence of desolation, punctuated only by the passing of cars, quickly enveloped and oppressed him, making the matter seem all at once more grave, if indeed it could be; yet, just as in the gloomy depths of night one must remind oneself that the bogeys that mutter in every dark corner are unreal, so my father set aside the eerie quietude that magnified everything – as a shadow cast in dimmed light is magnified beyond verisimilitude – allowing reason again to take the ascendency.

Behind him, the road led to Al-Mansoor; in front, to Al-Za'franiya. Al-Mansoor was only a small district, but he couldn't just go knocking on people's doors to locate our hosts if, indeed, we still remained with them. Moreover, he was keenly aware of the black mark against his name, as a suspected communist, and he didn't want to upset these Ba'thist men. They could cause him all kinds of trouble. For it was the prerogative of Saddam's high-ranking minions to get away with more or less anything they desired, as long as it was carefully concealed. It might appear a negligent, even cowardly act, but he convinced himself that I would soon weary of our escapade and return home (which, other things being equal, would have been the case). Knowing where we were gave him a sense of relief.

The silence was momentarily broken by the approach of a truck, the deep rumble of its engine making the car vibrate as it passed. Father's eyes followed its progress, as it cleaved the gently wavering corridor of vaporous heat that rose

200

from the asphalt, and was lost in the distance. Again, he reflected. Yes, he decided, the entire affair was no more than that of two young men having a bit of a carry on! Rather than rushing to an immediate decision, he decided that he would ponder the matter further. He could always return. So, he turned the key in the ignition, paused momentarily as if confirming his decision, and drove back towards Al-Za'franiya.

44

After my father left the house for the club, Zaid climbed to the roof of the villa to tend his pigeons. Gently undoing the peg that secured the avery's wire mesh door, he removed one of the birds from its perch, and softly cradled the creature in his arms. When things got hard, he had learnt to find great solace in his winged companions. They seemed so unconcerned, so untroubled by the difficulties men create for themselves. Foolish it may have been, but within those beady orange-black eyes, he could detect a placidity and innocence that can be found in the eyes of almost any animal, but never in man. He stroked the pigeon's wings, almost caressingly, then placed the creature on the back of a chair.

'What a mess it all is . . .,' the young man muttered, '. . . no one knows what's going to happen. But you. . . you just sit there, cooing to yourself, only concerned about filling your little belly and stretching your wings.'

Zaid retrieved the bag of feed from its shelve, took some seeds, and fed the pigeon from the palm of his hand.

From the lane below, Thameer shouted in his nasal voice and threw small pebbles onto the roof:

'Are you up there, Zaid?'

He stepped towards the edge of the roof.

'What do you want?'

'Khalid and I are going to The Rex. Do you want to come?'

Zaid considered his watch.

'I've only got until three, and then I've got to get back.'

'Come on then, that'll be long enough!' shouted Thameer.

'Give me two minutes,' replied Zaid.

Meanwhile the blacksmith's child leaned his great, sweaty bulk against the garden fence, amusing himself by plucking the heads off some of my deceased mother's lovingly cultivated flowers. Over the past few years this fellow – who had been the most profound disappointment to his father – had grown as fat as a balloon on the point of bursting. When they relocated to Al-Za'franiya, his long-suffering father, blackened by the smith's soot and scorched by the flames that licked from the ever-bright furnice, became greatly enamoured of the idea that his children would leave the paternal trade. He cajoled them and sought to infuse in their unresponsive minds an aspiration to some petty governmental post where, if things went well, they would be promoted through the ranks, and could retire on a pension that would spare them labouring until they left this world. But Thameer had not fulfilled his father's expectations. His performance at school had been abysmal; he seemed to miss the mark with painful accuracy. So profound a failure was he, in fact, that some even ventured the supposition that he failed on purpose. He bullied the other pupils, set himself up as a local vigilante; and was the beacon of gossip, the contriver of bogus tales. As for his brother, his star waned under the lurid glow of Thameer's nastiness. Equally a failure, all that was absent from his personality was that malicious streak that set his brother beyond all hope of redemption.

Khalid had joined the brothers merely as an appendage. The disengagement he felt as a child had followed him, like some starving dog, into his late adolescence. What once was raw boredom had developed, through numerous circumlocutions, into systematic ennui and angst. He found joy in nothing and followed, with preconceived resignation, even disgust, the escapades of his friends, as if to prove to himself that nothing could engage his interest in a world such as this.

'Let's go,' Zaid cried, shutting the gate carefully behind him.

Thameer quickly drew back from the decapitated flowers, and the three of them set off along the dirt track. By accompanying him to the Rex, Zaid sought to discover whether any hint of Zakiyah's accusations had seeped out into the open. If anything was in the air, then this unsavoury fellow would know about it; nay, he would most probably be its source. In a conversation of the briefest compass, Thameer was the first to speak.

'We haven't seen you for the last couple of days. You've missed out on all the fun.'

He then continued to relate some rather insipid tales that the remaining gang members – for many of them had since gone their own way – had got up to. Zaid nodded complacently, smiling as seemed fit, his mind preoccupied with other matters. The fellow bored him; even his appearance seemed distasteful to him, with the continuous cascade of sweat running down his forehead, his lank greasy hair and nondescript features.

Zaid did not know whether to wait for Thameer to introduce the subject of his brother or to venture forth himself. Usually one would not have to wait for the gossip to find easy access from his mouth, but for the first time, Thameer appeared apprehensive, almost prevaricatory. Zaid decided to drop a hint.

'I've been very busy these last few days, with all that's being going on. That's why I couldn't come out.'

'Must be very hard,' utterd Khalid, attracting both his friends' attention by the rarity of his speech. It was as if a voice had emanated from a stone.

'I'd say so . . .' replied Zaid, and then, tenatively looking at Thameer:

'Have you heard anything?'

'Well. . .,' he vociferated boldly, '. . . there's much that's been said, but I try to mind my own business.'

He was obviously embarrassed and wanted to change the subject.

'Come on, let's get going, the film will start soon.'

'What have they been saying?' queried Zaid, halting in his steps.

Khalid also halted, but Thameer kept on a few paces.

'It's nothing. You know, the usual gossip. No one really believes it.'

'If it's just gossip. . .,' Zaid interjected, '. . . and no one really believes it, let's hear what they are saying.'

'Oh, just some stuff about your brother; how he's been led astray a bit. Something like that.'

'What do you mean, "led astray a bit?"'

'You know, with that peasant lad.'

Thameer's matter-of-fact manner irritated Zaid. By the way he was speaking, one could tell that he believed what had apparently been circulating.

'You know. . .,' he continued, '. . . the boy from the village.'

'I know who you're talking about. But what's that got to do with anything?'

Thameer looked at Khalid imploringly, to see if the angst-ridden youngster would help him out, but he had wandered off, out of earshot.

'Let's just forget it,' he urged.

'No, Thameer, let's not forget it.'

By now the obese lad was starting to lose his temper. He felt that he was being particularly indulgent to Zaid by inviting him to the cinema, and now he saw his gratitude thrown in such a shabby manner back in his face.

'OK, if you want it straight: they're saying that your brother's a poof.'

Zaid edged up towards Thameer.

'Who's saying that?'

'Everyone's saying it!' he replied.

'And you, Thameer, what do you say? Are you saying the same?'

No doubt, attracted by the raised voices, Khalid returned, and sought to appease their growing wrath:

'Come on, let it lie. I thought we were going to the Rex?'

'We're not going anywhere,' interjected Zaid.

'You can say that again. . .,' offered Thameer, '. . . I'm not going anywhere with the brother of some poofter! Maybe you're one yourself!'

Zaid had had enough. Almost involuntarily he threw a mighty punch at the other's stomach, his fist sinking into the rolls of fat as if into a heap of feather cushions.

'Is that your best?'

The big fellow grinned malevolently, and hit Zaid back with interest, leaving him strewn on the ground. Khalid ambled diffidently between the two, at a loss what to do. He didn't want to upset Thameer, but at the same time he felt obliged to lift Zaid from the ground, and help him tend his wounds. When finally he got Zaid onto his feet, a small trickle of blood dribbling from the corner of his mouth, his assailant was gone. Such was the scene in Al-Za'franiya on Wednesday of that week.

45

It only took a couple of nights before the repetition of Khalil's gatherings began to cloy. How our hosts managed to sustain their interest, night after night, I could not fathom. Like anyone else, I was not one to refuse a drink and an evening of carousing, but I never did experience the enjoyment of repeating the whole thing every night. These fellows, however, Aziz, Khalil, and his other friends, always the same faces, enacted the same jaded drama every night without exception. I should have known by his guests' enervated, lacklustre faces, that, for them, any enjoyment they may have previously experienced had long since melted away. I suppose that when Khalil and his friend met us at the club, they felt that they had discovered some means of enlivening their soirees. As for Mohammed, he did indeed make an appearance as was required of a guest, but he always found an excuse to absent himself earlier than I did. In retrospect, I think he wanted to somehow test me, to see if I would renounce our hosts' company to be with him. He was still, now I know, suspicious of what Khalil and I got up to that day in the car, and wanted me, of my own accord, to follow him when he retired. But in this I failed.

Khalil's interest was solely in me. Though Mohammed was by far the more attractive of us (at least by my reckoning), my host liked the polish of city boys; no doubt, it had also occurred to him that it would be infinitely more difficult to cajole a peasant into bed. Depravity, after all, follows civilisation as a shadow follows a body. But this didn't stop Aziz trying his luck with Mohammed. No doubt, Khalil had boasted of his conquest and made his friend jealous, so he felt inclined to try and overcome the defences of a peasant lad. If things didn't turn out according to plan, he could just as well hasten our departure.

So, one evening, when Mohammed had retired to his room, Aziz left the party. He always went back and forwards, so his absence went unnoticed. I had sought to stifle my boredom by consuming more alcohol than was good for me, so my awareness was somewhat impaired. Upstairs, Aziz gently knocked on the door behind which Mohammed was laying on his bed drearily staring at the ceiling. Receiving no response, he slowly pushed the door open and greeted him warmly.

'You don't want to join the party tonight?' he began.

Mohammed sat up, somewhat defensively, on his bed:

'No thank you, I'm just feeling a little tired.'

'Oh, I'm sorry to hear that.'

'You don't have to apologise. We all feel a little worn down sometimes. I feel the same quite often.'

He gestured to the bed and asked if he could sit down.

'Of course.'

Aziz, who hadn't taken such a close look at Mohammed before, furtively looked at his profile, and found the young man more attractive than he previously thought.

'So, how are you enjoying your stay with us?'

'Oh, it's been very pleasant.'

'Good, that's good,' uttered the elder.

Seeing this aloof young man – an aloofness often mistakenly attributed to unsociability – Aziz had supposed that it wouldn't be difficult to make some abrupt transition to a line of conversation more suited to his objective; the lad, after all, was only a peasant. But it turned out that before him sat a very personable and polite fellow, and not the country bumpkin he anticipated. Unfortunately, this attracted him all the more to Mohammed, and so he let his hands take over from where his voice had began. He reached out slowly and placed his hand on Mohammed's thigh, easing it closer to his private area. Mohammed was instantly aghast and jumped from the bed.

'What are you doing? Leave me alone.'

'What's wrong Mohammed, I thought you and your friend enjoyed that kind of thing?'

'You're disgusting! Get out of here, you dog.'

'Come on, Sami doesn't mind it. He didn't say no when Khalil asked him.'

'You're lying. Sami's not like that.'

'I'm not lying, my friend. Ask him yourself. He'll tell you what he and Khalil were doing at the farmhouse.'

Mohammed ran to the door and rushed downstairs. Drawing the curtain aside, he saw Khalil sitting close beside me, the two of us laughing and drinking together. I didn't see him. At that moment he decided that enough was enough, and made straight for the front door of the house. It must have been about ten in the evening when finally he reached the highway.

209

46

I was too drunk to resist the advances of my host, and when he dragged me into his room, Khalil found me completely unresisting. It was enough for me to keep my eyes from closing. I don't even remember returning to my own room; perhaps I was carried there and thrown into bed like some discarded empty liquor bottle. When I awoke it was late. The shutters had been left open, allowing the sun to throw its blazing vesture over me. My head felt especially hot and my fringe was dripping with sweat. At once, seeing the bed beside me empty, thoughts of the previous evening flowed into my mind like water spouting through the sluices of a dam.

'Oh God!' I sighed, as my placid nightime soul became infused with the day's troublesome phantoms.

With mounting anxiety, I vainly sought my dear friend. But for the villa's expanse, and the possibility of his secreting himself somewhere, I would all the sooner have arrived at the conclusion that Mohammed had left. As it was, I couldn't believe he had departed. He had nowhere to go nor the wherewithal to get there. I left my room and ran downstairs. Within the villa's commodious confines, a clattering emanating from the kitchen led me into its precincts. Two elderly women, whom I had interrupted in the process of peeling a large heap of onions, stared at me, as if a stray dog had wandered in, fawning for scraps. They stopped what they were doing, each holding a small knife in one hand and a partially peeled onion in the other. I left immediately. Questioning them would be pointless, the pair of them appeared practically inorganic. On the first floor, I looked quickly into our room. Of course, Mohammed was not there. Everything seemed so desolate and empty. Had we arrived with some few possessions, simply checking for their absence would have revealed the true state of affairs. But we had arrived with nothing.

I ascended a further flight of stairs, leading to the second floor. This was where Khalil's office was. Such was my anxiety that I did not feel the least diffident encroaching thus upon his privacy. Moreover, he, if anyone, was responsible for this mess and, whatever happened, there was no question of us staying any longer at the villa. I knew where he was – I could hear his voice and that of someone else from behind the room at the end of the corridor, to the left – and so grabbed the handle somewhat aggressively as if seeking a reckoning.

'Where's Mohammed?' I demanded.

I had misjudged my position.

Khalil was startled, sprung from his seat, gripped me by the arm, and harshly escorted me from the room. It quickly turned into a very ugly affair.

'What are you doing coming into my private room like that?'

I was frightened, and tried to lie my way out of it.

'I knocked, but no one answered.'

'Come on, I let you into my home as a guest. I didn't give you the right to bother me when I'm working.'

'I was looking for Mohammed,' I interjected, 'I haven't seen him since yesterday.'

'I don't know where your little peasant friend has gone. Just go, I'm sure he'll turn up.'

I took a few steps backwards, wounded at the way he had referred to Mohammed. I had been used, and now there was no reason for my presence.

I then dashed outside, in search of Mohammed. What previously had been a vista of beautiful quietude, of sunny opulence, now became oppressive in its utter indifference toward me, clashing harshly with the turmoil I felt within. Its luxurious foliage grimaced malevolently at my straitened features; it smiled at my frowns, uncaring of my plight. Once again, I found the gardener grubbing away at the same patch of earth as before.

'Have you seen my friend, the fellow I was with?'

'No. . .' he replied perfunctorily, '. . . I've seen nobody.'

He smiled briefly, dutifully, then returned to his work.

I felt disgusted with it all. I wanted to get out of that place – immediately; I felt repulsion for prostituting myself to Khalil in the hope that it would somehow benefit me. If only I could go back and change things! Had it not been for my belief, although it now appears utterly incomprehensible, that my friend would somehow appear from nowhere, I would have left straight away without looking back. And I will not conceal that for a brief moment the entire affair appeared in a new light, and I even considered the position of Mohammed in my affections.

There is something about love that always leads to shame, debasement, and ruin. I longed for the security of my home; the loving-kindness of my father. It was time to leave and so I did. In fact, so hard did I run that whether my feet touched the ground must, to this very day, remain an enigma to me. The room, the staircase, the gate, it all flew by as if

I were seeing things from a distant train. Usually so concerned to avoid the sun's direct onslaught and remain couched beneath the shade, I propelled myself along the open road, my throat as parched as the dust thrown up by my vigorous stride.

'Liberation Square. . . Liberation Square. . .,' I muttered between teeth that stuck resistantly to my gums.

It was as if I were following a command arising from the depths of my consciousness; everything felt as if it was planned. From Liberation Square I could catch a connection to Al-Za'franiya. The thought of going home, of ending it all, came as an overwhelming relief. Everything would be resolved.

'Mohammed must by now have returned to the village,' I mused.

'But what if he hasn't?' I added.

But I didn't know what to feel anymore. I just wanted someone else to take responsibility for me, to tell me what to do and how to live. Even if it meant the worst, I would return home that day.

47

As I dashed along the road, behind me I heard a gentle, persistant rumble, indicating the approach of a large vehicle. I stopped, panting heavily. As the gap between us diminished, I could make out the torso of a young man, leaning precariously from one of the side windows of a mini-bus. He was soliciting for passengers to Baghdad. I had no money, but it didn't stop me waving the fellow down. To hell with it!

'Liberation Square!' I panted, as the vehicle came to a standstill.

'I can drop you within ten minutes of the Square,' he responded.

I nodded in agreement. He opened the main door while still hanging from it.

The drive was short, a lot shorter, in fact, than I anticipated. The bus made few stops, and rattled along indomitably. Cars shot past at apparently great speed. Through the dirty window, smeared with fingerprints, I saw, successively, the delapidated floodlights that oversaw the disused stadium; the road that Khalil and I had followed on our journey thereto; the summit of Khalil's farmhouse; and finally, the country club. As I approached Baghdad, the diminishing distance punctuated by the increasing frequency of road signs, it was as if I were regaining my independence, even my life. Strangely, I thought, it appeared to me as if it were those very relations that are said to oppress people – families, duties, responsibilities – that guaranteed a person's liberty. Without these constraints, life became a limitless desert, broken only by sleep and sensual pleasure, with neither freedom nor constraint.

The bus came to a halt, and I jumped out along with two passengers.

'Sorry!' I cried to the boy, 'I haven't got any money.'

Straight away my feet hit the ground, carrying me into the midday rush of pedestrians. I fought my way as if through a jungle of human bodies, forgetting the respect I was so wont to show toward my elders. I bumped into people, hastily apologising as I ran ahead; my elbow caught someone's bag of groceries, sending a rush of pomegranates and oranges across the pavement. Old folk grumbled, looking back disdainfully; children stared with bewilderment, as this mad stranger, dishevelled by several days' vagabondage, fled as if for his life.

At Liberation Square I had to wait about ten minutes for my connection. So many buses were relaying back and forth that it cost me immense mental effort to secure the necessary presence of mind. I felt dizzy, disorientated.

'If only I can get on that bus. . .,' I urged myself, '. . .it doesn't matter what happens after.'

I hadn't eaten since the previous day, and my legs were limp beneath me; intermittantly, my vision clouded over, fading to grey; the loud din of commuters ceased and again reasserted itself as my hearing pulsed in and out like an irregular heartbeat. I could not find a seat, so I sat upon the floor, certain that if I remained standing, I would soon fall unconscious. Passers-by stared at me as if I had just arrived from another world. So quickly does a person lose that imperceptible bond that unites a people together, and slip into isolation! Only a few days earlier I had walked among these people with a sense of belonging; now. . . who knows what had changed to transform me into a pariah? If I had not been so feeble, perhaps a combative spirit might of taken possession of me and demanded the answer to this question from one of these suspicious onlookers. But now I felt I had to conserve myself, to gather my mind as if into a solid and impenetrable ball, untouched by and untouching those around me.

A crowd of passengers, mostly military men destined for the army base outside Al-Za'franiya, elbowed their way onto the arriving bus. So dense and unorganised was the rush that I was able, without effort, to secrete myself within its mass, and sink in a corner of the bus unobserved. I lowered my head, like a convicted criminal awaiting the gibbet.

'How pleasant it would be simply to become nothing!'

No one can know the real and inimitable value of humility who has not lost himself in some socially unforgivable act, who desires only to be accepted once again alongside his fellows!

48

One should never presume upon the dignity of a Arab peasant. He will put up with much, but an affront to his honour he will never endure. In this, he far surpasses the city dweller. The most subtle slight affects him as keenly as salt cast into an open wound. When he feels himself treated disrespectfully, he is willing to submit that which he holds most dear, even if it means destroying himself. Following Aziz's overtures, and seeing me gaily drinking with Khalil, mindful neither of the time of night or the distance he would have to walk, Mohammed struck out onto the road. He didn't know precisely what would await him at home. He believed that neither his father nor Zakiyah would have revealed their secret to anyone. That, he thought, he could be sure of. He'd just have to throw himself on the mercy of Abbas, denying any truth in Zakiyah's assertions. For now, the future would have to take care of itself. Otherwise, his strength would leave him, and he would not be able to go on. But he couldn't remain at the villa, and there was nowhere else for him to go.

Mohammed continued to pace briskly in the direction of Baghdad. It had been more than an hour since he left

Khalil's villa. The sun had had now completely set. Very few cars passed, but of those that did, no one offered him a lift. There must have been something uninviting in his gait, or perhaps the late hour he was trudging along the road, that deterred anyone from stopping. Soon, however, a ramshackle cart, pulled by a old donkey with strings of saliva hanging from its mouth, ambled slowly towards him. It barely exceeded Mohammed's own pace. Driving the cart was an aged peasant. Beside him, a young lad munched from a large chunk of watermelon, a remnant from their earlier delivery to Al-Mansoor.

'Jump up young man!' the amiable driver urged in a thick rustic accent, 'it's a long way to go, wherever your going! You're lucky we're late today. We're usually home by now!'

Mohammed did not have to be asked twice, but straight away leapt into the empty cart, leaning heavily against its broken trellis side.

'Give the lad some watermelon,' the old fellow urged his son.

With a small, wooden-handled penknife, the young man cut a large lump of watermelon and handed it to Mohammed, who devoured it greedily.

'Have some more!' the old man cried, eager to engage his passenger in conversation.

It was a lonely drive, he explained, travelling back and forth, as he did every day at this time of year, along the same stretch of highway. Company was always welcome. As for his own lad, well, he said, a resigned smile indicating a small row of blackened teeth, he didn't have anything to say; he just sat there, eating watermelon throughout the journey, and spitting the pips at the donkey's ears. The old fellow struck the lad playfully on the shoulder, a little too forcefully, perhaps, than was warrented by his raillery. The other remained passive, his only response being a rather irritated expression.

Mohammed was glad to respond to the old fellow's humour. It felt good to be with his own people again, however strange a figure he might have previously cut amongst them.

'So. . .,' the driver began, '. . . you're on your way to Baghdad?'

'Yes. . .,' Mohammed replied, taking a large bite of watermelon, '. . . and from there, I'm going home, to Al-Za'franiya.'

'Well, you're in luck. We're from nearby. We can drop you quite close. And if it gets late, you can stay with us the night.'

'Thanks. . .,' Mohammed replied, '. . . that's very kind of you.'

'Well. . .,' the kind old fellow quickly interjected, '. . . that's what Allah created us for. To help one another. Nowadays, us old folk seem to be the only ones that remember that!'

With that he glanced sideways at his companion, who raised his eyebrows as if to say:

'Not again!'

The rhythmic trotting of the donkey was mesmerising. It could send a person to sleep. At the speed they were travelling, it would be a good couple of hours before they reached Karadha. By that time, it would be getting dark.

'Maybe you'd like to come on the run again tomorrow? It'd be splendid to have someone to talk to – I can't pay much, but you can have as much watermelon as you can eat!'

Mohammed uttered a noncomittal grunt. He was a lot calmer now, and had decided to go directly home and confront things.

The driver continued rambling, no longer awaiting Mohammed's response. It was a need just as pressing as

219

breathing itself; an accumulation of unspoken words that had to be discharged at the first sign of an interlocutor, even if he remained silent and unresponsive.

'You know what? I musn't say it, of course, but between us, our lot under the feudal system was better than it is today. Would you believe it? Of course, there's talk about the peasant getting this right and the peasant getting that right – but, if anything, our lot's not what it used to be.'

Mohammed, a barely imperceptible smile passing over his lips, stretched himself out. He reached for an old hessian sack, carefully and adeptly folded it, and laid it across his head.

'You see. . .,' the old fellow continued, '. . . it's always the same – just a change of masters – it's always the same.'

His postillion had now fallen asleep; his head rolled from left to right on his chest.

'Melons . . . melons . . . there's a business for you, son,' the old man continued, 'you should think about melons. With melons, a man knows where he stands.'

Here a short pause ensued. The driver looked round at Mohammed, who was now faintly snoring, and then continued with his monologue:

'What was I saying? Yes, that was it. . . melons, there's money to be made in melons, a modest income certainly, but one a person can rely on.'

The old donkey plodded along the highway. Baghdad came, and Baghdad went. Only the old man remained awake. Alongside the Tigris, he halted to give the donkey a rest. Nearby, a soft din of music could be heard emerging from the cafes alongside the river. The old man looked on, philosophically, as children chased one another around the brightly glowing lanterns. How short a time ago it was since he was a child! Yes, they were good times, he thought. He remembered helping his father out on the farm, the first time he was allowed to take hold of the cart's reins on his own; his ineptitude at market; the marriage celebrations; the birth of his first child, now a grown man in the army. And now the book of life was almost complete. He looked at the two young men, gently snoring in the cart.

'I don't know. . .,' he muttered, '. . . all that lies in the future for them.'

But he felt glad that for him the race had been run; he wouldn't want to be a child again.

'Oh no!' he said to himself, 'once is quite enough. Let Allah dispose of things as he will! Praise be to Allah!'

The cart once again hitched, the donkey plodded over Liberation Bridge, carrying the party to the far side of the Tigris. A hollow thud accompanied its weary tread, providing a rhythmic cadence to the sonorous cry of the muezzin. At Karadha the old man sprung from his seat, as lithe as a child, and gave Mohammed a gentle nudge.

'That's it, young man – we're here – Karadha, this is as far as I'm going! You'll be staying with us tonight?'

Circling around to the other side of the cart, he took hold of his son's arm and shook the young man.

'Time to get up, sleepy head!'

Mohammed reached for the ground with his toes, and fell heavily upon his feet. His legs were stiff.

'What time is it?' he asked, stifling a yawn.

'Time – it's somewhere around midnight,' the old fellow replied reflectively.

Once again the old fellow invited the young man to remain with him that night, but Mohammed was adamant that he would finish his journey. It would give him time to ponder things during the walk home. Anyway, from Karadha it was only a few miles to Al-Za'franiya, a distance easily traversed by a young man.

Mohammed decided that he would follow the Tigris as far as possible, and then, by way of Al-Rashid Military Base and finally Al-Hikmah University, he'd make a straight line for home, arriving there early in the morning. The whole journey would take no more than two or three hours. He bid goodbye to the old man and his companion, and looked around to get his bearings. Small, sepia lights glared from the outlying suburb; above, the stars, near and far, vied to outshine one another in the sable firmament. It was the calm before the storm, a beautiful calm redolent of quietude and bliss.

This was Mohammed's final opportunity to go back. But he would not go back. He had reached the end. For there is great solace to be found in resigning to the inevitable; in ceasing to struggle against an adversity to which one must yield or ultimately be destroyed. Cupping his hands, he drew a silken draft of water from the Tigris, splashing it against his stiff features. He was instantly invigorated. The water's clarity penetrated into his mind, quickening its sluggish prevarication into staunch determination. At once he set off, not at an ambling pace, but assuming the march of one ready to meet his destiny.

Upon reaching the military base, he decided to make a lengthy detour, which took him about a mile out of his way. Attempting to pass through the camp's checkpoints at that time of night would only bring unwanted nuisance, unanswerable questions. Better to circumvent its barbed wire fence, which struck out at a right angle, far into the distance, intermitted by the occasional glare of spotlights. Beyond the base, otherwise so alive with learned discourse, Al-Hikmah University maintained a voiceless presence. Silence, absolute silence. It seemed that even the chirp of the cicadas and the cooing of the pigeons had been eradicated by this concrete monster. Not a single beam shone from its precincts; the light of learning had been extinguished for now. Here was an intimation of immortality. Al-Za'franiya could now be vaguely discerned by its dark mass.

49

If ever there was a stubborn, dogmatic and authoritarian fellow, that fellow was Salman. Strength he conceived solely in terms of muscle; uprightness in subduing opposition. Yet, if one could imagine some physical organ corresponding to his sense of honour, then the slightest touch would have been sufficient to induce a spasm in it. But, for all that, he was an indefatigable man, and by his efforts he had established a small business selling paraffin. He sold fairly, at an honest price, and was thoroughly dependable, not taking a day off from his round even on those rare occasions when he was unwell. Every housewife knew him as 'Abu Nafot,' ('The Father of Paraffin'), and looked upon him with great respect. Always attired in the same dirty, paraffin-stained dishdasha, his approach could be detected ten metres away by the inimitable odour emanating from him. At the raucous cry of 'Paraffin! Paraffin!' accompanied by the bang of an iron rod on a metal drum, his customers would emerge from their homes, carrying old cans or some similar container. The liquid would be drawn off from a large matt black cylinder fastened to the back of his cart, upon which was roughly scribbled 'Paraffin.'

After years of wear, the lettering had become practically undecipherable.

One may, therefore, fathom in what grave terms he considered the 'nasty mess' (as he referred to it) at Abbas's household, by his inflexible decision to suspend his round and depart immediately for Al-Za'franiya, accompanied by Ahmed, Zakiyah's son. Remonstrate as they might, remind him of his obligation to his customers, neither brother nor sister nor father could deter him. Just when they thought they had induced some reason into the fellow, straight away he would hearken back to his initial standpoint.

'I don't care how long it takes, I'm going to sort this nasty mess out.'

Thus, one sees how a virtue so apt to prosper business, can be transformed into a veritable plague to those who would appeal to reason.

On the seat beside his own was Ahmed; behind his seat, he had gathered a few provisions – some small cucumbers, tomatoes, a cooked chicken (which he personally slaughtered the previous day) and some khubz – together with his most valued possession, his pristine rifle, threw a blanket over the top of all, and began his journey. The ride took him over some rough, and frequently pot-holed ground, even, at one juncture, requiring him to ford a snaking shallow stream. All this made his black cylinder of paraffin clank and rattle, and the liquid swish violently against its interior. He cursed and muttered against his unfortunate fate, which put him in a thoroughly foul mood by the time he had traversed the ten or so miles to Al-Za'franiya.

Abbas had been keeping a lookout for his guest much of the day. He knew Salman was a tough customer and, if truth be told, was even a little frightened at the thought of his arrival. They had never got on. It was as if a mutual hatred existed between them since first they saw one another.

Precisely what his brother-in-law was expecting to achieve by his visit remained a mystery to Abbas. But when he saw that Salman was wearing his egal crooked, he was greatly disquieted, and considered that he would have to watch the fellow very closely indeed. Even if he could not be present at all times, there were those around him who would be willing to keep him enlightened as to everything that occurred.

'Peace be with you, brother.'

'Peace be with you too.'

Salman's brief, curt, reply, his refusal to refer to the other as his 'brother,' summed up how he would comport himself over the next few days; that is, in a perfunctory, truncated fashion, uttering no more than was required to get the 'nasty mess' resolved. Abbas courteously invited his guest to be seated, and asked Salha to serve some food and boil the blackened kettle. Salman continued to complain and question his brother-in-law, and the fellows sipped tea until quite late into the night. It was clear that Salman knew everything.

The following morning, just before dawn, Abbas rose from his cot, did his ablutions, prayed, and threw his dishdasha about him, setting off for the fields with Salha and his sons. He wasn't altogether comfortable leaving his guest to amble about on his own, digging into everyone's business and embarrassing him, but he could not do otherwise. However, he could be sure that if anyone would guard Zakiyah's secret, he was the man. It was time to harvest the barley, and the work couldn't be delayed. He picked up his curled scythe, much worn but with a fearsome blade, and strode off, muttering some imperceptible words as he departed. Salman had already arisen from his cot – the fellow, it seemed, hardly needed any sleep – and sat cross-legged in his corner, no doubt considering what he would do. That previous night, he had harried Abbas for details of Mohammed's whereabouts, where he might have gone; and considered whether the old man might be holding out on him. The ultimate concern of their discussion, however, remained unmentionable, and the two of them had to employ a hundred different figures, epithets and allusions to utter what nowadays, at least in the west, can be uttered so candidly.

Shortly after Abbas departed, Salman slung his gun across his shoulder and left the hut. Outside, still hitched to the paraffin cart, he threw his donkey a handful of fodder, and patted the creature firmly on the head. At that time of day, the village was alive with the tread of peasants on their way to the fields. They filed languidly along the road, sometimes singly, sometimes in groups, carrying their tools in one hand and their lunch of khubz and onion, wrapped in a piece of linen, in the other. The presence of the stranger attracted their attention. Who was this tall, menacing-looking fellow, wearing his egal askew, standing beside the paraffin cart? What was he doing there? There were some who knew him as a relation of Abbas; he, they explained, was the only one who could put the fear of god into the old farmers' representative. They addressed him politely, and he reciprocated politely, almost as if not conscious of his words.

Much was going on in that stubborn head; most pressing for the moment was the direction he was to take – left or right? For Salman had no clear plan of action. Vaguely, he considered what his duty, as a man of dignity, was. He knew that what he had heard about his brother-in-law's son was true; for these were not words that could be bandied about lightly, as if in jest. No one would dare utter them without his being indemnified by their veracity. This, then, was the truth of the matter. All that remained was the question of its rectification.

50

Throwing another handful of fodder to his donkey, Salman strode off in the opposite direction to the peasants. As he drew nearer to the teachers' quarter, the influx of peasants grew sparser, until only the odd late-riser remained, pacing briskly by, to avoid his elder's tirade. Salman had never seen such a stark juxtaposition of poverty and middle-class opulence. The villas cut an anomalous figure beside the meagre dwellings of the labourers, one not altogether wholesome.

'These city people always bring problems,' he mused, 'whitewash their walls as they will, they'll never wash away their corruption. How and why they came here I don't know.'

This, he believed, was the source of Mohammed's undoing. The boy had clearly been ensnared by the city-people's wiles and now he had to pay the ultimate price for yielding to temptation. But whether Salman would be able to pull the trigger. . . the thought could not be envisaged in so straightforward and unencumbered a fashion. The whole affair was despicable; and to have to be the one to preserve the tribe's honour – really, it was a burden that any man would wish to shirk, if only he could. Best not to think about it. Anyway, come what may, he wouldn't leave until he had confronted the boy. With God's help he might be able to satisfy his honour without resorting to his gun.

'I'll come back later,' he thought, extending his long stride towards the peasants' village.

Having arrived at its furthest extent, he crossed the strip of deserted ground that circumvented Al-Za'franiya. To his right was a large heap of unused bricks, a shovel and cement-mixer, left behind many years before by builders. Beyond a knotty outcrop of tangled weed and wild orange trees, was the Tigris. On that day the great river appeared turgid, as if the mud stowed deep in its bed had been disturbed.

'It's different from when I was last here,' Salman pondered, 'only, I was very young then.'

He forcefully distracted himself from his more distant memories. They were too painful, as much of the past is. We often sentimentalise over bygone happenings: the bright landscapes, the cheerful faces of our friends and family; again, the laughter is heard, the voices of one's beloved, her inimitable smile – but the curtain soon falls away, a reminder that what followed was not what we had hoped for. The image fades as in a drama, leaving the viewer with fond memories that, in life, must ultimately perish as they are consumed in sorrow.

It was very peaceful there by the water's edge. It gets into one's blood somehow, and induces a gentle somnolence where even the heartbeat can be faintly deciphered. For Salman was not exempt from nature's charm. Neither was he a stranger to affection. Love once lived within the narrow confines of his breast. If in youth he had been an unlovable, even obnoxious, fellow, there was yet one who had loved him. Another he would never find. Now, committed to emotional solitude, he indulged in the pain that loss had brought him; in this way, he thought, some connection,

228

albeit tenuous, was established with his former love, even from beyond the grave. The pain he felt was the unbreakable thread that tied him forever to his beloved. Within this self-imposed misery, Salman was safe, submitted to the harshness expected of him, and was even its initiator. He would live like this for the rest of his days just to spite himself.

He looked inquisitively at the destroyed mill; only the outlay of the ground floor could be observed beneath its charred remains. The fire had been unable to consume the internal clay walls that demarcated its rooms. Everything else had perished. Salman cautiously stepped inside, and gently nudged some of the debris with his foot, as if he were searching for something. Leaving the mill, he wandered about for much of the morning, taking a few shots at ducks and other water fowl that skirted the Tigris. The man who despises himself will often tyrannise over nature's innocent creatures. Not only did he shoot birds; he shot at stray dogs and cats; anything, in fact, that inadvertently crossed his sanguinary path. Larger game he could only dream about, but dream he did. He would have loved to travel to Africa to fell an elephant or a lion. And anything he killed he left to be baked dry by the sun. He enjoyed shooting; that split-second as the finger gently depressed the trigger; it was almost as if it extended in both directions into eternity, a moment of infinitesimal extension, but infinite intension. It gave him the power over life and death, a power he so impotently submitted to at his wife's premature death.

That afternoon he returned to the villa, but no one was at home. He returned again in the evening. This time the front door was opened by my father, who politely greeted him, notwithstanding his own inner anxiety. Salman introduced himself as 'a relation of Mohammed.' But father already knew who this fellow was, and what he knew of him he didn't like. Still, he kindly invited Salman in to discuss

229

matters, but the other refused, convinced that to fraternise with the enemy – as he saw him – would be to leave oneself open to the charge of weakness.

'No, I'll stand here if you don't mind, brother,' was all he said.

Strangely, he hadn't thought about what he would say. Now he felt a little ridiculous, even embarrassed, which was saying a great deal for a man who had never been embarrassed in his life. A little put out by the other's discourtesy, he began:

'You're looking for information about the young fellows, no doubt?'

'Yes, brother, I want to know what's happened to Mohammed. I need to speak with him, to sort things out.'

'Well,' replied my father, 'I wish I could help you. I'm asking the same question about my son.'

'So you don't know where they are?' the peasant continued.

'If I knew where they are, I wouldn't be sitting here!'

Father didn't appreciate Salman's menacing tone, nor his suspicious glance. It wouldn't work with him, this bullying people about.

'Do you think I'm hiding them – is that what it is?' the teacher urged.

'I'm not saying that. It's only. . . you know the boys better than I do. Perhaps you know where they hang out. All young men have somewhere they go.'

'I don't know anything,' father replied, 'we all want this to end; and if you go frightening the young men off with your intimidating behaviour, then they'll never come back. I suggest you go home and sit and wait patiently until things sort themselves out.'

Salman had reckoned on a longer discussion, but nothing really remained to be said.

51

Abbas made it his business to know what Salman and Ahmed had been doing in his absence. Every intricacy thereof was disclosed to him by a network of interested peasants, who found therein a great source of delight. They fought with one another to provide the most comprehensive account of the stranger's movements, even adding material where observation fell short. But, for all that, there was not a great deal to be reported. Salman quickly became habituated to his new surroundings, and followed more or less the same route every day in his perambulations. What would happen when the young man reappeared was a particularly fruitful area of conjecture. Some there were who believed he'd give the boy a good hiding and leave it at that; others thought he'd take him away, and put him out of sight so his presence wouldn't remind people of the deed associated with him; others, again, were of the opinion that the fellow would shoot the boy as if he were a stray dog. However, Salman could not overstay his host's hospitality, and had to attend to his own farm, cattle and family. Accordingly, he left at first light, leaving his hand pistol, wrapped up in a gotra a white cloth, with Ahmed.

Mohammed himself reached Al-Za'franiya very early that morning. He had a good sense of time, and surmised that only a couple of hours remained until sunrise. Abbas would still be asleep and the young fellow considered that it would be better to wait until his father left the house, before he went in. He even thought of approaching his mother, Salha, first, but it would be very difficult to catch her on her own. If he could get to his father just before the other peasants set out for the fields, no one would see him enter the house. Otherwise, his presence would attract an unfriendly crowd and, no doubt, affect the old man's discretion by exposing him to the judgement of others. Abbas would then be expected to act according to precedent, and the matter would assume the guise of a public trial. He had to assume the worst: that everyone knew Zakiyah's story, and would welcome his downfall. This would give him some time to think the matter over. He would try to be as candid as possible with his father, but still he would have to deny Zakiyah's assertions. If he admitted the truth of her claims, there was no possibility of conciliating Abbas.

For the time being, Mohammed remained just outside the village, and sat down against the slender trunk of a date palm. A slight morning pinch suffused the air at that time of day, so he folded his arms about himself, and watched the last few stars fading beneath the onset of day. He felt numbed by it all. When he thought of the enormity of what lay before him, he could hardly believe that he was sitting there, as if he were awaiting the school bus.

Occasionally he thought of his friend. Certainly, those passionate feelings remained, but seldom surmounted the terror that brooked his heart. Anyway, he had been betrayed, and there was nothing else to do. This gave him a sense of sacrifice in what he was doing. Offering himself up like that, on the altar of love, he considered himself an oblation given over to a world at variance with himself, a world where only institutionalised love was accepted.

What caused our relationship to founder, beyond my obvious duplicity, was the uniqueness of the path we trod. He looked forward to the time when people of the same sex could live and love together as did those of different sexes. At times, prey to the prejudice of society, he felt that he had been lulled into a kind of madness. For whatever we do, however remarkable or even painful it may be, ultimately it becomes habitual, and ceases to burden the conscience or awaken the intellect. It is a quality of the will of each of us, that quickly catches up with every change in our life's course and invests it with the tedium of normality.

Passing the time in such manner, the rising of the sun now indicated that it was time to slowly make his way home. He quickly gained the uncultivated perimeter that skirted Al-Za'franiya, entering the suburb from the end of the teachers' villas. Looking around vigilantly, Mohammed scurried alongside the fences fronting the new development, keeping hard against the areas concealed by date palms, flitting from tree to tree. He would have passed by my parents' villa, but whether he stopped at this point, or continued straight on, I do not know, and leave it to the reader's own judgement. Crossing over to the peasants' village, he almost stumbled upon a small group of field workers. He hadn't noticed them from behind the date palms. Quickly, falling back, he regained the safety of the shade. There was something vaguely burlesque about this exploit that helped to alleviate his trepidation, and even brought a transitory smile to his face.

Allowing sufficient time for the group of farmers to proceed, he once again began to make his way, staying close beside the clay brick walls. The house of Abbas was now within sight. Hastily making sure that no one was around, he took to his heels with great vigour, not stopping until he reached home.

52

The previous night, Abbas and Ahmed had worked late into the evening. Barley is one of Iraq's major sources of production, and for villagers it is seminal to their livelihood. Abbas's forbears had been harvesting the crop for centuries, and this had given the task the reverence due all things of great age. For the period of its duration, everything else takes second place, and many peasants remain on their farms to catch first light, thereby avoiding the stifling heat that is characteristic of this season and is known by Iraqis' as 'the date heat,' when the dates ripen and fall to the ground. During the afternoon, the hottest time of day, they would retire to the barns, where the barley sheaths were processed, and the husk separated from the ear. But for all their hard work, it was one of the most pleasant times for the farmers. During the harvest, all hands were needed; the peasants brought their wives and children along, and they all remained on the farm. They ate there and spent their nights there. Every hand was given a scythe, to cut the strips of earth missed by the giant yellow combine harvester. Even employment was found for the little ones. The women sang as they cut the barley, and the fields resonated with the

sweet intonation of their voices wafting across the shim-
mering golden fields. The children threw handfuls of grain
at one another, frolicking as they are wont to do when
permitted some unaccustomed latitude, and the women
laughed as little Ali or Hussein rubbed the dusty husks from
his eyes. Truly, a bucolic moment!

Abbas, doubtful of when Mohammed would return,
decided to remain at the farm. He did not speak with his
fellows about what troubled him, and they didn't mention
anything as a matter of respect. Amidst the raillery of night-
time carousing around the fire, he was able to forget his
difficulties. Some of the older men recounted stories of the
past; they retold anecdotes as if for the first time; chided
the modern way of life, and sat reverently as one of their
number sang a lamentation telling of forlorn love and
rejected passion. They drank tea late into the night, even
though their bodies were aching, and tiredness fought ably
against their eyelids. Sleep? – there's enough time for sleep
when you're dead!

53

Mohammed entered the outer door leading into the yard, closing it cautiously behind him. His senses were in revolt as he approached, and he had to do violence to himself to find the strength to continue. Every step demanded infinite tenacity; every thought that threatened his resolve had to be summarily ousted; he let his body take over, submitting to each footfall as if it were the fall of a donkey's hoof and he a passenger. He put his ear against the door. Nothing stirred. Maybe his father was still asleep? Maybe he had left early? And then he remembered that it was the barley harvest. Perhaps the family wasn't even there? That was it, no one was at home. Expecting to find the house empty, he confidently opened the door. It was uneven, and its base scraped along the earth, requiring a lift at the same time as it was pushed. Inside he saw no one; his father's cot was empty, so too Zakiyah's and Salha's. He didn't notice that beneath a camel-skin cover, his step-brother was sleeping, so he strode into the adjoining animal pen, by way of completing his search. Of course, he found the animals quietly snoozing in their enclosure.

But not for long. One of the sheep awoke at his presence, greeting the young man with a voluminous 'baaaar.' Immediately, Ahmed roused from his sleep. The step-brother sprung up and grabbed his hand gun, which he kept close beside him. Making for the animal enclosure, he came face-to-face with Mohammed. The young lad was struck dumb, but in the split second that intervened, he rushed against Ahmed, knocking his pistol from his hand. It landed heavily on its handle, and fired, blasting a small whole in the roof. The shot alerted Abbas in the nearby field who immediately realised its origin. He ran as fast as he could to the house. A further shot rang out, as the two men struggled to reach the gun. Ahmed squeezed on the trigger while Mohammed again knocked the gun from his hand and ran towards the door.

But Ahmed caught hold of Mohammed as he tried to force his way past him.

'You disgrace . . . you son of a dog! Just let me finish this, so that I can hold my head high again.'

The young man shouted for his life. Ahmed grabbed Mohammed by the arm and swung him violently across the room. Thudding soundly against the wall, the young fellow felt as if his stomach had risen to his throat; his lower lip and tongue was bitten through, and a surge of blood ejected from the wound, running copiously down his neck and onto his shirt. The room turned about; his eyes rolled. Ahmed's anger was unappeased. Again, he grabbed Mohammed by the hair and threw him against the door and into the yard. A large clump of hair, with the scalp attached to it, remained in his hand. Mohammed was by now slipping into unconsciousness.

He knew that if he submitted, he would never awaken. If he could only make his way to the outer gate, surely he would be able to attract someone's attention. No longer aware of the pain, he dimly felt his way towards the door. Ahmed retrieved his gun. Nothing short of Mohammed's death would dispel his wrath. This was the end. The young fellow dragged himself across the yard, and reached for the handle and swung the gate open. It was enough for the peasants who had assembled outside to see that it was Mohammed, and that he was in terrible trouble. But before he could get beyond the gate, Ahmed grabbed hold of the young man's foot and dragged him back into the yard. A group of peasants tried to come to his rescue, but Ahmed aimed his gun at them and shouted. Nevertheless, their interference delayed the step-brother sufficiently to enable Abbas to reach the house. The old fellow finally arrived at the gate. He was not a young man, and the run made his heart beat fiercely; he panted, even stopping momentarily to catch his breath. He knew that the longer it took him to reach home, the greater the opportunity for Ahmed to harm Mohammed.

Only now did he realise how much he loved his son. It was as if a veil had been torn from his eyes. Everything appeared in a new light. Only the previous day, he thought he did not care what happened to Mohammed. Now he saw himself once again in his son, the life of his life, the fruit of his body. He could almost feel the blows that were being inflicted on the young man. He could see Ahmed viciously attacking his boy. He burst through the crowd that stood outside his gate. The gate was almost thrown off of its hinges. Abbas saw his son; heard the cries; the voice of Ahmed shouting frantically to his unreceptive son, whom he had by now dragged into the house. Without hesitation he dashed inside and took up his son in his arms.

'Get out of here! Leave him to me!' shouted Ahmed.

But he ignored Ahmed's admonition and lifted Mohammed in his sinewy peasant's arms, cradling his unconscious head against his chest.

'Leave it to me! Go!' Ahmed again shouted, this time louder and with greater menace in his voice.

The father continued towards the outer gate with the boy in his arms.

'Come back I say!' shouted Ahmed.

Abbas ignored the other, and reached for the latch.

'Back, come back or I'll lay you both out!' he shouted.

Abbas put Mohamed down and turned around to Ahmed.

'Give me the gun,' he urged, with a steadiness in his voice that defied the violence around him. He slowly approached him.

Confusion, utter confusion, overcame Ahmed. He had to act now; it was not a question of this one case only; he was defending an entire way of life; if he let this slip, the whole edifice would crumble. That couldn't be allowed to happen. With these last thoughts, he lifted the barrel of the gun and took a shot at Mohammed; the bullet missed, and caught Abbas directly in the chest. The old man fell to his knees, crouching over his son to protect him as he was giving up his last breath. A group of peasants ran into the yard and overcame Ahmed. Momentarily his eyes met those of his assailant. Abbas now knew that his son would be saved, and love suffused his dying glance.

Amidst all this hubbub, Ahmed was quick to realise that he had not only killed his step-father (which did not trouble him considerably), but a leading party member (which did trouble him). If he managed to escape a death sentence, he would have to spend the rest of his days in prison. But the end came more swiftly than anticipated. He could see that some party secret police were forcing a passage through the crowd. Guns drawn, they arrested him. He offered no resistance. The old order of honour killings had given way, at least in this one case, to father love and sacrifice.

54

A tremendous bustle followed, as rumour of the event swept across the village and neighbouring countryside. The fields were deserted by the peasants; the villas by the teachers; everyone made an exodus for Abbas's house. And when I say 'everyone,' it is not a mere hyperbole that I am employing. My countrymen will be well aware that every Middle Eastern man is convinced beyond the least vestige of doubt that he knows better than his neighbour how to deal with a situation. He is, moreover, avid to implement his knowledge, even if it means pushing aside someone who truly knows what he is doing. Add to this the necessarily insular character of village life, and it is not difficult to imagine the crowd that congregated that morning at the scene of the tragic incident.

Among the first to arrive was Salem Tahir, the local mayor. He wore the same outfit as when we first met him, only considerably more worn and patched. He set to organising the mob, while awaiting the arrival of the police and ambulance. Not to grudge the fellow his due, Salem Tahir excelled here. Within five minutes he had managed to disperse no less than half the crowd of onlookers and organise the remainder into a single, manageable, throng. A couple of peasants were allowed to remain with the injured man to stanch the blood that was oozing profusely from the opening in his chest. Every piece of rag or linen they could lay their hands on was foisted into service; but just as swiftly the material became soaked and unusable. The bullet, it seemed, had not pierced his heart; but he was losing so much blood that it was doubtful whether he would survive. Mohammed remained unconscious beside Abbas, yet no one offered to help or attempted to rouse him. The gates had been shut on the yard.

The crowd's attention was distracted by the arrival of an ambulance. The horde had to step backward as the rear doors were pushed open and two stretchers carried out. The crew made its way through the closed gate. The peasants watched intently as the ambulance-men ran backwards and forwards to procure supplies from the ambulance. Those who attempted to establish the status of Abbas's condition were ignored, or told to keep out of the way. Soon, the gate swung open and the first stretcher was hastily brought out. On it lay Mohammed, his face bloodied and bruised; an oxygen mask was attached to his mouth. He must have been suffering from some kind of shock, for he stared at the sky, his eyes wide open like two full moons, as if unaware of what was happening. The crowd waited attentively for the second stretcher to emerge. They thought that the old man would have been brought out first; his was the most serious wound. Again, the gate swung open, but not with the sense of urgency that the peasants anticipated. When they saw the stretcher bearing a white blanket covering Abbas's face, no more to see the sun's rays, they were as awestruck as the event was predictable. Seeing the old fellow laid out like that, some sought solace in the belief that this was Allah's will; others covertly remonstrated against their fellow's fate;

the women burst into tears, slapped their hands against their chests and heads, calling on Allah for justice and mercy.

When my father became aware that someone had been shot and that Mohammed had returned to the village, his earlier imperturbability collapsed beneath the tremendous blow. Awestruck, he cursed himself for his previous inaction. Hastily, he ran from the house in his shirtsleeves; he saw the ambulance, and forced the crowd aside to see whom was within – it was Mohammed. Then he saw the body emerge from the yard. God help him, was that his son being brought out? He ran over to the ambulance-men who were carrying the body, and pulled the sheet off the deceased's face. No one was going to push him aside until he had seen who was inside. When he saw that it was Abbas, his relief was tempered by the uncertainty that surrounded his own son.

The police had by now arrived and were trying to contain the situation. They had sealed off the yard behind the ambulance-men. And ten minutes later Ahmed emerged cuffed with hands behind his back, and marched by two police men on either side of him. When my father demanded to be let in to see if his son was inside, they perfunctorily confirmed that there was no one else within. The mayor then approached him. Not satisfied with their response, the teacher urged:

'Where's my son? Is he in there?'

The mayor confirmed what the police had said. Father then met Amineh at the scene, and the two of them returned to the villas. She offered to accompany him back home, knowing that what had occurred would be profoundly detrimental to my father's state of mind; she could provide some solace for him.

'No thank you, that's very kind of you,' father politely, as always, replied, 'but we'll be alright.'

55

When that day I arrived at a bus stop on the outskirts of the suburb, it was like an actor stepping onto the empty stage after the drama had long since unfolded. Following the debacle, many of the peasants had returned to the fields, where they again took up the theme of the incident between their labours; others, however, remained at the scene of the incident. Frantic, both Zakiyah and Salha, scooped up handfuls of dust, which they threw onto their heads. They beat their chests, all the time wailing uncontrollably. Among the men, some looked on, smoking, trying to stanch the flow of involuntary tears; younger folk assumed menacing features, vowing to seek revenge when they got hold of the 'city boy.'

Small suburbs are like that; and the protagonist in such a drama must often feel piqued when he considers that his tragic performance has become the theme of interminable and idle chatter. Everyone was now agog with expectation of my return.

On my way home, I took a detour through the peasants' village, hoping that I might catch a surreptitious glance at Abbas's house. I dearly wanted to know what had happened to Mohammed, whether he had returned as I anticipated.

Even more than propitiating my father, I wanted to straighten out things between us. Looking back, as I do now, on my thoughts at that moment, I can only presume that I was prey to some delusion. Truly, I believed that things would be resolved, and that Mohammed and I could resume our relationship – if not immediately, then surely some time in the future. I was naïve enough to believe that love would ultimately triumph; that people would forgive us for the sake of our love. But I did not reckon – though well I should have done – upon the many obstacles erected by human beings to prohibit the kind of emotions we shared. I say it again – I should have known better. But who knows better when passion veils perception of what is most obvious? It's an old story, one that will follow humankind until the end of time.

Those who have experienced these feelings – and who hasn't once loved? – will understand my anxiety when I arrived upon the scene of that morning's incident. The entrance to the yard remained cordoned off; a solitary policeman, smoking a cigarette, stood sentinel outside. Repudiating my earlier endeavour to conceal myself, I ran up to the policeman with great haste:

'What's going on? Has something happened?'

At first, the fellow tried to shew me away like a fly, but my persistence no doubt annoyed him, and he submitted to my importunities.

'There's been a murder.'

'Who?' I cried.

'Not quite sure, but there was some scuffle involving a couple of young fellows and an old man. More I can't say.'

I could only think the worse had happened.

'But who's been murdered? What's happened to Mohammed?'

'That's all I know. I'm just here to look after the place.'

I couldn't believe what was happening. The incongruity between this fellow's nonchalance and the gravity of the event struck me as surreal. Here was an event that surely heralded the end of my world, and this fellow was unconcernedly puffing away at his cigarette, and answering my questions with an indifference that bordered on absurdity.

'I must go inside,' I urged, stepping beneath the cordon.

'No you don't, young fellow.'

The policeman grabbed my arm, and forbade me to enter. If I continued to make a nuisance, he said, I'd be arrested. At that moment, the heated discussion I was having with the policemen, alerted some of the folk inside the mud hut, who exited en masse, as if to lynch me.

'Don't let him go,' they shouted, 'it's him, he's the one who caused all this trouble.'

The policeman roughly clasped my arms and pushed me to the ground. I was then mobbed by half-a-dozen furious peasants who kicked me, spat in my face, and shouted obscenities at me. Trying to control the situation, and fearing that the mob would beat me to death, the policeman forcefully lifted me up and thrust me onto his chair. It was not until he brandished his pistol that they were forced to stand aside. But I was in no way off the hook. The policeman, believing that I was somehow implicated in the murder, handcuffed me to the chair. All the time, the crowd continued to grow, becoming increasingly intimidating. My captor, however, did not scruple letting the crowd spit on my face, that continued throughout the episode. Soon the local mayor, Salem Tahir, thankfully arrived on the scene, managing finally to disperse the crowd and diffuse the situation. I could not have been more grateful to this good man, who explained to the policeman that the young man was not involved in the murder; and asked him to accompany me, for my safety, to his office, from where he fetched my father to collect me.

56

The period between the mayor's departure and father's arrival passed very quickly. I had expected to observe one of those much-described overnight changes in his aspect; those manifestations supposedly engendered by great anxiety. But nothing had changed. Still those same benevolent features, that controlled, almost magnanimous, expression. I stood up to receive him, my head hanged in humility. How surprised I was when my father threw his arms around me and hugged me closely to his chest!

'I've been so worried about you! Look at the state of you! I need to take you to hospital so that we can have your wounds looked at.'

'I'm so sorry father, please forgive me. Father, where is Mohammed? Is he alright?'

'He's fine, Mohammed's fine. Anyway, you've been eager to go abroad for some time. There's no better time than now. Tonight, we're going to stay with your grandparents in Baghdad. In the morning, we'll go to the British Embassy, to arrange your travel papers. Then I'm going to book you on the first flight to London.'

'But father,' I cried, 'I need to stay and see what's happened to Mohammed. I can't just leave things like this. I need to talk with him. I can't just leave. That'd be too cruel.'

'It's impossible for you to remain here, for your own sake. There's many people around here that would like to take the matter into their own hands. It wouldn't be safe.'

I remonstrated with my father to think again, at least to give me a couple of days before I must leave. Yet he was having none of it, and was adamant in his decision.

'OK,' I submitted resignedly, 'whatever's necessary.'

'Look,' he replied, trying to lift my spirits, 'you can start a new life in England – you've always wanted to go there – you've got your whole life ahead of you. You can continue your studies. I'll send you as much money as I can.'

'And Mohammed?'

'Mohammed lives in a different world to you. He'll get over all this eventually; he'll move on, and start again. Yes, it will take time for both of you. After all, some people would consider you beyond redemption for what you did. But let's not worry about that for now. Time will heal. It always does. I know. When you're in love, there's nothing like it in the world. It was the same with your mother and I. I thought I couldn't live and breathe without her. She was my everything. And then one day she was taken from me. My heart was broken – of course it was - I didn't think I could go on without her. I wanted to join her, beyond. But here I am today, thinking about the future, making plans. We must go on, Sami. We cannot just give up. We have a duty to one another and to your mother. What do you think she'd want you to do in these circumstances? Precisely as I have said. Believe me Sami, believe me, all this has just been a mirage; nothing is permanent; everything fades into the past; life is the affair of but a moment. So, do the right thing – by yourself and by me (and by your mother).'

Together, we departed from the mayor's office, and got into my father's car, where Zaid was sitting in the passenger seat. As the car drove off, my brother, who appeared very embittered, said:

'There's no one else to blame other than yourself for the mess we're in. You've brought shame on yourself and all our family.'

And I could not contradict what he said, for it was true. My father remained quiet. I queried:

'Are you not going to say anything, father? Ever since I was a child, I have always come to you to help me in my predicament. I confided in you that I was a girl – not a boy – but you did nothing. . .'

Zaid looked at me with apparent disgust.

'. . . You left the whole thing to my mother, who wasn't from here and didn't know what to do, despite trying to do her best.'

Father pulled up and stopped the car. Turning to me, he looked into my eyes:

'Sami, I knew all along about your predicament. But I just didn't know what to do. God is my witness, I spent many nights trying to figure out what to do for you.'

He paused, then continued:

'For this reason, I want you to go to London, where they can help you more than we can here. If you believe it's what you really want, you can live as a woman (I think they have some surgical procedure there), find happiness and be who you are. But you'll have to forget about us, Iraq, and whoever lives here. I may die without seeing you again, but at least I'll die happy, knowing that you are safe and accepted for who you are.'

We maintained silence throughout the rest of the journey to Baghdad General Hospital, where my wounds were attended to.

The following day, I completed the necessary paperwork with the embassy. I hoped that Zaid would come to see me off at the airport, but it seems the whole nasty affair had alienated his affection. Yes, he would fight to the death to save my reputation and honour; but he would not sully his hands even so much as to look at me. What strange and convoluted ways we humans invent, mixing love and hate so closely together!

I took a night flight to London. I would leave in darkness. For I could not find any light in all of this. I thought that Mohammed and I would somehow persist indefinitely – that love could continue beyond this world, beyond man, beyond time itself. But not so, not so . . .

Those few moments of love Mohammed and I shared together, can never be extinguished. They shall endure always. Let men do as they will, they will never succeed in annihilating the past. Far beyond this hoary matrix of space and time, beyond its aging expanse, our love will forever be stowed away; for make no mistake, this universe is shot through with moral import, and it is only when we love that we act truly in accordance with nature. All else passes into nothingness, never to return. How foolish, then, to regret those halcyon days when, from the bottom of life's void, we momentarily cried out to our creator and his ineffable features smiled upon us.

57

It was nearly dawn when DC Palmer finished reading Susan Green's book, the first light of day penetrating the curtains of his North London flat. Comfortably ensconced in an armchair, he was in that pleasant hypnagogic state, somewhere between wakefulness and slumber. Scenes from old Baghdad passed before his mind, broken into by a dim awareness of his current surroundings. It was not until midday that he was finally awoken by the bustle of life, the uniform din of cars and commuters, of people going about their workaday business.

The case of the architect had piqued Palmer's interest; but after perusing her book, he was like a man on a mission. He wanted answers. Without pausing for lunch, his first stop was the estate agent mentioned by several of the parties involved in the recent incident. It seemed to be the nodal point that connected all the threads of this narrative together. Accordingly, with much expedition, he pulled up outside the double-fronted shop of Jafari, a local property tycoon who, with great acumen, had speculated on central London properties in the 1980s. Nowadays, he had put away a sufficient pile to relax and put his feet up. Yet indolence was anathema to him. Those who suggested retirement were promptly rebuffed with assertions that such would lead to an early grave. One works; or one dies.

This middle-aged businessman had a stereotypical Middle Eastern appearance: heavy-set features, a large nose, dark unkempt and bushy eyebrows; all that remained of his hair was a border of grey, combed over the partition of baldness that dominated his scalp. When the wind blew laterally against his head, these long strands stood up perpendicularly, giving the most comic effect imaginable. He sat behind an expanse of desk, littered with all manner of documents. To left and right, two younger men, also Middle Eastern, were stationed. Two women were on the telephone, nattering away in foreign tongues. Palmer entered:

'I'm looking for a Mr Jafari. Is he here?'

'Who's asking?' came the suspicious reply.

Palmer displayed his credentials, and explained that he needed to ask a few questions. The estate agent was chary of giving out information (which he always believed could be used against him in some imaginary misdemeanour), but submitted to the detective's request. Together, they entered a small office, separated from the main shop. Adorned with expensive furniture, it was clearly used to impress important clients.

'Please sit down,' said Jafari.

'I'm making enquiries about the death of one of your workers, Ahmed Saraji. Can you tell me about how he came to work for you? Also, I need you to tell me what you know about Susan Green, the architect.'

'Ah, Miss Green! She's quite a star. Ever since she published her book and used this office as her address, I've had one problem after another. You know about the book, I suppose?'

'Yes,' Palmer responded, 'but tell me, what problems?'

'Well, for a start, that guy you mentioned, Ahmed, came into the office out of the blue with Susan's book in his hand. He introduced himself as a skilled worker. He told me how much he liked the Iraqi architect, and seemed to know that she was connected with the site in Kensington, but wanted to know when she would be at the property, and what she was doing there. I was tempted to tell him to mind his own business, but he was so insistent. And he was willing to work for a cheap rate, providing it was on the Kensington site. Anyway, I explained that Susan was designing the glass-work connecting the two adjacent properties. I just thought he had his eye on her or something.'

'Does she work full-time at the site?'

'No,' replied Jafari, 'she only visits the site on Thursdays. She does private work elsewhere. Oh, and she also teaches ballet at Kensington Hall.'

The estate agent paused for a moment. He was suspicious where all this was leading.

'I wasn't on the site the morning of the incident. It was an accident, wasn't it?'

Palmer was beginning to have his doubts.

'I don't know yet. . . Anyway, that's all for now. I'll let you know if I need any further information.'

With that, their meeting was at a close.

Next, Palmer made the short drive to Notting Hill Gate, where Susan's flat was situated.

'Miss Green,' the detective spoke into the building's intercom, 'this is DC Palmer. I interviewed you last week. Can you spare a moment?'

Susan was hesitant. She didn't usually like people intruding on her privacy, but she had been thinking about the incident with Ahmed the past few days, and wanted to talk with someone about it. She buzzed him through the door.

'I shall come straight to the point, Miss Green. Ahmed, the man who died on the site in Kensington last week: is he the same Ahmed you write about in your book, Zakiyah's son?'

Susan was taken aback and lost for words. But she soon realised the source of the detective's knowledge:

'You've seen my book.'

'Yes, I read it last night.'

'The whole thing has been playing on my mind. I wanted to contact you several times, but just couldn't find the courage to do so. So, in one way, I'm glad you've come. It saves me agonising further about what to do.'

They sat down at the dining room table. DC Palmer began:

'Miss Green . . .'

'Please call me "Susan."'

'OK, Susan. So, the Ahmed in your book, he is the same man?'

Susan nodded affirmatively.

'If there's anything you'd like to tell me, now's the time. You say in your book that Ahmed killed someone; that he was a threat to you and compelled you to flee to England.'

'DC Palmer, I'm not a vindictive person, and don't usually harbour nasty thoughts about anyone. Life's too short. But Ahmed, he was something completely different; something else. He was a man who thought nothing of destroying what was young and innocent, and all for some warped notion of honour. I've hated him for years, and cannot forgive him for what he did. In fact, to forgive him would be a crime in itself. Some things in this world should never be forgiven; neither should they be forgotten. Time, they say, heals. And I cannot deny that time has frequently sought to shroud Ahmed, the cause of my ill-feelings, so deep within the past that I had to make an effort to live that pain again and again. I could not let time deprive me of the abhorrence I felt for him. That would amount to betraying something that I carry close to my heart. Pain, DC Palmer, when occasioned by the loss of someone dear should not be hastily cast aside. It is pain that connects us to one who is lost. When that pain ends, the connection is broken forever. Why should life be allowed to continue as if nothing had happened. This is what I cannot understand. In a world so replete with pain: how can we all live and act as if everyone were happy? Shouldn't we be in eternal mourning?'

Susan paused for a moment, caught up in her recollections, then continued:

'You must think me a bad person?'

'No, not at all. You spoke of someone dear to your heart. I presume that's Mohammed?'

'Yes. With the same intensity that I hated Ahmed – for what he did; for what he stands for – with the same intensity did I love (or, rather, do I continue to love) Mohammed. Hatred and love, apparently so different from one another, are ignited by the same flame. Those who are incapable of hate are also incapable of love. The flame within, that in some people never goes beyond a gentle glow, in others blasts into a mighty conflagration that would consume the world.'

Interesting as he found her comments, Palmer saw that the conversation had digressed from what he had intended. Thus, he sought to bring Susan's outpouring to an abrupt end:

'Yes. What happened on the day of the incident?'

'I arrived at the site early on that morning, at around seven-thirty. Working on the site was a young Iraqi labourer, whom I asked to carry a square of reinforced glass up to the roof that connects the buildings, where it was to be fitted. I needed to test it, so that we could order the remaining squares of glass to replace the existing panes.'

'This labourer, did you speak with him in Arabic?'

'I don't like to revert to Arabic and prefer to speak English when in England. But he couldn't understand a word of what I was saying. I got exasperated with him and, yes, I spoke with him in Arabic. We need to move on, at least in some things. To me, speaking in Arabic meant reverting to the past. Moreover, I don't like to be questioned about the past. It's necessary to keep a distance with some people, who would otherwise intrude on one's privacy.'

She paused a moment, then added thoughtfully:

'It's odd that you should know that.'

'I've been doing my investigations,' Palmer retorted straightforwardly.

'You have, indeed, detective.'

'You just said that you don't like people intruding on your private life. I understand that. But why, if such is the case, did you go ahead and write a book, exhibiting your private life to the whole world?'

'Detective, there are more ways than one of concealing what one is. The book, which to others might represent a disclosure of sorts, establishes a wall, a boundary, between myself and the world. A narrative is both a disclosure and a mask; it reveals and conceals. And, then, of course, it is cathartic to empty one's self of so great a burden.'

Palmer didn't quite understand Susan's meaning, but was reluctant to enter into a discussion on semantics. The cathartic burden, it seemed, still needed to be unloaded.

'A book is like a second self,' she continued, 'it is sent out into the world and, in a sense, becomes an ambassador. Some people it provokes; others it endears. Unfortunately, my book has not been a very able emissary, and has provoked more people than it has endeared.'

'Such as?' Palmer interposed.

'To start, not so long ago, I had a visit from my brother on his way to America, where he currently lives. Now, there's a man in whom the flame I mentioned burns very low. In him, both love and hate have an insipid, phlegmatic, character! He lives without living, without passion or intent. Anyway, I hadn't seen him for some time. Clearly, he was ashamed of me, and very jealous of his reputation, his honour. Under a pretext of doing what was favourable to me, he sought to smother my book in its infancy. He told me the book would cause me problems; that Ahmed – that is, the painter who died on the site – had been released from prison by Saddam Hussein, who liberated all the prisoners prior to the invasion of Iraq by the US and UK in 2003. So, the story goes, he became affiliated with Al Qaeda or ISIS, or some such terrorist organisation. Then he disappeared from the radar. Some people said that he'd been killed; others were convinced that he fled to Syria (where his terrorist pretentions were employed) with a group of like-minded jihadists, crossed into Turkey, and then made his way into Germany. There the trail ended. Whether he would move on to England or not nobody knew, but Zaid, my brother, certainly thought that it was possible, and thought that in publishing my book I might expose myself.'

Susan hesitated, then concluded reflectively, 'It turns out that he was right.'

'What about Mohammed? Do you know what happened to him?

The architect's demeanour assumed an appearance of profound sadness and loss.

'I don't know. When I spoke to my brother about him, he seemed to shut down and change the subject. Shame dominates his way of thinking. Perhaps he's still in Iraq; maybe he was killed in the war; or he might have emigrated or gone to America like my brother. I don't know.'

Palmer observed a brief moment of solemnity in respect of Susan's sadness.

'I'm sorry to press you. You're clearly very moved by your recollections. I understand. What happened on that Thursday morning?'

'The Thursday? Yes. After the Iraqi labourer laid the square of glass, he returned to the ground floor. I was aware of someone painting, and hardly payed any attention at first. You know, when you're aware of something without it intruding on your conscious mind. But when he tossed his paint bucket aside and started to descend the ladder and come toward me, I became distinctly aware that I was in danger. A face like Ahmed's, or at least what that face meant to me, doesn't fade with time. I didn't know at that moment what his exact intention was, but I was quickly disabused of my ignorance. Speaking in Arabic, he said that I was an abomination in the sight of God, that I must be erased from the earth; and, finally, that he was going to throw me from the roof.'

'Did you try to reason with him or call for help?'

'I tried to tell him that his understanding of Islam was incorrect. Then he said that I had ruined his life; that I was responsible for the death of his stepfather, Abbas. Any response from me would have been pointless. He had made up his mind that he was going to kill me. Then I saw a way out.'

'A way out?' queried Palmer.

'Yes, detective. All that separated Ahmed from me was the glass roofing. The pane nearest me was the one that had just been replaced. All the others were unsafe and would not take much weight. Standing on the reinforced pane of glass, I goaded Ahmed, coaxing him toward me. "Come on," I said, "come and get me if you want."'

'And he assumed the other panes were safe?'

'Yes. And what followed you're aware of. There was no choice. It was either me or him.'

258

Palmer reflected for a moment.

'I have to report to my governor.'

'Am I in trouble?' Susan asked.

'I don't know. Leave it with me for now.'

Back at the station, DC Palmer knocked on DS Wood's office door to report his conclusions on the case.

'Come in Palmer. All finished?' Wood asked jovially, 'Any foul play?'

'Yes, all finished. No, there was no foul play. Just an accident.'

58

Shortly thereafter, a man entered Jafari's estate agent.

'Not another one!' the tycoon quipped, after seeing the stranger carrying a copy of Susan's book.

'Don't tell me, you want to know about Susan Green?'

The stranger was surprised.

'How do you know?'

'Let's say that I'm a mystic, I can tell the future! I've had it up to here with that woman and her book. Nothing but trouble! Last week I could have been closed down; I'm not joking. She's embroiled me in enough problems to put me in prison.'

He turned to his colleagues:

'Would you believe it! Tell him what happened the other day.'

'Yes, yes, it was quite an affair,' they echoed in unison.

'Quite an affair; that's a bid of an understatement! Quite an affair! I could have been locked up! All that nonsense about Ahmed. A man comes in here looking to do a bit of painting work, next thing I know he's dead. Anyway, I can't help you. I don't know anything.'

'Ahmed?' said the stranger, 'Ahmed Saraji?'

'None other.' Jafari was in a jovial mood and liked to dramatize things.

The stranger knew how to loosen the tycoon's tongue:

'I'm from Iraq, and have lived in America for some years, and I'm here looking to invest some money in property.'

'Why didn't you say so!'

Jafari rose from his seat and stretched out his hand.

'I thought that while we're talking business, you might put me in the right direction regarding Miss Green.'

'No trouble at all,' commented Jafari, 'Why didn't you say so!' he repeated, 'There's nothing can't be done for those who would only try. Now, about your investment?'

'If you could just let me know how I can contact Miss Green, we can talk business.'

Turning to one of his associates, Jafari urged, 'go and get Susan's card,' and, turning to the stranger, 'will that be good enough?'

'That'll do me just fine. I think we'll be able to do some business.'

'You bet we can!' responded the tycoon.

Seeing how much leverage his knowledge of Susan gave him, he threw in whatever he could on the matter:

'Yes, Susan's a great friend. Not a bad word to say of her. And she's not just an engineer, an architect: she's cultured too. Teaches ballet.'

'Teaches ballet, you say?'

'Yes, at Kensington Hall. In fact, she'll be there this afternoon. Why don't we take some details of your investment requirements, and then one of my people will drive you there. What about that?'

The stranger assented. Taking him into the side office, Jafari ordered one of his female employees:

'Bring us some tea! Tea for our guest! And some of those nice dates too.'

Jafari's rambling seemed to go on for eternity. Certain philosophers believed that time had only an ideal, not a real, existence; so too the common man is familiar with the compression or elongation of time according to the nature of circumstances. But it was not until that moment, however, that this hapless victim gained a really solid grounding in the ideality of time. Compressed within the confines of twenty minutes or so was a lifetime. It almost made his head swim; at other times he felt like he was going to pass out, and a dark fringe bordered the periphery of his visual field. He had to take random swigs from his cup to keep himself awake.

'So,' Jafari concluded, 'I can see that you're as excited as I am about this investment. Things are certainly looking good in the market place.'

When one of the tycoon's employees came to take him to Kensington Hall, and he passed through the doors of the estate agent, it was as if he were levitating. Never had his feet felt so light upon the ground. He was positively gliding along. It must be like this, he pondered, for disembodied spirits.

At Kensington Hall, Susan was demonstrating certain techniques, pirouettes and the like, with two or three students. The stranger paused at the entrance, drinking in the splendid peace and quietude that suffuses a person who, after a search so painful and so long, he realises that he has finally come home; behind him are the harsh, tempestuous seas, the dead calms, the torrid squalls that sought to sink his fragile bark; the harbour awaits; the journey is over.

A tear broke loose from his eyes, and tumbled down his cheek. There, before him, was the summation of his life; the why and wherefore that accompanied his every coming and going.

Completing her demonstration, Susan became aware of the presence of the stranger. Were her eyes deceiving her?

She did not know. Was this possible in this theatre of pain and illusion? She did not know. Could she trust her eyes? She must needs come closer; as Mohammed himself closed in upon her.

'Is that you, Mohammed? Is that really you?'

'Yes, it's me. And you, Susan, that's quite a transformation!'

They embraced, and recalling those days of old at the watermill that bordered the Tigris, they danced the pas de deux from Swan Lake, to the applause of those present.

This work of literary fiction was delayed by more than three years due to a violent hate attack sustained in Cannes, France, that caused the author serious injuries, while attending an industry event in 2015. The team at Diversity Books is immensely proud to see it finally published. *www.diversitybooks.com*